HOLY GROUND

Darren +
Mom
Please, enjoy!

Nick
Williams

Holy Ground

Mark Williams

Holy Ground

ISBN: 1453730184
EAN: 9781453730188

Special thanks to the editing and advisory team-

Nancy McCurry, NancyMcCurry@cox.net
Rosa Cays Editing
Diane O'Connell Literary Services, New York, NY
Jerry Simmons-Indi Publishing

Front cover photo: Dallas Ryan Photography Ltd.;
Los Angeles, New York, Scranton
Cover Art graphics: Bob Ryan Studios; Phoenix and
Paradise Valley
Cover location: Wally's American Pub and Grill, Phoenix.
Owner- Wally Collins
Back Cover photo: Joni Miller Photography Ltd.

Tactical review:
Kenneth R. Bucy, MSG (RET) USA
Special Agent John Wagner, Ret.
Agent Cheri Oz, DEA
Sgt. Travis James-Leroy Williams, USAR

To John Lynch for his support, protection, and
encouragement

Dedication

I want to dedicate this book to those who have once stood or who are currently standing in, The Gap.

And to one specifically-

63rd Regional Readiness Command
11th Military Police Brigade
422nd Military Police Company
2nd Platoon, 3rd Squad

Charlie Team Leader

Currently deployed somewhere in the throat of the Dragon

Foreword

Mark Williams writes his heroes the way God probably sees us. We find them stumbling around in their own personal battles: grizzled, failed, weary, tough and cynical. They have a great heart, but it's had the life nearly kicked out it by failure, pain or rejection. They drink too much scotch and employ language usually reserved for dockworkers and pirates. But near their lowest, they find themselves inexorably drawn into *a life altering, life revealing chain of events.* From somewhere within, they discover themselves responding with bravery they didn't know they possessed. I think that's how God probably sees us all: messed up and full of compromised sludge, without the slightest awareness that our moment to shine is waiting, just around the corner.

His hero is usually encouraged and reminded of his purpose by a partially-sane vagrant, or some such sketchy character. In speaking wisdom through them, his books give strange and wonderful dignity to the forgotten, misplaced, rumpled and ignored.

Smack dab in the middle of the most dangerous scenes is where you discover some of the best humor. And oh, there is humor! There are one-liners in here worth admission to an overpriced Vegas buffet!

Toss in his ability to seat you in a neighborhood bar-where undercover cops swap war stories...or an evacuated office where you learn horribly close-up how trigger pins detonate explosives-and you've got a page-turner like few others.

Mark has this great ability to show the invisible thread woven throughout each of our lives-giving meaning to every moment; especially the ones that presently make no sense.

He has become a writer worthy to stand with the "big boys of fiction." He tells a story you don't want to end. I think it's because you're not reading a rehashed plot a ghost writer has reworked for an author who has run out of good ideas. Mark's letting us into how he sees life. He somehow convinces us that this life, in all its pain and ugliness, is still worth hanging around for. *Because that moment is coming*...where all the unraveled threads form a tapestry...where the good guy's unseen courage gets displayed...where you finally see that your day to day life actually counts...where the garbled mess of real life turns on a dime, just when you'd feared it was all a random hoax. And he hands this gift to all of us who read along with him. You're in for a wild and delightfully redeeming ride. Enjoy the pie!

John Lynch
co-author
True Faced and *Bo's Cafe*

YOU KNOW.

1120-150

Mark Williams

"People sleep peacefully in their beds at night because there are rough men and women ready to do violence on their behalf."

—George Orwell

Holy Ground

Late December, 2003

The old man played his bagpipes on the hill until the vehicle went out of sight. His friends called him "Old Silverback," like the Silverback gorilla, the wisest and strongest of the family. He liked that term—*Silverback*. He took pride in it. The other bagpiper had come out of the church ahead of the casket and played as it was loaded into the hearse. The old man echoed the song of the lead piper. The song was ancient, used to bury the warrior dead a millennium prior. His intent was to bathe the crowd, to soothe them only the way the pipes could.

On this day, for this man, the crowd not only filled the church but some of the parking lot. No one turned and looked at the old man, even though he was just a few dozen yards away. He stood on a small hill, just outside the front of the church, on the other side of the parking lot. It was only a few feet high but it made the old man the tallest thing in the area, and the sound of his pipes launched into the air from there, right onto the throngs of people coming out from the church.

First came the immediate family, then co-workers. The outside crowd parted to let them through. *It had been a good day to die*, the old man thought.

The melodic sound of the pipes carried over the church and across the street, as if it were chasing the hearse as it pulled away. Finally, the old man stopped playing and pulled on the ends of his curled mustache, making sure the wax tips were still in place. Tucking the bagpipe under his arm and, while holding the chanter in the same hand, he reached down into his sporran, the small satchel hanging from a chain from his belt in front, and freed the small silver flask within it. He uncorked it with his thumb and, after toasting the vacant street where the hearse was last seen, took a long pull on the container, letting the drink slide down his throat. The man in the hearse would have liked the drink as well, a long pull on a fine scotch—especially with the old Silverback.

"They all done?" a young man asked as he walked up behind the old man. The old man knew he was there, but didn't look over at him. He nodded his head.

"That sounded good," a second young man said, coming up on the other side looking in the direction of the departing hearse. "They're on their way to the graveside?"

The old man shook his head. "Naw, the boy wanted to be cremated. There's nothin' in that casket but air, there is."

"We're heading out," the second said as he and the first young man turned to leave. A third man had come up. He was older than the other two. He had a mustache and wore a bright Hawaiian shirt. He had a small paper plate and a plastic fork and was eating a slice of strawberry pie. He said nothing and simply nodded to the others. He stood for a minute. The old man looked over at him and gave him a small grin. The man in the Hawaiian shirt winked at him, then turned and followed the other two.

"Aye, right behind ya," said the old man.

He looked over at the crowd. The old man knew them all and saw the news crews trying to get a late interview with anyone who would talk to them. The endless questions comparing this to 9/11; everything seemed to be compared to that day, even if it wasn't. His upper lip rose as if to snarl, but no sound came out.

Most of the mourners would never know the cost paid by the man they came to honor. Most didn't care about those final weeks leading up to the explosions and the killings. The old man knew what the news wanted and it wasn't the truth, just improved ratings. He put the flask away and walked off the hill, looking one last time into the throat of the crowd as he found his way down. He watched them for a moment. A smile came to his old gnarled face; slowly, almost without him knowing, a wide grin formed, then a slight laugh. *Nope, they'll never know the cost.* The old man stood there a little longer, and then turned and walked away, down the short incline following the path of the other three, off the short hill. In a few steps, around a far corner of the church, he disappeared from view.

CHAPTER ONE
The purpose of life is to fight maturity.

—Dick Werthimer

———————————

March 20, 2003

Cooper woke up, lying on his back, to the clock radio.
"The second invasion of Iraq started early this morning...."

He kept his eyes shut and his breathing slowed. His hand moved up to his face and to rub his ear. He felt the whiskers on his face then down to his chest and his testicles, freeing them from the boxers he had on that spun tight as he rolled over.

He was breathing like he just finished a run. His pillow was soaked with sweat. "Oh, god," he groaned. His right shoulder hurt him. If he laid on it long enough, an old high school football injury flared up. As a matter of fact, it had gotten worse. Now, the other shoulder hurt from laying on it so much, so he would roll to his back. He couldn't sleep on his back. His fifty-five year-old body was becoming a wreck. He was sore from osteoarthritis, from years of running on hard concrete streets trying to keep his fading body somewhat in shape. He was losing that battle. He smoked too many cigars and drank too much scotch at Moreno's Bar, usually to the point of becoming a stumbling pile of goo. His blood pressure bordered on hypertensive, and the rib-eye steaks he allowed himself to eat helped his total cholesterol to reach the nice round number of 260.

He got up and felt his way to the bathroom, peed, and then turned on the shower. He had a shower radio and he turned it on, adjusting the station from the music station to NPR. "Sorry Waylon, can't sing with you this morning." He stood there with his arms crossed, as if he was hugging himself, just letting the hot water run over him. *A cheap man's Jacuzzi,* he had called it. After fifteen minute of soaking, shaving, most of which he had done with his eyes closed; he got out and dried off. *Huh, probably should wash this towel,* he thought, the smell similar to that of mildew long since gone to seed.

In the base of his brain it could still register sound. He listened to the radio and the reports of the invasion.

"Early reports coming from those journalists imbedded with...."

Cooper's ruddy complexion was highlighted with close-cropped, salt-and-pepper hair and a gray mustache. His face was filling out from the high consumption of alcohol in the last few years. His face had taken on a reddish tint, especially his nose, from hours in the Arizona sun and was marked with broken capillaries, just above his cheeks. His lips were thin; if it wasn't for the mustache, his face would almost appear mouth-less. Jowls were forming below his jaw line. His ears seemed to sag, like the rest of his body, which after years and years of abuse, sloped down as if he had carried a heavy rucksack and never taken it off. His whole body, under a load of weight that had been there for so long, no one noticed it anymore, especially Cooper, worked on the joints and muscles.

He went into his closet and pulled out one of five tan jumpsuits. He slid on new underwear, throwing the ones he was wearing onto a pile in the corner of the room. It was a sizable pile.

"...numerous fires are being reported from downtown Baghdad...."

He felt his stomach and his growing waist line. His abdomen, which at one time was cut into six muscular sections, began to push on the belts holding up his pants when he would get dressed. The flight jumpsuits were much more comfortable. Surprisingly, in some regards, his body still depicted health. But if one looked, they could tell. Even though he went to the gym and ran three times a week, his body was still writing checks it couldn't cash. All in all, Cooper William Gardner was a physical wreck waiting to crash. In a few years, if he kept up his lifestyle of self-abuse, he would drown in his own life, probably in his own toilet.

He was a helicopter pilot for the Phoenix Police Department. Cooper was the senior pilot and part of the development team that employed the aircrafts when the trend in police work called for it years ago. After his tours in Vietnam, he came back home and joined the department. He happened to be at the right place at the right time when the city decided to start an air wing. He was part of the initial six who made up the section. He was also the only one with any helicopter experience. All the rest were street cops the department sent to flight school. He loved it.

He looked over at the top of his dresser and at the pictures hanging on the wall behind it with him in younger days. He had trouble focusing from the bed so he rubbed his eyes and his face again; pictures of him on graduation day from the academy. He joined the department and then shortly thereafter married his first wife, Torin, and just as quickly divorced her after a year and a half. The job and the old dreams consumed his life and that of his marriage. Torin made the mistake of saying she would wait for him to come back from Vietnam. She did. They married. But neither of them were the same person they were before he left for the war.

"God, you're such a cynic!" she would call him.

"Oh, really, well I guess that makes you a bra-burning feminist!" Cooper wasn't quite sure what all that entailed, but it was the talk of the time and it wasn't meant to be nice.

The marriage lasted until he had been out of the police academy for almost a year. He came home one day to an empty closet and a note on the counter saying she was tired of the silence. That was fine; he didn't want to talk to her anyway.

He went over to the edge of his bed and sat down while he put on his flight boots.

"...coalition forces started in the darkness with air and cruise missile strikes at the nation's capital of Baghdad...."

"'Bout damn time," he said as he reached over and shut off the radio and then wiped some white stuff from the corner of his mouth, transferring it to his bed sheet.

He went to the closet, pulled his Glock and three magazines from the gun locker on the top shelf, stuffed it into his shoulder holster after first instinctively putting one of the magazines in the butt of the gun, slamming it in, then charging the weapon. The other two magazines he put in the well worn magazine pouch just above his waist on the other side, opposite the holster. He grabbed his keys and headed out the door. It was the start of another beautiful day for Cooper Gardner.

Mark Williams

CHAPTER TWO
Fear is that little darkroom where negatives are developed.
—Michael Pritchard

Scottsdale, Arizona, 1971

"The itsy-bitsy spi-der, climbed up the water spout. Down came the rain and washed the spider out," Jodi Hawkins sang while she sat in the back of the closet, behind the clothes rack. Jodi was five and wore pretty dresses and had long, dark hair, just like her mother. Her daddy loved her dark hair. As a fact, she had never gotten her hair cut. He liked Jodi's mother with long hair, too. Jodi liked the back of the closet. It was safe and warm, like a den where big mother bears go and take their young and make them safe and comfortable. It's where Jodi liked to be when her parents argued. When her father hit her mother, she liked the very farthest part of the closet. She couldn't hear her mother cry or scream way back in the back, especially when Jodi was singing to herself.

Still, Jodi could hear some of the conversations, especially when words were screamed. "You're pathetic!" the mother said.

"Me? Look at yourself. What have you done to yourself?" Jodi's father slurred back. They both had their share of liquor and it almost always resulted in a war. They were just another couple on one of the more affluent east side streets in the Arcadia area of Phoenix. Large, rambling houses with large, rambling yards, was all that existed here. He was an investment manager for Gerstin-Shwindt. Mother was part of the tradition of the time; staying home, taking care of Jodi, and making life look good.

"I am what you made me."

"—out came the sun—"

"Look at your hair. *God,* why don't you wash it at least once a month?"

"Because you want me to wash it! Jodi and I grew our hair because her *father* 'loves long hair.' Does *she* have long hair too? Does your *whore* have long—" There was the clear sound of skin on skin that penetrated the walls of the closet. Jodi sang louder.

"Leave Vanessa out of this and don't you ever call her that. Don't you ever call her that, or—"

"Oh, it's *'Vanessa'* this week. Between your daughter and your whores—what are you going to do? You going to hit me again? You can't leave me. You can't leave the *image and the success* that I've brought you. Your status among your friends—what would they say?" Jodi could hear her mother begin to laugh at him. Jodi, even at her young age, knew Daddy hated it when Mommy laughed at him. Jodi had seen him clench his teeth when her mother was like this. Jodi could hear her—in her state she kept laughing. It wasn't just Jodi's mother who would cut; Jodi heard her father too. Both of them would cut each other to the bone, but her mother could cut Daddy open—wide and deep with her sarcasm.

"—and dried up all the rain—"

The sound of something being thrown against the dresser and then the sound of breaking glass, like that of a lamp, impacted the wall which Jodi had her back to. It caused her to flinch and cover her ears. Her eyes were already closed.

"Oh, god—"

"Yeah, bitch, god ain't here. You aren't going to laugh at me again with that filthy mouth of yours." There was a muffled sound of deep flesh being impacted by something. The sound was deep and guttural.

"—the itsy-bitsy spider crawled up the spout again." She sang the song until she fell asleep between the clothes in the bear's den.

It was a sunny day the following morning. The day was beautiful and the spring morning hadn't grown too warm as it had a tendency to do in Arizona. The scent of orange blossoms from the still standing groves around the homes in the neighborhood was carried across the home and into Jodi's room. Jodi had overslept. She had anticipated another melee when her parents went out to a black tie function the night before so she had moved from her bed with her favorite blanket and pillow into the closet after the baby sitter left. Nothing woke her. She slept straight through until she woke up the next morning.

"Mommy?" she said as she came out of her large closet and into her room and then the hall. Nothing. "Mommy?" she called again. The wood floor in the hall was cold so Jodi went back into her room and slipped her Bugs Bunny bathrobe and matching slippers on and skated back into the hall and down towards her parents' room. "Mommy, where are you?" she called. She thought she heard something in the kitchen so she turned at the hall intersection and moved in that direction. There, next to the kitchen counter, and just on the other side, the television was on in the neighboring den. "Mommy?" she called again. It was unlike her mother not to answer.

She moved back towards the bedrooms. It was a long hallway with four large bedrooms, the master at one end, Jodi's bedroom, then a bathroom, and two other bedrooms on the other side of the bathroom. She was an only child, and the two other bedrooms were converted into a craft room and father's office. She stood for a moment at the intersection of the two halls. She thought for a moment as to whether to go towards the office, or into her parents' bedroom. The door to the bedroom was almost closed. She moved towards it and pushed the door open slowly. "Mommy?" She heard water running. It was coming from the back, where the bathroom was. She moved slowly in that direction, carrying her favorite blanket. "Mommy?"

She got to the bathroom door. It had a full length mirror on it. There was a crack on it from a fight from the prior year. Something had hit it. It went from the top center of the mirror to the right side, about seven inches down. For some reason, it hadn't been replaced.

Jodi pushed on the door to the bathroom, slowly opening it. She looked at her reflection in the mirror while she opened the door. As it opened, she could see her mother standing in front of the larger mirror over the sink. She was still wearing her dress from the night before. Makeup had run down her face and neck and dried, staining the top of her blouse a dark gray, making her look like a ghoulish clown. She had a handful of hair she had just cut away from her head with a pair of long scissors. Her mother saw Jodi in the mirror and began to turn.

"Mommy?"

CHAPTER THREE
I know how men in exile feed on dreams of hope
                    —Aeschylus (525 BC-456 BC)

March 22, 2003

"Something's percolating tonight, Joe," Cooper said to his co-pilot. He and his attack flight of five Huey gunships were listening to the ground traffic from the base.

The dreams were back. Cooper hadn't had them in years, thinking they had gone for good, but they were back and they were louder than ever. When he got back from Vietnam, he had trouble sleeping, eating, driving around corners, having a distinctive fear that someone was there with a gun. Eventually those dreams and conscious thoughts became part of who Cooper was. He couldn't go to counseling; that *wasn't done*. It was just a part of going to war. It was just life. After decades, the dreams faded, sometimes not appearing in the night for months, sometimes years. But it didn't take a lot for them to return. His mind just needed a reminder. The Iraq invasion was another war of gunships and fast movers followed by more boots on the ground. He had been listening to the radio reports coming out of the Middle East for the last couple of days and his brain was connecting to old files.

They varied in form and time but they almost always started at the same place—January, 1968.

Cooper and his attack group had gone airborne from their base in southern Binh Tri Thien Province in southern Vietnam after the air unit had received a call that a marine firebase was getting hit. Shortly after going airborne, other traffic started to come into his headset from other locations. When they were about fifteen minutes out, they heard the last call from the base requesting a "Broken Arrow." It chilled him. Cooper knew that for a commander of ground troops to call for that, things had to be in a world of hurt. "Ordering an airdrop on your own house, yep, something's a percolating tonight," Cooper repeated.

From his location, he couldn't see the lights of the fight yet. Cooper and his flight were at the treetops and moving as fast as they could. He had been flying the gunship for the Army in country for nine months. They had done everything, from close ground support to mail runs. The helicopter had taken everything from ground fire to people throwing rocks. There was even a bullet hole in the windscreen to Cooper's right that came in then out the overhead window. Right below it, written in a black marker, Cooper scribed, "Missed me, bitch."

Joe Torre, Cooper's co-pilot, had been flying with him for two years after both served time in infantry units. Ever since they went to flight school together, the two had been driving the equipment. Neither of them said much. Sometimes they would talk, but tonight was different. There was a feeling, a knowing, a response to the sound on the radio that the world that night, their own section of the world anyway, was about to explode and get messy. Cooper was young, just turning twenty-one years old, but looking like he was forty on this night. He had lied about his age and enlisted at seventeen. The air was thick with the smell of jungle, and every once in awhile, the smell of detonated explosives would waft into the cabin of the Huey.

They flew through the night with all their lights out with the exception of the amber glow of their instrument panel lights, routine procedure to not give the ground troops any good targets as they flew as close to the trees as possible, using them for cover. The exterior navigation lights were out and they flew in a loose formation, following the silhouette of each other to the show. All was quiet until a line of trees was cleared, dropping down a couple hundred feet to a lowland area.

"Crap," Joe said as he saw the lights of the firefight in his windscreen.

"Crap's right. They are getting their asses kicked. The whole area is sparking," Cooper responded. He keyed his microphone button on the handle of his control stick. The aircraft were following in a line, one behind the other, with about fifty feet separating them. "Able Flight Lead, to flight. You can see them in front. Stand by for approach and fire directions."

They could hear radio traffic from the base as well as other locations throughout the work area. They were about a mile out.

Joe pointed to their eleven o'clock. "There's the base."

"Got it," Cooper said. Flares looped out and lazily fell out of a central location of inky darkness and ignited over the base. They could see flashes and streaks of light of various sizes outbound, likely the howitzers and mortars. Returning rounds couldn't be seen. Cooper and Joe figured the NVA were launching mortars from the woods. The flash of the mortar launches were obstructed by the jungle.

"Shit," Joe said.

"I think I just did," said Cooper. He again pushed the microphone button on the control stick. He took a deep breath before he spoke. "Fire Base Tango, this is Mud Pounder flight. We are less than two clicks east of you in-bound to your locale. Where do you want us?"

The voice on the other end was clear, firm, with an edge of fear in it. "Mud Pounder, this is Tango. Forward units on the northeast have been over run.

Units to the south are taking heavy fire. Many NVA—repeat—many NVA in all quarters—wire compromised."

When he opened his gray, bloodshot eyes on that Sunday morning and stared at the ceiling, it took him a second to realize where he was. There was a moment he thought he was still flying the mission. His right eye was actually stuck shut and he had to reach up, find his face, and pull the skin down under his eye to pry it open. Sometimes, when he wasn't sleeping and after the dreams, he allowed himself to lie in bed and go back in his mind to a particular day. It was like yesterday instead of over thirty years ago. Sometimes, there was a comfort in the thought. He knew who he was then. He again, closed his eyes.

The neighbor's dog started to bark at something and brought Cooper back to his bedroom. He was lying crooked on the bed when he finally returned from his dream and thoughts, which disoriented him. He laid there for a minute. *Why, do I do that?* He thought. *Why the hell do you like to go there?*

He rubbed his knees. "Jesus, I feel good," he said sarcastically to himself. "Cooper, you are one lucky som' bitch."

His face felt as hard and worn as the rest of his six-foot frame. He frowned at the taste in his mouth as he caught the first gasp of outside air. Something had definitely crawled into it, had offspring and then died, he thought.

After his hand freed his eye, he slid his palm over his face again, stopping at his mustache. There was something in it. *My god, boy, what's growing in your face?* It had dried there and Cooper couldn't tell, nor could he remember what it could have been. Food, phlegm; he didn't know. Hopefully, it would be one of the major food groups from Moreno's Bar from the night before and not something that had crawled in bed with him.

He felt around his side and found one of the four pillows on his bed that he routinely slept with. He pulled it over his face as if to block out the light of the new day. He pushed it away after a few seconds. It smelled like mildew and dried sweat. He looked at it, holding it up enough to where he could focus on it without his glasses. It was an off-white pillowcase; at least that's what his eyes reported. He got the pillows when he left his second wife, Allison. He could see a large, dried stain in the center of the pillowcase, as if something had spilled on it and it dried in a circular pattern. He tried to remember the last time he had washed his sheets. He couldn't. He couldn't remember if he ever did. He made a mental note to strip his bed and wash the sheets this week. He sniffed the pillow again; a slight stench of ammonia filled his sinuses. He wondered if the neighbor's cat had gotten in and marked his pillow again. *Oh, well, the smell wasn't too bad.* He looked around from his bed and his eyes fell on the back arcadia door. It was stuck. *I need to fix that,* he thought. He could hear the dripping bathroom sink. It reminded him of the burned-out light bulb next to his bed which reminded him of the two others in the house. Oh, he remembered, he still needed to do last Friday's dirty dishes—or were they Wednesday's?

He finished surveying the room, his eyes falling on the pictures hung over the highboy. A couple of them were old and faded, ones of him in Vietnam with his crew. They were next to two newer photos of him with the Chief of Police awarding him the Medal of Valor. His dress uniform was starched and perfect in the picture. Now it hung in the back of his closet.

He had stayed single for years after the first marriage train-wrecked and then married Allison, one of the dispatchers from Glendale whose voice he fell in love with during his graveyard rotation, when he would listen to traffic from neighboring cities. "You don't understand," he started to explain to his friend, Moreno, when they both worked patrol. "She has this deep, sultry voice on the air."

"Most of the dispatchers have that voice," Moreno responded. Male, along with a few female officers would find an excuse to go to the dispatch center in an attempt to get a look at the voice in the darkness. Most were disappointed. Cooper wasn't. He talked his friend into going with him to put a face with the voice.

"Holy crap, my friend," Moreno said as he peaked around the corner and into the heart of the dispatch center. He found Allison by her name on the desk cubical. "You do not deserve such a woman. She needs someone who is sophisticated, cultured, and good natured. You are none of those things."

"I can be—wait, what the hell you talking about? Are you my friend or not?"

"I am just trying to keep you from hurting your spirit. She is very fine. She does not want to go out with someone such as yourself. She needs someone of her own culture."

"You?"

"Of course I have not thought of this, but since you have brought it up—"

"You bastard, you think you should date her? Your wife would be pissed. She'd gut you in your sleep. You think you're the one who fits those categories? You're the 'sophisticated one?'" Cooper said, using little air quote marks because he knew Moreno hated little air quotes. "You smell your underwear to see if it can make one more day before you change it."

"Frugality is a virtue," Moreno said, placing his hand over his heart.

"And Chlamydia is an STD."

Allison's ancestors were Peruvian farmers. She had the slight frame of an Inca and an olive complexion with deep green eyes. It was lust at first sight for him, and he was a pilot for her. They lived together for awhile, and then decided to get married. He never had a jealous streak until he met her. She never had anger issues until she met him.

"Why did you smile at him?"

"What? I can't be friendly?"

"How friendly do you want to be with him?"

"Oh my god, you're pathetic."

"Yeah, well—"

Both found within a couple years of their union that theirs was a trampoline experience. There never seemed to be calmness in their home.

After five-and-a-half grueling years, she, too, left. Years later, after a particularly over-indulgent nights at Moreno's, after Moreno retired and opened his dream bar, Cooper would call Allison at work from the pay phone in the corner of the bar. The end was almost always the same; she would hang up on him.

"Look, I know I was a son-of-a-bitch. But I don't think we should've ended it so fast—"

"Coop, we've gone through this. We've talked about this—for years," came her calm voice. "It was my fault, Coop. I was too weak to deal with what we had to deal with."

"What the hell is that supposed to mean?" he said in a slur. Cooper knew she couldn't win—ever. He always had to have the last word, no matter what his state of mind was. Eventually she would hang up.

Cooper would follow the call with a double shot of scotch and a long night.

After a while, he quit calling. He had scabbed over. He did wonder why she never got a restraining order on him for calling her at work or why she never reported it to her supervisors, not even to her new husband. He heard she eventually married a United States Marshall who apparently fell in love with the voice as well. Cooper was always expecting a big man with a star on his chest to come in to Moreno's and kick his ass, but it never happened. Maybe, he thought, that was her way.

Because of his seniority, he managed to stay on the defense instructors' rotation as a training officer at the academy. He would go down two times a week and teach ground fighting techniques an officer could use if they found themselves on the ground. Cooper had actually perfected a leg-scissor sweep; an officer could bring an attacker down if they got close enough.

"You—Recruit, on the mat," he said as he pointed to one of the recruits from Class 6554, one of two classes at the Phoenix Regional Academy. "Hold the bag right next to your knee there on the side." Cooper would adjust the bag and its holder for the demonstration. He then got down on his back while talking to the class, just before kicking the bag with the side scissor kick. "Now, whatever you do Recruit, don't move the bag," he said as he continued the instruction. He could hit the nerve bundle on the side of the lower thigh and send a lightning bolt of nerve impulses up the leg and collapse it. The training command had to be careful practicing this maneuver because it had the potential of breaking legs or tearing ACLs, especially if Cooper was the instructor. He was tough on them. But the train wreck that was his life was coming. He knew it. He just didn't care.

Mark Williams

After his flight, he did all the paperwork; he assumed the other officers would screw it up. After he filled out the flight report, Cooper would go back over the aircraft, even after the ground crew had checked it.

"No, I got it. You'll just ..." he started to say to each co-pilot he would break in. The sarcastic tone in his voice was always apparent. Cooper chewed up flight crews. He was, as he told Allison, a 'mean sonofabitch'. She, eventually agreed with that particular point. He'd check the craft again and make any notes about it in the maintenance log. He'd then go in and change out of his flight suit and into civilian clothes he carried in his jump bag, move his Glock from his shoulder holster to his hip, and ride home on his 1984 Indian motorcycle.

Cooper pulled into his garage and park the bike next to his 1994 F-150 extended-cab truck, a truck he used on rainy days or when he needed to go anywhere out of the city. He walked into the house via the inside garage door. He'd check the mail and made a quick stop to the bathroom, after first tossing his keys in the brass ashtray with the Army Air Calvary emblem in the base of it as it sat on the side table by the front door. The mail he checked went next to it. He dropped anything he had with him on his unmade bed, remove his holster, stuff it under his socks in the top left-hand drawer of his dresser then wander back to the kitchen where he would unconsciously open the refrigerator door. An open soda can, a very black banana, and two containers of yogurt were all that made up its contents. He looked at his watch and walked back to the front door, pick up his keys, and walk down the street three blocks to Moreno's Bar. He had lived this same routine every day since Allison left.

Holy Ground

Phil Moreno's Bar was a public place; at least that's what the business license said. Unofficially, it was a safe place for cops, fire personnel, and military—anyone who stood in the gap. Those who found themselves there would be heard to call it 'sacred.' Their families were safe there too. Veterans from wars or non-wars wandered in on a routine basis.

The bar was attached to a small restaurant that served comfort food, probably the best comfort food anyone had ever tasted—meatloaf and mashed potatoes with some of the skin still left on the potatoes, spaghetti and meat balls, barbeque chicken, raspberry pancakes the size of the plate, turkey sandwiches sliced from a real turkey, with a salsa dressing that made eyes roll back in your skull as you bit into it. Cooper loved it and told Moreno so every meal.

"You're feeding me horse meat again."

"I do not own a horse," Moreno would reply for the five-thousandth time.

"Not anymore. You made entrees out of the old nag."

"It was not a 'nag.' It was a stallion!"

"Figures—it's chewy," Cooper always said when he was eating.

Moreno tended the bar and his nephew, Fernando, worked the kitchen. Fernando was Moreno's sister's oldest son, and had been arrested for possession. The arresting officers knew who he was and took him straight to the bar. Moreno told him he could work for him as long as he stayed out of trouble or he, himself, would take him to jail after first shooting him in the kneecap as a reminder to never ever embarrass the family again. Fernando had been straight ever since, about six years.

At Moreno's, weight gain, or diets were never topics of discussion, especially when it came to eating Moreno's homemade pork chorizo rolled in a fresh tortilla and topped with enchilada sauce, cheese, and sour cream. The smell was like no other. 'Heaven in a tortilla,' Fernando would call it. The whole thing was the size of a baby's arm. Phil, Americanized from 'Felipe', made it himself from a recipe his Nana gave to him. Anyone who finished it, got a free shot of tequila, served straight up or over ice. Most of the winners of mind over stomach took it over ice because their insides were already on fire. Nana's secret recipe for the chorizo not only included a shovel full of paprika and chili powder, but a shot of hot mustard melted in a cup of tequila—hence, the tequila as a reward.

Phil Moreno was a thick man. Everything about him was thick—his chest, his arms, his hands. His young, powerful physique had given way to comfort weight. His neck was so thick it disappeared, causing his ears to rest on his shoulders. He had been a cop for thirty years and finally retired at seventy-five percent of his last salary.

"You know," Cooper started in one day when they met for lunch right after Moreno retired. He remembered they were sitting on the bench in front of the bar before he owned it. "You've done all the retirement things one does when they first pull the pin. You and Sonya, took a cruise to the Mexican coast to see 'your ancestors.' Your wife told anyone, and I mean *anyone* who asked, even though you, my friend, truly think your ancestors were from Europe."

"So? She is proud of our heritage."

Cooper continued. "You tried to play golf, bocce ball, and racquetball at the Y. You took a cooking class at the community college, a painting class at the community college; you even took a class on Medieval

24

Chinese History at the community college. Now, you are about two years into this retirement when you found out the old Do Drop In Bar was for sale."

"Sonya has said I always wanted to own a place like this," Moreno nodded toward the burned out wreck behind him.

"A restaurant, not a bar," Cooper said, pointing to the sign.

"What's the difference? You're going to serve liquor at the restaurant or food at the bar," Moreno said to him.

"You have married a smart woman my friend," Cooper said to him. Cooper knew for years Moreno had wanted to own his own restaurant, but when Cooper told him most restaurants failed in their first eighteen months, and that bars, especially low-overhead bars tending to the working class were cash cows, Moreno's eyebrows went up. "I can serve all the food I ever want to serve at the bar, plus have the cash cow."

"Do I drink for free?" Cooper asked with a look of seriousness.

"No, you have to pay double. A gringo in my bar—all of you have to pay double."

"Figures."

The Do Drop In was a piece-of-garbage watering hole that had been occupied by at least two different biker clubs before Phil got to it. It burned down during the second occupation from a meth lab that was concealed in the back room next to the industrial refrigerator. The same refrigerator where the police found body parts during a search warrant on the bar when the first motorcycle gang occupied it. When the meth lab fire was extinguished, and the fire investigators continued searching the site for point of origin, there was the refrigerator. When they opened the large, stainless steel door, they found another body. This body was missing major parts, as well as the head. When it became available, Moreno took this as a sign, a sign from God that he was to own a bar, not just any bar—this bar. It sat empty for almost two years before the owner, presumably the bank, put it up for sale to rid itself of the liability.

"I found it," Moreno said, during their lunch on the bench.

"Found what?" Cooper responded.

"A bar, er, restaurant."

"Thank god. Maybe now you'll move on."

"Move on?"

"Your wife."

"What about her?"

"Tell me she did not gently take your face in her hands and politely and lovingly tell you that you were driving her crazy? I have heard her tell you 'Go, enjoy your toy.' Do you remember her hands? They were folded, like she was praying."

"It's going to take some work, and some paint," Moreno said.

"That's nice. Don't expect me to help, unless I drink for free."

"And some drywall."

"Why?"

"It kind of burned—in a fire."

"Jeezus, which bar?"

Moreno grinned. "The one behind us. We're sitting in front of the future site of 'Moreno's Bar'!"

Cooper looked, rolled his eyes. "Holy mother of god."

"I know, isn't it great?" Moreno said and smiled.

Cooper remembered the bar and the fires. There was something in the fire, the act of the fire itself that perked his interest. It didn't destroy the

26

building, although there were sections wiped out. He read the article about the fire over and over again. He clipped the articles and eventually gave them to Moreno. He looked at the black-and-white picture of it in the paper, a fire investigator holding open the refrigerator door, another photo showing the inside of the empty refrigerator. It was as if the fires had cleansed the place of its evil, and it was appropriate that Moreno, once one of the good guys, own what once was a tabernacle to all that was evil in the world.

Cooper knew, Sonya couldn't have agreed with him more. Frankly, he knew that if his friend had asked to be the lead Prima for *Swan Lake*, dressed in a tutu and prancing around in front of throngs of thousands, she would have said 'by all means.' He was under foot. Since he had retired, he had dragged her across the world and back. Cooper knew he needed something to pour his life into again. His wife, Cooper knew, needed him to pour his life into something again.

The price was right. He spent the next year fixing it up with the help of his off-duty friends from both the PD and the fire department.

Moreno's Bar opened on November 11, Veteran's Day, an appropriate day for a bar like this. It was the ideal design and finish to a building originally the site of many years of pain. "Yeah did good Phil," Cooper said fingering a low ball of scotch on opening day. "This place use to be a piece of crap. Now it's a place for good scotch, cold beer, and comfort food served to people sitting on red tufted seats at polished wooden tables. If I didn't know better, I'd think your were gay," he said tipping his drink. Moreno smiled. There, in the corner of the bar, was the refrigerator. Moreno found new glass doors for it and at a second-hand restaurant supply store, he found a lighted

Guinness Beer sign that he put on top. Now the symbol of death was the symbol of the bar, holding all the Guinness Moreno's Bar served. It too, had been reborn.

"I like this place because I can walk here," Cooper slurred one night. Moreno's place was just a few blocks off Central Avenue and was located in a strip center that used to be a dope-infested cesspool until the Gang Unit concentrated on it for about a month. The city fathers decided to deem the surrounding neighborhood, 'historic', as part of their redevelopment plan, right after The Do Drop In burned down. Now, the strip center was a pleasant place that good people could go get their groceries, fill up their bottled-water jugs, and buy nice shoes.

Cooper showed up after work at about the same time, five days a week. The bar itself was long, about thirty feet, and it made a turn at the end for another six feet. The dark wood shined from years of polish and reflected in the mirror behind the bottles of liquor on the back wall of the bar. Cooper would sit at the end of the bar, just as it made the turn. It gave him the best view of one of the two televisions.

One television dangled over the pool table at the other end of the bar from where Cooper always sat. The one he watched was tucked up in the corner, right in front of him and angled back toward the length of the bar. If he was working the swing shift, which he usually did, he got to Moreno's around eleven. If anyone was sitting on Cooper's stool, Moreno would make them move. There were many regulars, each had their own habits and Moreno allowed that. When he could, he would honor those customs and patron seniority by moving people who did not have that seniority. There was a pecking order, and people would follow it or be told to leave.

"Hey, you old bastard," Cooper called to Moreno as he entered and made his way to his stool.

"Who you callin' 'old'?" Moreno said and came back with a Glenlevit in a low-ball and placed it in front of Cooper on a napkin. Moreno looked at his watch. It was nearly eleven. He picked up the T.V. remote and changed to a cable channel that broadcast old television shows. The "Burns and Allen Show" with a young George Burns and Gracie Allen was one of Cooper's addictions. He'd watch it with the intensity of a child watching their favorite kid show. Moreno knew Cooper, for whatever reason, liked the old black-and-white show. Cooper watched it whenever it was on, and at the end of every show, he always mouthed the words along with George Burns. "Say goodnight, Gracie." After the show, Moreno changed the channel or turned it off, depending on the time of night; He knew Cooper was done with it.

Cooper would have another double and either a platter of nachos or chicken wings, or one of Fernando's rib-eye steaks and a baked potato the size a of ten-year-old boy's foot, complete with a half stick of butter and sour cream, or any other combination of food groups consisting of starches, fats, and protein.

"What am I feeding you tonight, amigo?" Moreno asked.

"You got anymore of that horse meat?"

"I think I have some from last week, yeah," Moreno said as he poured some ice in a drink for a customer.

"Nachos, I think, with Fernando's deep-fried chicken," Cooper said taking a sip of his drink.

"One order of nachos with last night's cock-fighting loser," Moreno said. "What's going on with tonight's show?" Moreno asked, thumbing toward the television.

"I don't know. It just started."

"That Gracie, she's a pretty *mamacita.*"

"Careful, don't you be talking about her that way," Cooper said. "She's not 'hot,' she's pure, lovely, sweet, all American, and a virgin."

"Aren't those two married?"

"Yeah, so?"

"How can she be a virgin if she's married?"

"Come on, this is the fifties. No one of any value had sex in the fifties. I bet she never took her clothes off in front of George—ever."

"How disappointing," Moreno smiled and walked back to the kitchen.

"Ah, those were gentler times. All of our sins, like equal rights, domestic violence, and the homeless were all underground. It wasn't polite to talk about. Nope, sex was repressed and saved for Columbus Day and New Year's Eve. That seemed fair. Life was easy then. Yep, you let Pandora's Box stay open, crap's going to leak out all over your shoes," Cooper said to Moreno's back as he took another sip of his scotch.

Every night, he watched the show and sipped his scotch. Moreno returned with his food and laid out a cloth napkin in a triangle shape in front of Cooper, a technique he saw at another restaurant and thought it would be classy to serve food in such a manner; he placed the nachos on it. When the show was near the end, George and Gracie came on stage and bantered back and forth. Whatever Cooper was doing at the time, eating or drinking, he would stop and listen until George and Gracie gave the famous sign-off line. Moreno, without words, would come down and use the remote to flip it back to ESPN.

"You want to know what your problem is, my friend?" Moreno started in after Cooper and refreshed his drink for the third time.

"You not pouring my drink to the rim of the glass *is* my problem." Cooper said hunched over his food. "You not keeping the toilet paper holder filled in the men's room. You not reminding Fernando, your cook back there, that I take my steak medium rare! Now, you'll probably tell him and he'll under-cook my chicken and I'll have stomach cramps for three days and won't be able to walk five feet away from the toilet. You'd think after these many years of me coming in here, he'd quit either burning it or serving it raw. The hemorrhoid issues I've been having since I've been eating Fernando's food? Any of those problems match your list of problems I have?" Cooper said with a grin as he stared into his glass.

Moreno smiled. "No, my friend, none, and frankly, there is nothing wrong with Fernando's steaks. No, your problem is you have ghosts in the attic," he said tapping his own head. "You were a hotshot pilot in Vietnam and you're an even better one now as an old white dude. When you are in your ship, flying over the city, lending air support and flying like some crazy person, landing and jumping out to help some officer just so you can lay hands on some piece of slug crap and then taking off into the wild blue like Buck Rogers, people know; there is no one like you. You flying high cover for them is like having their own guardian angel who is just as likely to come down and slap the shit out of them for being dumb as you would slap the shit out of some scrote-bag."

"You say that like there's something bad about it."

"I ain't done. I was just catching my breath."

"Oh, sorry; please continue singing my anthem," Cooper said as he dipped his finger in the glass of scotch and pulled a hair out of it. He looked at it and flicked it on the ground after frowning at Moreno. He then drank a hit from the glass.

"You'd fly in and out of power lines, trees; hell, you flew into a tunnel once. You would go where other men didn't think to go. Some people, myself one of them," Moreno held the bar towel he was using to wipe down that end of the bar, and placed it over his heart as if he was making a pledge. "That music, oh. When you come up on a scene that's active and required a little music, that ship and the job, they are a part of you."

"Hey, I.A. cleared me of that. A few neighbors of this big piece of work the ground units were hooking up started to get out of hand with some other friends and family complaining I had rock music while I flew over their house. Come on, why would I do that?"

"I ain't done."

"Jeezus, Mary, and Joseph."

Moreno continued, "You push the ship, your co-pilot, and yourself to the limit. Some of the crap you do, you ain't even suppose to be able to do. You still doing loops?"

"I've never done a loop."

"Uh-huh, you lying bastard. You know, McDonnell-Douglas really doesn't condone what you say you don't do." Moreno looked at him again. "You know, amigo, on gratefully rare occasions when officers found themselves trapped and ground backups were minutes off, there were rumors they could hear music coming from the sky. They are mostly too young to even know the song—what is it? Oh, yeah, '*Born to be Wild.*' They don't care about that, bein' too busy getting shot at, beat, spit on or some other violation of their life. They just wanted air cover to light the night and chase the demons away—for good."

Cooper looked into his glass. Moreno had moved away from him and couldn't hear him say to himself. "They don't know what I know."

"You will kill yourself, or worse yet, someone else who's trapped with you in your death wish," Moreno called back to him from the other end of the bar. "You still chew those pilots up. No one wants to go the distance with you because they think you will get them killed. Frankly, they're right. Flying under power lines or into tunnels or doing loops will get them killed or worse, sooner or later."

"What could be worse than dead?"

"Not dead and crapping in a diaper for the rest of your life."

Cooper looked into his empty glass. "You done?"

"Yeah, you old bastard. I'm done—for right now."

"That's all I live for, the right now. So, if you're finished chewing on my ass, pour some more of that good stuff in this glass. The glass is lonely."

By one or one-thirty on most nights, Cooper would get up from his seat, pay his bill and leave the same way he came in. He would walk home, enter through the front door, place the keys back in the brass ashtray, and wander back to the bedroom. He'd strip to his white boxers and t-shirt, go into the bathroom and throw his dirty clothes on the pile, brush his teeth before shuffling back to bed. He kept Plato's *Republic*, and a pair of reading glasses on his nightstand. He would lie in bed and read a page or two from wherever he left off the night before. After a couple of pages, he slid the book back on the table and the glasses on top of it and flipped off the light.

The next day, he would do it all over again.

CHAPTER FOUR
*The perfect bureaucrat everywhere is the man who
manages to make no decisions and escape all
responsibility.*
—Brooks Atkinson

November, 1991

"I love you," Joe said.

"I love you too," Jodi said back while looking away, throwing a soft smile in his direction. She was going to dread this night, she just knew it. It was going to be like the others.

Jodi Hawkins eventually grew up and married Joe Campbell. She lived with her aunt until college and the intense therapy she received as a child for what she witnessed seemed to calm her mind. The one noticeable, lingering symptom was the establishment of security through wealth, at least to the degree of immediate comfort. It was a deciding factor in her career, personal life, and marriage. Her life needed order and her husband helped provide that.

It was this that drew her to Joe. Early in their dating, just about the same point as always, when Jodi would get cold feet and torpedo the relationship, thinking it was better to be alone then to travel down the past again, Joe changed her mind.

On this night, early in their dating, he took her to the Capital Grille at the Biltmore. The dining room had large semi-circle booths with buttoned leather. In the booth next to them was another couple. They were arguing. Joe noticed Jodi almost crawl into a make-believe shell. He could tell their arguing, although low in volume, stung her. She had tap-danced around her parents' death with him, avoiding the details that only she knew about and never shared, but it didn't take a doctor of psychology to figure it out and make the connection.

"You know, my parents did that," he said looking at his steak while he cut it.

"What?" she said as if waking from a dream.

"What that couple is doing. Dad would accent it with a slap or two, especially if he drank, until mom and the county sheriff made him leave."

She began to stir her potato with her fork. She was distracted. The voices caused her to go back in time. This was her fear. It wove its way into every relationship she ever had and eventually choked the life out of it before it had a chance to bloom. She feared it was here—again.

"What's wrong?" he asked.

She took a deep breath. *God, I hate this.* This very issue Joe had, she was sure would seal it. Her past destroyed every relationship she ever had. "You know, there is a tendency that children take on the character traits of their parents like that."

He nodded in agreement. "That is true, but not me," Joe casually took a bite of his steak as if there wasn't a care he had in the world.

She looked up. "Why can you be so sure?"

He smiled. "The key to that *co-dependency* trait you are talking about and yes, I have looked into it, obviously, is awareness. I'm aware of that trait. It is never really far from my brain. I've even been through therapy on it—lots of therapy. But there is something else to help set your mind at ease about me."

She looked at him, waiting for the answer.

"First, I love you and would chew off my arm before I hurt you—in any way."

She looked away.

"But, there is something else."

She looked back.

Do you see a drink in my hand?"

It took a second for what he said to register with her. Jodi looked at the table and remembered he only ever drank tea around her. She looked back into his eyes.

He was smiling.

Years later in their marriage, he would still check with her.

"Are you happy?" Joe would sometimes ask her, usually whenever she was staring out of the car window while they were driving somewhere after they got married.

"Uh-huh," she would say, followed by a smile.

They were part of the young professional world of educated, sometimes highly educated, people who were starting careers and families. They could drive the nice cars and live in the new high-rise condos the city was pulling out of the ground or own a home in the choicer neighborhoods. They didn't drink coffee; they had fresh-squeezed juices and green tea. When they did want a coffee product, it was never one they made themselves but from the ubiquitous coffee retailers around town. They ate salads as entrees, and when they felt like slumming with the rest of society, they would go see the Phoenix Suns play basketball wearing their designer shirts with the collars pulled up.

"Honey, we have to be at the party by seven tonight," Jodi said from down the hall as she got ready for work. She was brushing her long, long hair. She stopped and reached down and adjusted the three small ceramic jars on her counter which held some of her makeup and cotton balls. They were slightly out of alignment.

Both were civil engineers in their own small firm and specialized in general site development as well as road and freeway development. Her training was in grading and excavation of large sites and he was the 'gutter pan' guy, who made streets and curbs match and look like, well, streets and curbs.

"I know, I know. The meeting with the city council should be over by then. We have the whole zoning issue on the PADD Project to redo."

Jodi stuck her head out from around the corner and looked down the empty hall. "I thought we took care of that."

Joe looked out from the hall bathroom as he adjusted his new Jerry Garcia tie Jodi had bought him from Neiman Marcus for his birthday. "We did. But one of the new advisors to the mayor wanted another look. It shouldn't be a big deal, but we have to keep the politicos happy, and at the same time, put it to bed or the project is going to be off track. Are you going to get to the gym today before the party?"

"Of course. You know I get grumpy if I don't get in my Pilates," she said as she put on her earrings and single strand of cultured pearls that matched her creamy white linen blouse. "Besides, I put on two pounds since our trip to Cancun and I want to make sure it's wiped off the map."

"Good idea," he said. "Hey, a package came for you yesterday. Did you get it?"

"Yes, thank you."

"More of that shampoo from Paris?"

"Yeeeees."

"I will never understand why you have to order your shampoo from Europe," Joe said.

"Nope, you probably never will," she said in a hushed tone.

They traveled and played all across North America and parts of Europe. If they could predict a finer life, they would struggle to think of one. Jodi was safe. She was happy and safe. Joe liked her hair long and she was happy to supply it.

Ten years later, people still couldn't tell Jodi was thirty-six, and Joe, or 'Joey' to his friends, at thirty-nine had seventeen percent body fat, on a six-three frame. They had his-and-hers stationary bikes and Joe would often hop on the bike after his morning run, getting in a couple of miles with his wife as he watched the stock report.

"You want some more tea?" he asked Jodi before he climbed on his bike. The sun from the skylight filled the room with natural light. The Boston ferns in the corner loved it. The 52-inch plasma flat screen in the corner had CNN on talking more about the war.

She looked into her glass in its holder on the handle bars and saw she still had some. 'No, I'm fine." She then stood up while she peddled.

They found time in their schedules to have a baby they named Anthony. He was a Christmas Day baby and along with everything else the Campbell's had, this was a perceived blessing, anointing to their lives. They painted the third room of their home light blue and forest green and trimmed it in six-inch-wide crown molding. They hired a muralist to paint ducks and geese on the walls, and an Elmer Fudd doll sat in his crib and then later in his "big boy" bed.

By the time he was ten, Anthony was making straight A's at Phoenix Country Day School; a school whose tuition outstripped most total household incomes. They were the epitome of the twenty-first century urban family: a dual career, success, and knowing and being known.

Holy Ground

"Did you send the thank-you letter to the mayor?" Joe asked as he navigated the Land Cruiser through the Biltmore Hotel where they went for their traditional Sunday brunch with some of their friends.

"Way ahead of you. I took care of it last week." Jodi said as she peered into the drop-down mirror on the sun visor. "Did you tell the nanny we'd be back after brunch?"

"Did it."

"You're sweet," she said as she pursed her lips and then closed the mirror.

"Of course I am," he said.

Their assets were tied up in their business, their mortgage, car payments, and vacation deposits. As part of their contracts with the cities they worked for, they would include family insurance, 401K funding, and other traditional employee residual earnings as part of their employment packages. They were paid handsomely and the extra benefits were set aside for those rainy days, a prediction that was never given its true time of day. After all, they were doing so well, living such a happy life. They told their financial planner to invest even more.

That was until the head-on car crash with a city trash truck killed Joe and eventually, their son.

39

CHAPTER FIVE
*Be courteous to all, but intimate with few, and let those
few be well tried before you give them your confidence.
True friendship is a plant of slow growth, and must
undergo and withstand the shocks of adversity before it is
entitled to the appellation.*
—George Washington

August 2003

Cooper had been flying the MD-500 since
McDonnell-Douglas first produced it for
civilian work.

There were even rumors that, on occasion, the
MD-500 did loops, but totally against the protocol of
the aircraft designer and just general safe flying rules.
It wasn't done a lot, and no one, including Internal
Affairs could ever prove he did loops. His co-pilots
never gave him up; they just put in for a transfer. It
was fine with him. It got harder and harder breaking in
'newbies'. They were young, at least younger than
Cooper, most by a full generation. Even though they
were qualified, they never measured up to Officer
Gardner's *standards*. He wished he could fly the ship
alone. The older he got, the more removed he found
himself from other cops. A newbie had just transferred
out last week. Cooper figured this week would bring a
new one. He was right.

"Gardner, I need to see you for a moment," his
sergeant said as Cooper passed by his office. He
stopped mid stride, let out a heavy sigh and turned and
walked in.

"What's up, Sarge?"

Ben Sargelli was the shift sergeant. He was
about fifteen years Cooper's junior and a graduate of
the university; an educated man on the fast track for

rank. Cooper had bothered him, with his attitude and ancient ways, for as long as he could remember.

"You're breaking in Jackson, starting today."

"Jesus, Sergeant, I just got done with one last week. He didn't make it and now we're throwing another weak link into the batter?"

"Close the door," Sargelli said. He waited until Cooper turned back around. "Look, Cooper. These pilots are complaining about you. They're saying you're not safe—"

"What the hell they talking about? Most of these tweaks don't even shave yet."

"Listen, officer," sergeant said. "You will train this pilot I am giving you. You will not abuse him. You will not berate him. I want to make this perfectly clear, Officer Gardner: If I get one more complaint about the way you fly, the way you teach, the way you sneeze, I will transfer you to Evidence where you will live out your days in the basement, handing out old blood evidence samples to detectives young enough to be your grandchildren. You want to play with this, Cooper? I have had it covering for you."

"You can't threaten me. I'll talk to my rep—"

"I already did, Officer Cooper. Want to know what your union representative said?"

"Yeah, yeah, what did he tell you?"

"Let me quote him." Sargelli cleared his throat and picked up a piece of paper as if he was going to read it. "'It's about time.'" Sargelli tossed the paper back on his desk. "Now you have heard it straight from the source. You screw this one up, Cooper, you are through. No more. Do we understand each other? You train them and turn them loose. We aren't flying bush in the jungle anymore. We're in the big city with big politicians who—and I agree with—see you ancient dinosaurs, and those like you, as a liability to this city.

You either fix it or I will. That is all." The sergeant went back to his desk and began reading a folder. He was done with the conversation; all Cooper could do was leave.

The week before Cooper's conversation with his sergeant about the new co-pilot, his trainee was getting the word of his own transfer.

"Jackson, starting next week you're flying with Cooper Gardner," his patrol sergeant said in passing as he walked by his office door.

Paul backed up and stood in the door. "Cooper?" He repeated back to make sure he heard right.

"Yeah," his sergeant said.

"Next week?"

"That's what I said. You wanted air duty so here it is."

Paul nodded and started to walk on.

"Jackson, come back here."

"Yes, Sergeant?"

"Don't you want to know why?"

"'Why' what, Sergeant?"

"Why I put you with Cooper."

"I'm sure you have your reasons."

"Yes, I do."

"Is there anything I could say to make you change your mind?"

"No, probably not."

"Is it a black thing?"

"A what?"

"A black thing, you know, you putting me with him because the LT or the Chief or someone has some Oreo thing?"

"No."

"Are you doing it because he's an old man, worn hard? You putting me with him because he needs some dressing up with some good-looking cop like me?"

"You ain't good-looking," Sergeant said, sitting back in his chair while Jackson stood in the door frame.

"Now, that hurt. You putting me with him so I could give him some tips on flying or stock tips? So when his ugly, ancient ass retires, he won't be living with you in the spare bedroom in your converted garage?"

"You wish you had half his flying skills. As far as him living with me, I got a carport."

"Well then, no, I don't have any questions."

"Get your ass out of my office."

"Aye, aye, sir."

CHAPTER SIX
You got to ask yourself, do ya feel lucky? Well, do ya—
punk?
—Dirty Harry

———————————

Paul Jackson was about the same height as Cooper, but nineteen years his junior and as black as Cooper was white. He came from a family of eight, growing up in the bayou country just west of central New Orleans in an area between Kenner and Rivertown. When anyone asked he liked to say "I'm from da- Bay-u." The family instilled value and God in each of their children, and failure by quitting, was not an option.

He ended up spending eight years in the Navy, five of those years flying Sea Stallion helicopters for Navy Seals black operations in parts of the world most people never knew about and could never find on a map. When he got out, he didn't want to go back to Louisiana. He wanted to go where it was dry and warm, somewhere he didn't have to check the front porch for snakes before he went out to get the paper. Phoenix was where he met his wife, Doris.

They met at the grocery store, on aisle ten, both looking for cereal. "Excuse me," she started the conversation. "But could you reach that box?"

"This one?" he said, distracted from his list of things that he always forgot to get at the store.

"Yes, thank you," the small framed woman said with a coy smile. Doris was a pharmacological representative for a major drug company with a dual degree in chemistry and microbiology. Paul Jackson, sworn bachelor and devoted lover of many women, fell in love in a food aisle across from the cheese in a spray can and just down from the salted pork.

Paul was an easy going man. The fact that Cooper was almost twenty years his senior didn't disturb him. The only thing that bothered Paul was the attitude. So, when he found out he was going to be flying with the old man, he snickered. It was going to be just a walk in the park.

Paul couldn't decide if it was the luck of the draw he'd gotten to ride with Cooper for the last four days, he wondered to himself as they flew from one end of the city to the other, answering calls. The unit was working four tens so Tuesdays were the team's Friday. Other than work-related conversation, they hadn't said more than a dozen words to each other the entire time; almost all of them spoken by Paul. He had heard the guy was not a big conversationalist, yet he still expected more. That was actually all right with him. He had also heard Cooper was a real ball-buster. He would chew on pilots just for fun. Paul was expecting that and was prepared for it. What he wasn't prepared for was the silence.

The second week flying together started about the same; no words other than communication about the job. They didn't even talk about the radio traffic as most pilots would. A hot tone would sound and Cooper turned the ship in that direction. Paul gave up after the first couple of days; he had tried to start conversations and break the dead silence by using the events they were listening to on the radio as a conversation starter. Cooper either ignored him or answered in one or two-word grunts. But it was a new week. Paul had spent the time with Doris and so he was feeling good about himself and his life. She always made him feel better. He'd try to engage his partner again—one more time. *What did he have to lose? This will be fun, trying to drag the old son-of-a-bitch out of his crusty old shell.* "So, how long have you been with the police de—" Paul started as he looked out the Plexiglas.

"Coming up on thirty-three years," Cooper said with an obvious sigh, as if he had been asked that for years.

"Thirty-three years, huh?" Paul repeated.

"Yep."

Paul took a long breath. This was going to be harder than even he imagined.

"How long have you been fly—" Paul began to ask.

"About twenty-seven years, on and off."

"... flying—twenty—"

"Seven."

"Seven," Paul sighed. He smiled. "You were flying when I was in sixth grade." Cooper didn't say a word. "Is there something wrong? Did I do something wrong, something to piss you off?" Paul asked.

Cooper looked over at his co-pilot with a somewhat surprised look on his face. "Yeah. You're alive." Cooper paused. "No, why?"

"Well, you're acting like you're mad at me or something. I didn't make this assignment. The sergeant wanted you to check me out in this thing. I didn't ask you to do it."

"You just got lucky, huh?" Cooper said with a frown.

"Yeah, I guess this is my lucky week," he said as he looked back out the window adjusting the radio volume in his headset. Time went by again in silence. Paul was surprised when Cooper started to talk.

"Look, it's nothing against you. I'm sure you're a good cop and all the other fraternity B.S.. But up here there is no forgiveness. I've trained every pilot the city has had in the last twenty-one years. I've flown every piece of equipment this city and every other city our size has, and it isn't getting any easier. My sergeant said I need to be nicer to the officers I train. I'm too mean, too reckless. I'm a 'danger' to society."

"Yeah, I've heard all about it," Paul said. "You're an asshole."

"They keep sending me children that—"

"I'm not a child."

Cooper rolled his eyes as if he got caught saying something he shouldn't have. "—can't find their own asses when they're sitting on it—"

"I know where my ass is."

"—and don't give a shit about the job anymore. The cops today aren't like the cops from before most of your class was born. The job still meant something. A lot of the officers today are afraid to get water on their web gear or be the first one into a bar fight. They don't want to get their mug busted up because they're afraid they're going to get knocked back on their pockets."

"Or maybe because they'll get their asses sued. God, this is going to be a long night."

"Hey, you brought it up."

"I did not. I just asked you how long you've been doing this. You're the one who got all ramped up like a parking garage." Paul shook his head. "Look, I was just asking to try to get a little conversation going. You know, you have a jacket of being a real asshole. Has anyone ever told you that?"

"Yeah, I've heard that. You just told me twice. No one ever told me directly though, other than my sergeant."

"Just my luck—well?"

"Well, what?" Cooper said looking over at his co-pilot.

"Did you listen to him? Do you want to go through life being likened to Attila the Friggin Hun?"

Cooper was silent for a minute. "I'm that bad? I thought I'd been pretty nice."

"No," he said shaking his head. "You have an earned reputation of being a real shithead. Like elephantiasis-sized shithead. I think you would be surprised where your pilots came from. You never let them stay long enough to find out, did you?" Paul said looking out the window again. The radio traffic was quiet. There were no distractions other than flying the aircraft and looking at the city lights.

"So, you're from Louisiana?"

Paul nodded.

"What happened to your accent?"

"What?"

"Your accent? You don't have an accent. I thought everyone from the south had an accent."

"I had mine surgically removed."

"I didn't know you could do that," Cooper said while he looked out his side window while initiating a turn. There were a few minutes that passed before he spoke again. "So, where did you learn to fly?"

"What?"

"I asked, 'where did you learn to fly?'"

Paul was somewhat taken aback by Cooper's tone. It was friendly, or at least maybe it was Cooper's attempt at being friendly "I, ah, learned probably with the same company you did, only mine was the Navy.

Cooper snorted. "Too bad."

"I did my share of roof jumping. Give me the stick and I'll show ya."

Cooper snorted again. "No thanks."

CHAPTER SEVEN
Friends may come and go, but enemies accumulate.
—Thomas Jones

———————

The world that stayed outside the upper-class home and the iconic schools and lifestyle rolled into the Campbell's lives like a tsunami wave. It literally consumed two-thirds of the family and threw the third member into a world that was only seen in movie dramas. Jodi had no real adult experience in this world. In a matter of seconds, her family was all but destroyed. Their ideal world of peace and prosperity and the American Dream was crushed, never to recover. Her past was back.

Jodi arrived at the hospital after she got the call from the police. She went alone, not thinking of calling anyone or even telling anyone where she was. She was only told by the police officer on the other end of the line that her husband and son had been in an accident.

"I'm Jodi Campbell. My husband and son were in a car accident and were brought here," she said to the receptionist. Her hand shook as it held her car keys.

The receptionist picked up the phone, dialed four numbers and then waited. She softly told whoever she called, "Jodi Campbell is here."

A few minutes later a doctor and a nurse in light blue surgical scrubs came out to the waiting area.

"Hello, Mrs. Campbell?" the thirty-something doctor said as he reached out to offer his hand.

"Yes, I'm Jodi. How are my husband and son?"

"I'm Dr. Stredson, this is Nancy Turley, my nurse. Come, let's go sit down and I will fill you in," he said as he finished shaking her cold, clammy hand. Instead of sitting in the waiting area, he directed her to a corner room with a door and two couches. There was a door on the other side of the room.

Once they were inside the room, the doctor waited until the door was shut before he spoke. "I'm going to speak frankly, Mrs. Campbell. Your husband and son were in a car accident with a very large, and very fast moving city trash truck." He took a deep breath before he continued. "I'm sorry to say Joe died instantly. Anthony is alive and we have him in intensive care. Even though it appears he was belted in, he was seriously injured." The doctor was kind and left out the details about Anthony being thrown forward and hitting the collapsing dashboard, shoving the airbag into his head, along with the dashboard and engine compartment. The wreck was so violent the airbag wasn't of much use.

As he finished, Nancy had moved to Jodi's side and put her arm around her shoulder while the doctor continued. "Your son, in addition to the trauma of the accident, has some severe brain injuries. The next few hours are going to be critical."

Jodi's knees began to give out as she reached up to her face as she listened. She felt like she was in a well; the final words from the doctor saying "We are not confident he will live until morning." Nancy caught her and directed Jodi to one of the couches.

Anthony didn't die right away. He lingered for months.

She took another blow to her psyche when she had the first conversation with the investigating detective, Charlie Roven, and he told her what had happened. "The trash truck was full and at its maximum weight. What your husband and the rest of the drivers on the road that day didn't know was the truck was being driven by a tweaker named Jerome

Glulitte who was out from Chicago after serving time for a series of robberies of small markets."

The detective filled her in on his background. He wanted a fresh start and warmer weather. So, Jerome moved to Phoenix, got high and stayed there. Somehow, he landed a job with the city and in the post-accident interview, after he floated down from receiving two milligrams of Narcan from the emergency room physician to counter the drugs in his body. He then talked to the accident investigators. It surprised the detective that after he read Jerome his rights, he was willing to talk.

"So, you want to tell me what happened, Jerome?" the detective asked, sitting across from him in the county hospital room where Jerome was taken. The bed was in the jail wing.

"I was in an accident."

"We know that, Jerome. Why were you in an accident?"

"I was, ah, a little high. I thought I hit the mother lode and could fence the truck for enough dope for a lifetime." As he thought about it, he hadn't quite worked out the details of fencing a truck he was assigned to as a work vehicle.

"Did you see the police cars behind you?"

"No, were there police cars behind me?" he said with a sarcastic smile. "Apparently, I must have failed to consider the ten police vehicles and a helicopter that circled me as I sped through the city streets, bouncing off of one car and then another as I made my way through the city." He smiled again.

"It does not appear to me you give a shit about the people you've injured or killed today," The detective said. He moved the tape recorder that he had placed on the table a little closer to Jerome's bed.

"Nope, I would say your observations are just about right."

"Maybe when we charge you with murder, then, maybe you'll care."

Jerome rotated in his bed, looking the opposite way from the detective. "Nope, probably not."

One of the drivers involved in the accident managed to use his cell phone to call nine-one-one and the chase was on, although it wasn't much of a chase. Jerome wasn't much of a driver. He rounded the corner at Camelback and Central and took it wide, unable to control the turn at the speed he was driving. It took him right into the face of the Campbell's car.

Jodi's pain only got worse with the bureaucratic nightmare that continued for months.

"The news isn't good, Jodi," her lawyer told her, after he came out of the city hall, human resources hearing room. "The City denied all claims. They said it wasn't their fault, it was the driver. They denied any responsibility. Of course, we thought they would."

Jodi was numb. She looked at him as if he was speaking a foreign language. "There's something else," he said. He swallowed and shook his head as if he couldn't believe it himself.

"What?" was all she could say.

"Apparently Jerome was so high he didn't feel the impact of being thrown through the front window of the truck and landing on what was left of the hood of your husband's SUV before rolling off and onto the asphalt. He was actually able to get up and begin to run as if he hadn't just gone through all that. His face and arms were cut and he was bleeding profusely, but he was able to maintain his pace for a block until arriving officers cut him off with their cars. He flew over the hood of one, landing on the street again, when the officers got out of their cars and hit him with their Tasers."

"So?" she said. She felt a sickness in the pit of her stomach. The cramping was working its way up to her skull.

He sighed before he spoke. "Apparently, he is suing—he is claiming his seat belt in his company truck didn't hold him in and the officers used excessive force to subdue him."

"Like I said, so?"

"I am getting a sense from the city's lawyer they will settle with him."

Jodi couldn't think. She was tired. She had been dealing with this nightmare for months and now it was taking a macabre twist. "Wait. They won't pay for our expenses. The insurance won't cover because someone else should be paying, and that someone, the city, says they won't pay, but they will pay the guy who started the whole thing? Do I have this right?" Her voice broke.

"I'm sorry, Jodi, but that's just about right. Look, I'll keep working on it, but it doesn't look good." He left her there, alone in the hall. She turned to leave, her legs like iron, barely able to move. She bumped hard into someone.

"Watch it, lady," came a voice to her right. Jodi looked up. It was a police officer. She couldn't respond. It was just another slap, one she didn't expect and couldn't respond through her numbness.

It was Cooper.

He had been subpoenaed on an old case. Their court rooms were next to each other. He kept moving down the hall shaking his head about the ditzy woman standing in the middle of the hall, blocking his way.

Jodi never had time to grieve. Anthony was taken to a rehab center for the first six months after the accident; after his life looked like it wasn't going to get any better and whatever insurance was left was running out, they sent him home. There was nothing more the staff could do that couldn't be done at home. Anthony's care absorbed her. Home care was not covered by insurance and it drained their financial resources quickly. Business fell as well; income fell, resources fell. The world was free-falling with no ground in sight. The city that supplied them with their lives, she felt, was responsible for taking it away.

Anthony eventually died, drowning in the fluid that filled his own lungs. They rushed him back to the hospital but the outcome was expected. Jodi felt guilt as she sat there holding his hand, praying for his death, and at the same time, wishing he would live.

Within three months of him coming home, almost a year after the accident, Anthony Campbell, a day from his eleventh birthday, died of pneumonia. Jodi's fears turned to anger and then to hatred. Everyone seemed to have forsaken her and her family. As every day passed, she thought the entire city should be there, in her nightmare, taking the place of her husband and son.

Jodi got word that Jerome pleaded guilty to the lesser crime of driving under the influence instead of vehicular manslaughter. He would be out of jail in two and a half years.

No one knew her heart was screaming before its emotional death. It was her childhood again— insecurity of losing a mother and father and the loss of safety it brought. Even through the fights, there was still the safety of a home, shelter, food, only now it was her own life. The bottom had fallen—again. The nightmares came back, only this time she was awake when they arrived. She found herself in the bathroom, staring into the mirror. She looked down and straightened the jars. Then, she looked back to the mirror, deep into the mirror.

"Mommy?" She remembered the call to her mother.

Her mother turned to her, holding the scissors. There was red on them and on her mother's hands, trailing up her arm and dripping from her elbow. Hair her mother had cut from her own head, was sticking to the liquid on the scissors.

"Come here to mother," she remembered her mother saying. "Come here to Mommy."

Jodi's hands were clammy as she remembered. The images were back. The smell and feelings were back. She could feel the cold tile of the counter as her mother lifted her and placed her on the counter. "Mommy is going to cut your hair like Mommy's." She could smell the stench of day-old booze and sweat. "Mommy is going to cut your hair."

She couldn't remember if she struggled, but remembered a pulling on her head, the roughness of the scissors, of her mother's hands holding her hair. Then—there, through the open bathroom door, she could see her father's side of the bed. The white sheets were red. A lone arm hung out from the side and there was a dark liquid running down it and dripping on the floor, forming a puddle. "Daddy hates our hair now. We need to cut it so he likes it again." Those were the last words she remembered her mother ever saying.

After the hair cut, it was her mother's turn to leave, with the help of some bourbon mixed in a tall glass of milk, and a bottle of meprobamate. They found her on her side of the bed, next to her dead husband after Jodi's aunt alerted the police.

Her aunt found Jodi in the closet two days later. She had carried in the family cat's bowl of food and water. The twin bowls were empty.

Now, Jodi gazed at herself standing in front of her own mirror. She had a long pair of scissors and opened them up as she grabbed a hand full of hair and cut it off. She smiled and the makeup from her tears ran down her face, her neck, and stained her own blouse. Her heart was dead.

She built a wall around it. It was frozen, cold— still. Someone was going to pay for the misery her family suffered, the misery she was now suffering— again. Someone was going to pay dearly.

CHAPTER EIGHT
Criminal: A person with predatory instincts who has not sufficient capital to form a corporation.
—Howard Scott

———————

For third shift, the night patrol was Unit Adam eighty-seven. They worked the warehouse area just south of downtown Phoenix, between the America West Arena and the streets just south of the railroad tracks. The tracks traveled east and west next to the arena. The two-officer unit was now the norm for Phoenix ever since an officer was shot in an ambush the year before. The two officers in Adam eighty-seven, Tony Del Rosso and Julie Elizabeth, had each been with the department for six years. The two had actually gone through the academy together, or almost together. Tony was in the class right behind Julie. They graduated approximately one month apart. They had gone to different precincts when they graduated, but both ended up at "six-twenty," the main headquarters for the Phoenix Police Department, 620 W. Washington. The two had been riding together for the last year and a half. They were partners and knew each other, in some ways, better than their own families. Cops had to; their lives depended on it.

"All I'm saying is we just didn't hit it off. That's all I'm saying. I'm not saying anything bad about your brother," Julie said as she drove the car around the east side of the second of three warehouses in a row, just before bouncing over the railroad tracks that led into the Jackson Avenue housing projects.

"But you don't want to go out with him again? If you liked him, you'd go out with him again."

"I knew this would happen," she said, shaking her head.

"What? Nothing's happening. Look, I just wanted to know what you found so bad about my little brother, that's all," Tony said gesturing with his hands. "You know what he said about you? He really liked you. He was really hoping you'd go out with him again." They drove for a few minutes in silence. The neighborhood seemed quiet this time of night. "So what was it that bothered—"

"He picks his nose," Julie whispered, flinching at the same time.

"He, what?"

"He—he picked his nose and then he looked at it!"

Both of the officers were looking out their respective windows. "Okay, well, that is pretty bad. Did he do it at the dinner table or at—"

"Does it really make a difference? He did it on our first date. That's not a good thing to do—anytime."

"Come on. It's not that bad."

Julie looked at him. "Are you kidding me?"

"What about after marriage?"

"What about 'after marriage'?"

"Well, if you got married and your husband did that, you wouldn't leave him, would you? I mean, it's not divorce warranted, is it?"

"I'm not going out with your brother again."

The radio cracked to life. "Any unit for unknown trouble, twenty-five twenty-three East Roeser."

"Thank god," Julie said as she turned east toward the call.

"Adam eighty-seven responding," Tony said into the mic, then turned back to his partner. "Okay, I can understand that. That might have been a little hard to watch, but still; I can't see you dumping the guy just because of a little social inappropriateness. He's a nice guy."

"He wiped it on the underside of his chair. Can we drop it and worry about this call, please?"

"All right," Tony said. "Still, I don't think that disqualifies him," he said in a low tone.

"Tony."

"All right."

The radio cracked again. "Adam eighty-seven, caller stated they thought they heard glass breaking in an apartment next to theirs. The suspected apartment is number thirty-two. The call was from a pay phone at that address. The caller then hung up." Tony looked at Julie.

They both knew these calls had the potential to be a setup to ambush the police as they arrived on the scene. The units were one level, older and worn, with low riders parked on the dirt originally designed as a lawn.

Tony keyed the mic again. " Adam eighty-seven, we're coming twenty-three now. Where was that pay phone?" It was then the front window and Tony's side window exploded, throwing glass everywhere. Julie instinctively veered the car to the left away from the sound and impact of rounds coming in the front and passenger windows. The right side of the car was exploding with bullets as they moved through the door and side panels of the car. The car hit the far curb of the driveway, bounced off the front of an older model Impala held together with more Bondo than steel, then careened into the side of a Mulberry tree while still drawing gun fire.

"Get out on your side! Get out on your side!" Tony screamed to Julie as he climbed over the center console of the car. She opened the door and fell to the ground as he came out behind her. He reached over

Mark Williams

and pushed the officer emergency alert button on the car's mobile data terminal, or MDT, before he too, fell out of the car. Somehow the two of them made it out without getting shot. Each took up a position opposite of where they thought the gun fire was coming from, trying to keep the engine block between the gunfire and themselves. "Adam eighty-seven, nine-nine-nine. We are taking gunfire at twenty-fifth Street and Roeser. We are pinned down by what appears to be automatic-weapons fire coming from the south of our location," Tony said into the mic, crumpled down behind the rear wheel of the car.

The helicopter was just about twelve hundred feet above the ground. The cockpit was quiet except for the occasional call coming through the two pilots' headsets. They heard the first call for Adam eighty-seven but didn't think anymore about it. There was no need. The interior glowed with amber lights from the console and the city lights outside.

"Aren't we getting a little low on fuel?" Paul asked looking at the fuel gauge.

Cooper looked over at the indicator. "Yeah, we could probably start to head in that direction. Go ahead and tell 'em we're coming in."

Paul keyed his handset. "Air Twenty-four."

"Air Twenty-four," came the seductive female voice in the black box. Cooper knew the voice. "We're heading back for one-oh-five," Paul said just as the hot tone sounded off. The oscillating high/low tone signified an officer was in real trouble.

"All units, hold for emergency traffic. We have emergency traffic from Adam eighty-seven. We had a partial voice contact with the sound of gunfire in the background. Unit last reported coming twenty-three at a call located at twenty-five twenty-three East Roeser." There was a pause in the broadcast. "We just got a radio call of a nine-nine-nine. All units, we have a triple-nine at that address." Cooper turned the ship in the direction of Roeser Avenue without saying a word.

"Tell radio we are engaging, ETA one minute," Cooper said, as he held the turn.

"We got fuel for this?"

"We have officers in trouble," Cooper said. "We'll use it as a ram if we have to."

Paul looked at his pilot. He was thinking the same thing.

Julie was looking right at Tony when his hip exploded. She picked up her microphone, which had fallen from its clip on her shoulder. "Nine-nine-nine. Officer shot, my partner is shot!" Adam eighty-seven, officer down. We have been ambushed. Automatic-weapon fire from an area south of our unit!" She reached into the car and turned on the car's red-and-whites before they started to receive more gun fire. The lights exploded as the shooters turned them off with their gun fire.

The lights weren't visible for long, but long enough for the air crew to see them. "There they are—one o'clock, low," Paul said pointing toward the flashing lights.

"They want to kill us," Tony said, trying to hold pressure on the wound as he leaned against the car. He sounded almost normal; the shock of being shot hadn't registered in his voice.

"Ya think?" Julie said sarcastically as she slid back down next to him. Bullets started to shatter the overhead rack of lights, raining colored plastic on their heads.

"Yep, that's what I think. I think you pissed them off or something. It must have been your driving," he said, clenching his teeth. Blood was oozing through his fingers. Julie looked at the blood pooling on the street. She thought the round hit something important, like an artery or a vein.

"We've got to buy them time until the ground units get there," Cooper said as he pointed off to the west and saw several police cars answering the call. They were at least a mile away. He pushed the nose of the ship down toward the downed officers. He could see five silhouettes heading toward the police car. Muzzle flashes preceded them.

Julie leaned up over the hood of the car and laid down five quick rounds in the direction of the approaching bad guys before she received return gunfire. She slid back down next to Tony. "Look, you've got to hang in. I will get you out of here, but you've got to give me some time. Can you fight?"

Tony nodded.

"Okay, all you have to do is look for anyone coming from your left. I got everything else. Can you do that?" Again, Tony nodded.

Julie cued the microphone on her shirt. "Adam eighty-seven where's our backup? I have an officer in need of evacuation now!"

Cooper pulled a small cassette tape from a cushion between the seats and handed it to Paul. "Put this in the cassette player and turn on the public address."

"I heard about this."

Cooper keyed his mic. "Adam eighty-seven, Air Twenty-four is coming twenty-three. We see you. Keep your heads down." Cooper looked at Paul. "Let's step into some shit," he said with a smile.

"Roger that," Paul said. In the glow of the console lights, Cooper thought he could see a grin on Paul's face.

Julie saw the approaching shadows trying to flank the car as she leaned up over the hood again. They had stopped. Something was distracting them. She took the opportunity to shoot one in the side of the head. He dropped like a duffle bag full of laundry. She cleared the magazine and loaded another fifteen rounds into her gun and dropped the slide. It was then she heard the helicopter blades and engine, but there was something else. "What the hell is that?" she said to Tony as she looked around in the direction of the noise, still aware of the men trying to flank the car. She couldn't tell what the noise was. Tony stopped for a minute and tried to focus on the sound. The music screamed over them just as the helicopter passed above the treetops and headed for the remaining men. 'Magic Carpet Ride' by Steppenwolf came out of the speaker from the belly of the helicopter as its body headed toward the two men circling to the north. "That's Cooper and Steppenwolf," Tony said. His voice was starting to shrink.

The helicopter pivoted to the right. Two flashes of light followed by two audible pops of what Julie could tell was the sound of the police Glock, came from the left side of the ship. The pilot was apparently shooting at the shadows. Two men fell and didn't move. For a moment, Julie was stunned by the accuracy, two pops and two people drop.

"Nice shootin' Tex," Paul said in a matter-of-fact tone.

Cooper stuffed the gun under his leg and turned to Paul as he prepared to land the ship within twenty feet of the ground unit. "Get this ship some air. Let radio know backup is on the ground."

"Let me go. You take your own ship—"

"Get my baby out of here. Don't you dare let anything happen to her," Cooper said as he got out. The aircraft jumped off the ground like it was on springs and flew off. Within a few seconds, the music was gone.

"Tony, Tony!" Julie said as she put her hand on his shoulder and tried to rouse him. He was fading. There were still men out in the dark; those left were hiding now. They sought the cover of dark shadows, trying to figure out what just happened.

Julie watched the man from the helicopter, instead of moving toward her, he was walking toward the two shadows stopped behind a car, not far from where she was. She watched him, the pilot. She stared at him. He wasn't running. He was almost out for a Sunday stroll, except he had his Glock by his side and his helmet on. She had heard about Cooper but had never met him. Her ears were ringing from the concussion of the shots resonating off the metal of the police car she used for cover. She could swear the pilot was talking to the two men. She couldn't hear what he was saying until just before he started to shoot. His voice grew louder. He was clear. He was calm and very direct.

"Police! Lay down your guns or die as the filthy vermin you are." He then raised his gun and delivered four shots as he walked forward, toward the hiding men.

Tony coughed and Julie turned to him. He was mouthing something. She got down next to him. "I'm right here. What are you saying?" Tony coughed and then whispered. "It's Coop, partner. Our cavalry has arrived." He opened his eyes and looked at her. "You gotta give my little brother another chance. I'll talk to him about booger-picking." He was somehow able to give her a feeble wink just before he closed his eyes. "I'm going to make it."

Cooper turned toward the police car and walked at the same lingering pace over to where the officers were. He crouched down next to Tony. "We're getting you out of here. Just hang on for a few minutes longer."

Tony opened his eyes and then closed them again. "Jesus, Coop, you still have the tape?"

"Yeah, you like it?"

Julie heard something again and looked over the top of the car and saw movement again, lots of movement. "I counted about eight."

"Yeah, maybe ten. I couldn't tell from the air. I don't think they were all armed. There are two less now," he said as he nodded toward the two bodies laying in the street. Just then, the officers received gunfire from the corner of the street. Cooper and Julie ducked and covered Tony, sheltering him with their own bodies. Cooper unsnapped one of the Glock magazines on Tony's web gear.

"By god, that will be enough!" Cooper said as he got up, firing three quick rounds in the direction of the gunfire. Another silhouette dropped to the ground, motionless.

"Cooper," Julie said, still covering Tony. "What are you doing!?"

"Stopping this noise." He moved toward the shadows, using the Impala next to the patrol car for cover.

Julie could hear the sirens coming. "I hear our backup. Wait, Cooper, wait for the damn backup!" she said almost in a scream.

"Tell Radio to put me out with you," Cooper said over his shoulder as he walked into the darkness.

Julie watched him as he went around the car and out of sight. "Radio, this is Adam eighty-seven. Air Twenty-four pilot is on the ground and is twenty-three with us. He is walking to the south from our location and engaging the suspects times at least six. We have one officer down who needs immediate evacuation with a GSW. Repeating, officer down and shot, need evac." Her voice was calm. She let go of Tony long enough to check her magazine, taking Tony's other unused magazine and readied her gun. The race was on as to whether they were coming for her and her partner or if Cooper made them stop and think long enough for the ground units to get there in time. She was sure they could hear the sirens as well.

Julie heard the radio repeat her transmission. The dispatcher asked her again for their location. Air Twenty-four had called in and said it was over the scene. Julie could see Cooper at the back of the Impala. He turned to her and took off his helmet. He keyed the mic on his collar. "Air Twenty-four."

"Air Twenty-four," came Paul's voice.

"You see them to the southwest?"

"Ten-four, I was watching the ones to the southeast. You got three on the southeast."

"Shit," Cooper said under his breath as he changed his line of sight to the other side. Sure enough, there were three more.

"They're running in your direction, Coop. I got the light on them."

Cooper lowered himself and turned to Julie. "Watch that side in case they try to flank you. Watch your breathing and get a good sight picture."

"What are you going to do?"

"I'm tired of this. I'm going to see how dumb these bastards are," he gave her a smile before he got up and moved to his left, toward the front of the car.

Cooper took a few steps then stood perfectly still, shooting six times in two-round bursts at each of the three men who were running at him from the southwest. All three fell and didn't move. He then turned to the others and started to move in their direction, keeping the Impala between them. "Hey, shit for brains, you're under arrest. You want a piece of me? Come and get your heart eaten, you piece of crap." He stopped and took a knee, reloading his gun while looking in the direction of the threat. The area was lit up by the million-candle power light on the helicopter. He slammed the magazine into the butt of the gun before standing again and moving forward. He fired another three rounds before he spoke again.

"Come on, children. You want to kill a cop, now's your chance." As Julie watched Cooper, he didn't seem concerned, but he wasn't sloppy either. He shot off another three-round burst and then moved, three rounds and moved. He was buying time. He just needed enough rounds until the other units arrived. He changed his magazine and fired, moving and firing and reloading three more times.

"Radio, Air Twenty-four. Step it up," Paul reported.

Cooper's gun was empty. "Air Twenty-four, I'm out." They all knew what he meant. His gun was dry and there was no help arriving on the ground. He did the only thing he could do. He continued to pick a fight.

"All right, you little bastards. I'm all out of bullets." He pulled out his expandable baton from the zipper in his pants calf pocket and charged it by spinning it down and away from him, stopping when it came up to his ear.

Paul couldn't believe what he was seeing and he had seen a lot. Cooper was armed with a stick, an expandable baton against guns. "Air Twenty-four get back behind cover," Paul ordered firmly into the radio. There was no reply. "That crazy old bastard—you've got to be kidding me," Paul muttered to himself. He knew almost immediately the old man was drawing the threat

67

away from the wounded officers on the ground. In that moment, he realized he was watching real bravery— mixed with, he was sure, some kind of psychotic behavior. "Jesus, here we go." He swallowed his gum and pushed down on the left rudder, causing the copter to yaw sharply to the left. "Roof jumping, here we go." He remembered the last time. He had just made site of the targeted buildings in the distance after flying over hundreds of miles of very flat and very dark desert.

It was 1991, on the eve of the invasion, and downtown Tikrit was on the horizon. He could see one of the three palaces Saddam owned.

"I can't believe this son of a bitch," Charlie Donaldson said. He was Paul's co-pilot.

"What?"

"This bastard has three palaces in his home town; one for mom, one for him and his wife, and one for his mistress. That takes balls."

They had a squad of SEAL operators in the back and they were coming in 'low and slow' as the boys at the stick liked to call it. The lumbering Sea Stallion was the largest helicopter in the American arsenal and it was his job to plant the team within reach of Saddam. Intel thought he was home. The team was going to try to snuff him before things got too messy.

Paul brought the ship in on the western border of the town, near the airfield in the Salah Ad Din province. The desert was so flat and non-descript, depth perception was a severe problem. He reached up and adjusted his night goggles and could see the green hue of the ground and the dust he was kicking up. The landing was harder than he liked or practiced, a slight sign of nerves. It seemed only seconds he was hearing the door gunner over the intercom reporting the team was away and they could dust off. He and his two escorts stayed low for three miles before they gained some altitude. For the next three hundred miles, they would take sporadic small arms fire from the ground. Once they landed, they quickly refueled and stood by to go back and get the team. They didn't have to wait for long. Saddam wasn't home.

"Couldn't we just have called?" Paul remembered his co-pilot asking as they landed to extract the team.

"Where's the fun in that?" he said. They were flying low across country they knew was occupied by bad guys.

"Where's the fun in this?" one of his gunners said. That was just as the front wind screen exploded and Charlie Donaldson's neck began to leak out all over the inside of the cockpit.

By dawn on the first day of the invasion, Paul had flown into the throat of the dragon twice. He had to make the three hundred mile trip back with Charlie in the seat next to him. For the first fifty miles, Paul had to listen to Charlie gurgle in his own fluid until his heart finally stopped beating because it ran out of blood to pump. Now, he was in his home town, appearing to do the same thing.

"If you want to rumble, the least I can do is play too," Cooper said towards the shadows.

Three men came out from where they were hiding and were, themselves, bathed in the light of the copter. They didn't care who saw them. Cooper figured they were long-time bad boys who wanted to make their bones killing a cop, maybe even two or three. They would be heroes to some in this neighborhood; to others, it would be the final death blow. They would solidify their grip on an already terrorized community. He watched as three men came out of the shadows and into the bright light, each carrying some type of handgun. It was then Cooper heard music—loud music. ZZ Top's "Sharp Dressed Man" was coming from the heavens.

Cooper looked up, past the approaching men. "Oops, too late," he said. Just then, the helicopter came over the far row of houses and headed at the three men, four feet off the ground at about sixty miles an hour.

"Every girl's crazy about a sharp dressed man..." Paul sung out loud just before the words played. He noticed his accent was back while he sung.

"Every girl's crazy about a sharp dressed man ..," screamed over the PA as the helicopter came in and nearly struck the three men who stood in close proximity of each other. It then climbed for the trees, pivoted on a vertical axis and dove at the men again, right over Cooper's head. The men were distracted with the helicopter. They began to shoot into its sides and belly. Cooper used this time to close in on them. He came up behind the first man and landed a blow to the back of the man's head and shoulder with the expandable steel baton. It was a strike that would not be within company policy, but since the man was trying to kill three police officers and since Cooper's report would reflect the man "ducked" as he was throwing the strike, everything would be fine. The man fell straight to the ground. Cooper was quick to pick up his dropped gun and point it at the other two men who also had their backs to him.

Paul noticed Cooper was armed again. Instead of dropping down one more time, he stayed high and gave Cooper light.

"Hey, you little ferret bastards," Cooper called to the two. They turned and stood facing a really pissed-off cop with a gun pointed at their faces. "Grab some asphalt, shitums," he said as he pointed the Taurus nine-millimeter at the two. They dropped their guns and lay face down on the ground. Just as they spread their arms, the first of five initial ground units arrived. Cooper signaled the officers to handcuff the two on the ground. Cooper trotted back to the police car where Julie and Tony were.

"Air Twenty-four, find a hole and set it down. We need to evac this officer right now," Cooper said into his shoulder mic.

"Air Twenty-four, copy."

"Okay, let's stuff him and get him out of here," he said to Julie. "Grab his feet." The two struggled with Tony until another officer came over and helped them with the dead weight. Paul set the ship down thirty yards down the street and waited for his partner. Cooper jumped into the back and the other two officers fed him Tony's body until he was in. Julie stood watching after she let go, but saw Cooper signal her to walk around to the front of the copter where he was sitting, holding Tony up. "You're his partner, right?" he called to her over the roar of the rotor blades. She nodded her head. "Then you're going, too. Get your ass in and hold him while we drive." The two exchanged places and once she was belted in and given head phones by Cooper, he jumped back in the left seat. "Radio-Air Twenty-four. We are ten-eight, ten-nineteen to St. Joseph. Please notify them we are bringing in a wounded officer who has at least one GSW and has lost a lot of blood," Cooper said as Paul got the aircraft back into the air.

"I thought I told you to get this thing up and get some air?" Cooper asked. The ship jumped into the air as he finished buckling his seatbelt.

"I forgot what you said and I was coming back to clarify," Paul said as he pushed the stick forward and skimmed the tops of the trees. "If you looked closely, you would have noticed I came from the air, so I actually did what you told me to do."

There was a moment of silence while the two pilots formally exchanged control of the ship. "You have the ship?" Paul asked formally to Cooper, still keeping his hands on the stick until he heard the correct response.

"I have the ship," Cooper said as he placed his hands on the controls and his feet on the rudder pedals. He paused before speaking again. "Thanks for not hearing so well. Where did you learn to fly like that?"

Paul looked over. "Saddam's back yard. I was part of a SEAL team that got to the first show early."

The radio interrupted their conversation. Paul answered the call for flight status. "Phoenix, Air Two-four, we have two officers inbound to St. Josephs with at least one GSW. Could you make the call for us? ETA— two minutes."

The radio operator acknowledged the transmission in the usual cold and calculating voice.

"Yeah, I bet you were in the Army, huh?" Paul asked flatly.

The indicator was reporting the ship should be out of fuel.

"It's my delicate demeanor, huh?"

Paul just smiled. "You know you guys couldn't get anywhere unless we carried you there in all those pretty gray boats."

"You young pukes don't know what it's like to jump on the trees and stay there. The NVA would shoot us down with rocks," Cooper said with a smirk.

"'Young pukes'? You old piece of crap. You ever fly into a sandstorm—at night— with no lights, and no stars, and you look fucking down and your artificial god-damn horizon is spinning like a top? Hell, Hajji didn't need rocks. He'd just wait until our air intake clogged or we'd friggin' crash flying upside down, thinking we were right side up, somewhere in ten-million square miles of sandbox."

"Huh, you did that?"

"More than once," Paul said nodding his head, holding his own smirk.

Cooper was shaking his head.

"The the hell you doing shaking your head?"

"Nothing."

"Come on, out with it."

"Well, it's just like the Navy to fly into a sandstorm."

"You really going to throw down with this old 'Army versus Navy' bullshit?"

"It's a well known fact about Navy pilots."

"Well known fact about what? Oh, and we're called 'aviators' not 'pilots'. You're called a 'pilot'; along with crop dusters and everyone flying in the French Air Force."

"Well, you are at sea for long periods at a time. No one but other men and the occasional—,"

"We're about ready to crash because *you* ran us out of fuel and you're talking about me?"

"It's a well known fact."

"I think I'm going to find time to piss on your grave when you die tonight."

"I'm, just saying," Cooper said with a smile.

"Head stone, too," Paul said. He looked out the window. He was smiling, as well. Paul knew one thing, the reason he was welcomed home as a hero, the reason people came up to him on the street, random people, after his tour in the Gulf was because the veterans from Vietnam made it so no service person would ever be treated like they were—ever. He knew he had this 'old piece of crap' to thank for that.

Cooper just smiled. "Yeah, or if those Air Force boys hadn't flown us over the Big Pond. We'd have to walk the whole way." A moment passed—worth a couple of heart-beats. "Thanks for coming back."

"No problem. I just wanted some extra stick time. By the way," he started as he looked at the fuel indicator. "Are we going to crash?" Paul asked with the complacency of a man asking about the price of a new drill.

"I hope not. We're already going to kill a whole forest writing the report for this one."

"Yeah, if we live to see the forest. Sitting down writing a long report seems like a nice thing to do right about now," Paul said in a calm voice. "Crap, flying in a sand storm doesn't look too bad right now either. There's the landing platform." He was pointing out the window to the hospital landing pad for the medi-vac helicopters. Within thirty seconds they were over the pad and setting the ship down. There was already a medical team standing by just inside a pair of glass doors, away from the down-wash of the rotor blades, waiting with a gurney to take Tony inside. The surgical team waited in a nearby surgical room. The ship sat down like it was just another day. Cooper feathered the blades. Paul was out and opened the back door. The emergency team didn't wait for the blades to stop. They quickly approached the ship and moved the wounded officer to the gurney and Julie followed. After the two officers were unloaded, the pilots flew the helicopter to a nearby parking lot and called in for a fuel truck to be sent to their location.

It was about thirty minutes before another officer arrived to just be with them after the shooting. He was in civilian clothes assigned to the Human Resources Bureau to handle just these types of events.

Paul called Doris and told her he was all right but going to be a little late. It was an hour before the first of five detectives arrived and talked to the two of them separately. Just in general terms at first, to get the basics of what happened. They took Cooper's gun but immediately gave him another to replace it. The detailed interview would be back at the station the next morning. There was no rush anymore. It was time for calm and to allow the body to slow down. By the time the initial detectives left and the fuel truck pulled away, four hours had passed. Another crew came and flew the helicopter out and back to the airport.

Cooper and Paul went back to the emergency room, through the door directly across from the parking lot where the helicopter set down, to check on the two officers. The room was filled with people in uniforms, friends and other members of their squad. They stayed just long enough to find out Julie was fine, just a few scrapes and bruises from the exploding glass. Tony had just come out of surgery. He was alive; that was always a good sign if you've been shot.

"What did you find out, Commander?" Cooper asked Commander Travis Lawrence, the ranking officer in the waiting room and who was in contact with the investigation team at the site.

"From what the shooting investigation team is saying, two gangs, each vying for control of the same neighborhood, tried to set up each other with the police ambush. Bastards. The only kills were the gangsters, the oldest was seventeen. We've hooked eight people so far." The commander looked at Cooper. "You two got him here just in time," he said gesturing with his thumb in the direction of the operating room.

Cooper and Julie were placed on administrative leave for three days, typical for officers involved in shootings. Paul was also given three days. He was called in by the air-wing sergeant and asked if he wanted to stay or change partners. The sergeant thought he knew his answer; after all, everyone else had transferred out. He figured Paul would want the same. Sgt. Sargelli told Paul it would be the final pin needed to have Cooper removed. He had to hear the answer twice when Paul told him he didn't want to change partners. *Nope,* he thought. He found a home with this old piece of crap.

CHAPTER NINE
The end excuses any evil.
—Sophocles, *Electra* (c.409 BC)

_____

October 2003

Jodi Campbell wasn't nervous. She could walk and talk and laugh with friends now, if she did laugh at all. Most people, when they looked at her, still saw a grieving widow, but she seemed to be doing better than expected, her friends thought. Her movements and actions were nothing out of the ordinary, and some of those actions were simply signed off to a wife and mother, who had lost her family and was gallantly trying to find life again. So after a few months, when Jodi Campbell's friends thought her eyes contained a hint of a fire, that life for her was still possible, no one considered anything out of the ordinary. Her eyes didn't seem sad or painful anymore. Her friends even began to like her short hair. But who was to judge Jodi Campbell, people thought? After a while, her friends talked about how she almost seemed as if life was filling her again and perhaps she might, through her apparent personal strength of sinew, live to a ripe age and mentor others who had lost children, possibly even marry again. That's what people thought about Jodi Campbell.

The real fact was, Jodi Campbell had snapped.

"They said we aren't worthy, they said we're no good ..." Jodi sang as she drove her car, sometimes for hours, around the city months after Anthony's funeral. She would have the radio on and incorporate her thoughts into words in time with the melody of the song. *"No, one's going to live, they're all going to pay. In the end, we will all laugh and play."* Jodi Campbell had a

mission, a destiny, a new drive in her life. Her friends were right, there was a hint of fire in her eyes. Hatred.

"First things first," Jodi said out loud, seeming to arrive at an answer on Camelback Road, just under the Nordstrom's overpass at Scottsdale Fashion Square. "We need to go shopping, don't we boys?" she said smiling. "Anthony, you love to go shopping with your mommy, don't you, sweetie?" She looked in the rear-view mirror to the empty seat where Anthony had always sat. "Honey, we'll look for a new shirt for you," she said as she patted the passenger seat where the Joe in her mind was sitting. "I know we don't have a lot of money, but it'll be okay. "First though, we need to go get some supplies. It's okay, you two can wait in the car. I'll only be a moment," she said as she winked at the empty passenger seat.

In the evening, the business was lit by a single street light, hanging on a temporary construction pole. The light was partially blocked by the edge of the construction office. Jodi had done engineering work for the small mine. This being so far out of town, there wasn't much human life that crept out at night here. She knew where they kept the cordite locker. After all, she had designed a good portion of the excavation for this part of the reactivated Klevox Mine, a crushed-granite mine, which literally made little rocks out of big rocks. They used small amounts of high explosives to do the initial demolition of the rock prior to putting it through the crusher.

"Joe, you remember these folks, don't you?" she said as she parked and looked around. "The storage is around the back. No, I'm sure, honey. You wait here."

Jodi still had keys to the lock on the front gate and the bunker where the explosives were kept. She had used it before to get in and oversee soil samples and run compaction tests for the small mining operation. She parked around the side of the main gate away from the light, walked casually up to the front gate with latex-gloved hands, and opened the lock with her key. She slid the gate open, walked back and got in her car, pulled it just inside the entrance, then got out and shut the gate. She drove to the back of the facility, next to a large berm of dirt wrapping itself around it, was the steel shed containing the items she wanted. The fire diamond symbol, with the word "Explosives" written in the middle of it was hanging in the center of the door. She pulled out the key to the round lock shrouded in steel connected to the steel door on the side of the steel building. Jodi didn't care if the company noticed it was missing. In fact, she knew it would be awhile before they did notice. Their schedule to excavate more ground was a month down the road.

"Look what I got?" she said as she got back in the car. "I needed the blasting caps and a few feet of detonation cord. I took some of the cordite to get things started, but the rest I figured would be Ampho—you know honey, diesel fuel and fertilizer." She paused as if to reply to the comment in her mind. "I know, but you know I like gardening. I can make it myself. It'll give a much bigger splash and it's just easier to get. We can get those at the neighborhood garden shop and gas station." She started to dig in her purse for a notepad. "I almost forgot. We need light bulbs for the bathroom." She started to make a list, calling it out as she wrote, "light bulbs, ammonium nitrate, some flowers for the front porch, five gallon gas can of diesel."

She paused and looked at the list. "There. I think that's it for now, oh, no wait. We're out of tea and cottage cheese. Joe, honey, looks like we have to go to the store after the home store."

Jodi turned the car around and drove out of the site, locking the gate behind her. She looked back at the facility. No one could tell that she had been there. Her tire tracks blended in with all the others.

She rounded the last turn on the dirt road that led to the facility. Just before she came up to Central Avenue, she slid a CD of Handel into her car's CD player.

Jodi felt hungry and her mind turned to what she might like to eat. She thought about going to the Biltmore and having some calamari salad at the Bamboo Club. "I'm hungry. You two, hungry? We can go to the Bamboo Club, then look around and see what we want to blow up first." The CD changed tracks. "After we eat, I really do need to shop for a new purse, something I can carry my wallet and a small explosive and timer in. Something that will go with that blue dress you like." She looked over at the empty passenger seat.

After deciding her next order of business, she relaxed in her seat and turned up Handel's minuet from *Water Music* and allowed it to fill the car with the melodic sound which only comes from Handel. There was a good deal of contentment—having a plan. She was going to sleep well tonight; she thought to herself. Tomorrow—the garden shop some light bulbs, and tea.

CHAPTER TEN
Part of being sane, is being a little bit crazy.
—Janet Long

M oreno wiped down the bar. He snickered at Cooper's latest fiasco. "Boy, Coop, you flew your butt out of that one. You come in here and it never surprises me what you have done. Just stay away from the bar with that helicopter, amigo. I don't want you crashing into it. I just got it to where I like it."

Cooper took another sip of his scotch. He lost track whether it was his third or fourth. "It wasn't me. Not all of it, anyway."

Phil kept wiping. "You breakin' the cherry on another one? Hombre, didn't you just do one?"

Cooper looked down at his plate, which held the remnants of his meat lasagna and a side of French fries. He found one of three remaining fries, dipped it in the ranch dressing next to the plate, and snapped it into his mouth. "That was a while ago. It didn't work out."

"None of them seem to work out. What's that now, about five in four years?"

"Four in two. And why are you counting, *hombre*?"

"Now, why would you say that word like I'm cutting your lawn? They couldn't all be that bad," Moreno said.

"Yes, they could." He raised his head toward Phil. It wobbled a bit on its axis, but found the man who was talking to him. "Have you ever flown a helicopter?"

"I've seen 'em fly overhead to report the traffic," Moreno said.

"Sonofabitch," Cooper said. Moreno knew how he felt about traffic reporters. It twisted his stomach into a knot the size of a volleyball whenever Moreno brought it up. Cooper thought they weren't pilots; they were circus workers who performed for money.

Nights played one into the other and about every four months or so, Cooper would drink enough and think enough to walk over to the pay phone in the corner of the bar and 'drunk dial.' He never used his cell phone and in his well-oiled logic, why would he? He didn't want Allison, his ex, to know it was him calling, although after receiving a dozen or so of his calls from Moreno's Bar as it came up on the caller ID, she figured it was him calling—again. Tonight, was another one of those nights. "You calling a cab again, amigo?" Moreno queried him.

"I don't need a cab," Cooper slurred.

"I wouldn't drive if I were you," Moreno returned without looking up.

"Lucky for me, you ain't me. I walked here, remember?" Cooper mumbled under his breath.

The second marriage crashed, and it took years to put out the fire and carry away the wreckage. It had been years since the final disillusionment and eventually, Allison remarried. This one also didn't want kids and was a federal Marshall who traveled three days out of the week.

Cooper would sit and let old thoughts of Allison come to the forefront of the lubricated brain pan. Random thoughts of old times, old things, old ways. He never called her before midnight. That would be too convenient. He always knew the husband's schedule, whatever his name was, so Cooper missed the inevitable confrontation. Allison never told him her ex-husband had been calling in the middle of the night over the past few years. Why—she never said and

Cooper never asked. He dropped the coins in the phone and dialed. She picked up on the fourth ring. "Hello." Her voice was gruff. She cleared her throat and said it again. "Hello."

It took a second for the voice to register as hers. She sounded different, and for that second, he thought he had dialed the wrong number. "Allison? It's me."

"Coop?" She sighed. "Of course, it is."

"I was just calling to see how—"

"Do you know what time it is? You've got to stop calling here."

"No, I didn't know it was late. Hey, I'm sorry okay? I thought I'd just give you a call. I, ah," He paused for moment. "Just wondering if you still had that baseball I caught at Candlestick Park when we were on our honeymoon. I remember you had on that green paisley dress." He had to come up with something to talk about, and this subject came to his mind between the third and fourth scotch.

"Baseball? You called me to ask me about a baseball?" She opened her eyes to look at the time. It was 12:34 . "I don't know. I don't remember any baseball."

"You don't know?" There was a sense of frustration that his wife—his *ex*-wife— didn't remember the baseball he caught on their honeymoon. "I thought it was on the bookshelf next to the pictures of—"

"That was years ago, come on. There are different people living here now," she said with a cut. "It's late—is that why you called? To ask about a damn baseball?"

"Yeah, I guess it is a little late, no, no. Look, I'm sorry all right? Jeezus, why does everything have to be a battle with you? I don't care who I'm waking up ... Hello? Hello?" He thought for a minute about calling her back. He always thought about calling her back. After all, it was just a simple question about a baseball, *his* baseball. It wasn't hers. She didn't catch it. She didn't care about it. She didn't need to be rude about him calling, he thought. Yeah, he was sorry it was so late, but it's not like she couldn't go back to sleep. He went back to his stool.

"You call her?" Moreno asked.

"She doesn't care how my day went."

"She cares about you, my friend."

Cooper nodded while he held his glass with two hands. "Nah, I stomped on her heart too many times while we were married for that. The only thing she wants to know is when I'm dead."

"You underestimate that woman."

"You underestimate this man. Now shut up and pour. I can still feel my lips."

CHAPTER ELEVEN
If you cannot get rid of the family skeleton, you may as well make it dance.
                    —George Bernard Shaw

———————————

Cooper woke up hard the next day with something dead in his mouth. He usually woke up hard after drinking. He never drank during the day, and it was never a problem when it came to work, but after work, when the world was off to the side somewhere and he didn't have to deal with its toilet for a few hours, he liked to share the moment with a lowball, no ice, and a padded stool. He stared out the window as the sun cut through the curtains. It was about nine in the morning and the sun was cooking the day away already. He rolled over and stared at the ceiling fan listening to the *sht-sht-sht* sound as it rotated. "I need to fix that," he said. Then he really smelled his breath. "Oh, god."

He really needed to wash the sheets. He rolled over and tried to filter his breath through the sheets, but that wasn't much better. He pulled the covers up under his chin. They were cool to the touch, and after a moment he fell back asleep. He had a feeling *they* would show up again if he went back to sleep. He was right.

Cooper was monitoring the radio traffic. He heard the request and it confirmed what he thought. The NVA were regrouping for another run at the base. They wouldn't wait long to release the tide they had built. Even though they were being mowed down like grass, the enemy felt victory was at hand. The *Boogieman* had to strike while they had the momentum; the copters had to strike while they had them retreating. "Okay, flight, you heard 'em. On my go, we'll finish our orbit and come straight at the tree line just about when they decide to get brave again. We'll rocket them clear back to Hanoi."

Much of the dream was the same as before. Bits and pieces would be different. Sometimes they were short; some seemed like they never ended. But there were some parts in every dream.

He remembered a face of a soldier. He couldn't have been more than a teenager. He was in the back of the helicopter during the evacuation of the wounded from the base. His face was ashen but their eyes locked. He was laying on his back between the pilots seats. There was a look the boy gave him. It was only a moment, a flash then he had to fly but the look—it jarred him hard awake.

He woke up breathing hard. He placed his hand on his chest. He was soaking wet from sweat. It had only been about fifteen minutes since he had fallen back to sleep again. His eyes opened. His brain was on; switched on as if it had been awake for a while. He rolled to his right, reached down and opened the night stand cabinet and pulled out a shoe box without looking.

From memory, he reached inside, with his eyes closed and pulled out a piece of paper. He opened his eyes and read the words on the citation: "... *for actions taken above and beyond the call of duty....*"

He slid the paper back into the box. Cooper closed his eyes and tried to push the thoughts away. He fell back asleep again.

Jodi loved working with her hands. Even before she was married, she painted and worked with clay, making coffee cups and vases, then painting them.

During the winter, she would knit; a craft her
grandmother taught her when she would visit during
summer. She enjoyed creating things and seeing the end
product of her work. She also enjoyed the snipping of
wires and the molding of the explosive into the half-
gallon plastic milk containers filled with marbles.
Mixing the fertilizer and diesel fuel was like potting a
plant except for the strong smell of diesel and fertilizer.
She loved the smell as she busied herself fitting the
mixture into the three containers and lavishly pitting it
with additional ball bearings in clay on its sides then
placing each into its own grocery store bag. She worked
without gloves. The gloves were bad for her nails, she
thought. She liked the feeling of the chemicals on her
skin, the way they started to tingle at first, then burn.
She was leaving lots of finger prints. If they could find
any after the explosions, they deserved them, she
thought.

"Look, boys," she said to no one present, as she
held up one of the containers. "Isn't it nice? Big, too."

She washed her hands in the kitchen sink, then
went back and admired her work. She could walk into
any store and no one would know what she was
carrying. She had collected bags from some of the stores
from the mall. She smiled.

She spent the day before shopping at Paradise
Valley Mall and finding just the right bags to transfer the
explosives into. They had to be pretty, with handles.
They also had to be tall but narrow. It couldn't be just
any bag. They had specific functions, all three of them.
They had to fit inside the opening of a public trash can,
the type with the lids on them with a smaller hole in the
center.

She went into a candle store and told the sales
person she was shopping for birthday presents and
needed her purchases separately bagged. The candles

were large, just the right size and fit perfectly into their individual bags—with handles.

Each explosive had a specific yet random function. Once they went off, she knew they would be grouped together. That was what she wanted. She wanted them connected to things later. She wanted the city to know there was someone, an unknown someone, who was making a statement. There would be no note, no phone call. It was all in the action.

Her finger prints weren't in the main computer system, but she knew they would find her. They had been taken for her engineering license years before, but there was no guarantee they were even in a folder let alone a database somewhere. By the time they found her, it would be too late. Her full plan would be complete.

She finished the trimming of wires and placement of each explosive in their own bag. The timers would be added when she arrived at the mall, where she would set off her first statement of anger; only she didn't think of herself as angry. She was righting a wrong. They, those people who did this to her and her family, would have to figure it out on their own.

She sat the three shopping bags on her bed and looked at them, finally pleased with herself. They looked like gift bags. From the outside, no one could tell they were anything other than that, even if someone looked inside. She didn't like that she could see the wiring and the tops to the containers if she looked down into the bag so she went into the hall closet and found some tissue paper she had used on the prior year's Christmas presents. *"I think they'll like what we bought for them, I think they'll wonder what comes next ..."* she sang as she worked to some random tune.

She stuffed some tissue paper down on the top of each bomb, leaving the wires for the timer hanging out the side of the bag. She could easily plug in the timer with its own battery and slide it under the paper while no one was watching. She stepped back and examined her work again. "Oh, guys, I really think we have done a wonderful job with the gifts. Don't you two think? When the timer is in place, you won't be able to see anything." She stopped and looked across the room as if something drew her attention there. "Really? You think so?" She looked back at the packages. "I think you're right. That would make them look extra special."

She walked over to the side table and picked up some ribbon. Each bag was a different color. She had to make sure she had the right ribbon to color coordinate with the corresponding bag. She tied the ribbon into bows around the two handles of the bag. She stood back and looked again at her creations. They looked like three presents for a party. She smiled. "There, that looks nice," she said.

Around ten o'clock Cooper finally woke up. He slid his legs over the side of his bed and hung his head, his chin almost touching his chest. It was going to be a long day. After a shooting, the departments always made officers ride a desk. He had a tinge of remorse for getting Paul involved in the events of the day before, but they quickly faded. Paul was a big boy, he thought, and if they hadn't done what they did, two officers would more than likely be dead. He smiled for a moment, remembering the flying Paul did. He thought this one might stick around. He might like him to stick around.

He pushed himself up and walked down the hall to the kitchen, where he started a pot of coffee, then retrieved the newspaper from the front sidewalk.

Jodi picked up the bags and walked out of the bedroom and down the hall into the kitchen, where she had laundry piled up on the edge of the kitchen table. She put the bags down, after first pouring herself her second cup of tea and began folding the towels that made up the majority of the laundry. Music was playing from the stereo in the living room. She hummed a few bars from *Madam Butterfly*. She walked over to the kitchen counter next to the sink and opened a drawer. She put away three dishtowels and a couple of freshly washed dish sponges she had used the day before. She looked up at the three-by-five-foot corkboard hanging above the counter. It was covered in newspaper clippings about people suing the city of Phoenix or any of the surrounding cities for whatever people sue governments for. She picked up two newspaper clippings laying on the counter, just in front of the towel drawer and added them to the board with a couple of pushpins. She leaned back against the kitchen island and looked at the board. She picked up her cup of tea and she took a long sip, never taking her eyes off the board.

Cooper leaned back against the counter and sipped his coffee. The newspaper was open and laying across the sink, resting on the faucet. This allowed Cooper to look and see out the kitchen window while he caught up on the day's news. He liked the morning. He enjoyed the time just before the sun broke the horizon. Even though it was late and the sun was well overhead, it was the morning which lent some peace to his life.

On the windowsill, over the kitchen sink, were two photos, one of Cooper and Allison in happier days. They were hugging each other on a sunset-lit beach in Avalon on Santa Catalina Island. The other picture next to it was of him and Allison with his sister Peggy, his brother-in-law Lindy, and his nephew Luke, all standing on the steps of the Lincoln Memorial. It was taken on a beautiful spring day; at least he thought it was spring. It could have been summer. He couldn't remember.

She wouldn't say so but Cooper needed Peggy as much as she needed him in those early years. Even when her family moved to Arlington when Lindy got transferred from Luke Air Force Base to an office in Crystal City near the Pentagon, they kept in touch at least once a week. It was harder for him than it was her, although he never let her know. She married in her thirties and had their son in her late thirties.

He helped her pack and saw her and her family off at the airport, then cried his way back to his car. He was now totally alone. The thought overwhelmed him, burying him even deeper in a hole of despair. That single event, Peggy and her family moving away, was enough for Cooper to contemplate ending his life. He toyed with the idea— how, where, when, then threw the idea out when he remembered someone would have to identify the remains, probably Peggy. He only found relief from the despair when he worked. Work freed him; at least it occupied his mind. The loneliness and despair would give way to work. Life would work, it would have to.

He looked at his watch, closed the newspaper, and walked over to the phone to call his sister. He wanted to hear her voice. He had a rare moment of loneliness that morning. It flew in and flew out, but it was enough to want to hear her voice.

The phone rang three times before she answered.

"Hello?"

"Sis? Coop," he said, smiling at hearing her voice. "Yeah, it's me. How's my favorite sister? Well, I know you're my only sister, but that doesn't change the fact you are my favorite sister. How's Luke and Lindy? Luke's birthday is coming up, huh? Peggy, I surprised you? You thought I would forget my nephew's birthday? I bet you think I don't even know how old he is, do you? He's thirty-three, Peggy." He snickered for a moment when he heard his sister laugh at the comment. "That's right, you had him when you were eleven, oh, seventeen? Well, that's what you convinced the hospital people to say." He talked to her for awhile. She brought him up to date on the family, then the conversation turned to harsh reality. "How are you doing, Sis? The chemo's going all right? You aren't working too hard, are you? You tell Lindy if you get too tired, he can carry you to the bathroom." He waited for a minute, "I know he doesn't need to dear, but it will make him feel important." They both laughed for a minute. He brought lightness into their lives. Ever since Peggy found out the cancer had spread to the other breast, he felt as if he couldn't hear her voice enough. They were always able to make each other laugh.

Luke, their twelve-year-old boy, loved his uncle and whenever Cooper went back to visit them or on business, he took Luke out to throw a ball around with him and his father. Sometimes the four of them would have a picnic down by the Reflecting Pool on the south side, under the trees bordering the pool from the Lincoln Memorial toward the Washington Memorial. They would spread out a blanket and find peace there. They would watch people pass by on their bikes or jogging, and they made fun of foreign tourists who stood out with their cameras and ill-fitting baseball caps. He cherished those times and memories, even when Allison went with him. They did have good times together, plenty of good times. Sometimes, in all the business of living, it was difficult for Cooper to find them.

Holy Ground

Jodi walked down the mall, casually window-shopping, carrying her bags with her. They were heavier than she thought they would be. After a while, they felt like they were cutting her hands. She smiled at the pain.

She went in and out of the stores, looking at clothes, trying on shoes, or sunglasses. She liked a pair of Ray-Bans she saw and bought them. She wandered in to a high end outdoor outfitter store next to the sunglass boutique. She tried on a sweater she spotted on a lower shelf in the back corner of the store. She didn't like the color on her so she put it back on the same lower shelf, along with one of her bags. She found it opportunistic and modified her plan to place the devices in the stores rather than the cans. She did the same at two other stores. By the time she got to the end of the mall, she had replaced the three bags she brought in with three new ones with actual clothes.

Jodi sat in her car until it happened. She was listening to NPR, giving an update on the war. "Do you hear that boys," she said to the empty car. "We're taking the war to Evil everywhere!" She shuttered. "This makes me feel so patriotic!" She said patting the back of the front seat with her right arm and checking her lipstick in the mirror. After about twenty minutes, she saw the first group of people run from the one of the main exits to the mall, followed by another group and then a stream of people. She didn't hear the explosions; she didn't expect to. The looks on their faces told her something had happened. She heard the sirens starting to arrive. There was one, and then three, then she couldn't count them. They were coming from every direction. She didn't smile. She just started her car and drove away.

CHAPTER TWELVE
*I have always thought the actions of men the
best interpreters of their thoughts.*
—John Locke

"**Y**ou knew this was going to happen," Cooper said to Paul as they walked down the hall toward the shift commander's office. Cooper and Paul were instructed to report to the lieutenant's office upon their return to the station the following early afternoon after their three days off. It wasn't uncommon to be called in multiple times to the office after an event like this. The shooting they were involved in was so rare, not because of its violence but because of the extensive involvement of the officers and the length of the fight. Only the Bank of America shoot out in Los Angeles in 1996 had something this violent. While most police gunfights lasted only three seconds, this one lasted minutes. Cops involved make the news—everywhere, as well as wind up in some lieutenant's office.

"Yeah, yeah, I know. This isn't going to go away anytime soon," Paul responded.

"Nope, I think we're just getting started, partner."

"Oh, boy," Paul said with a deep sigh.

"By the way," Cooper said, chewing hard on the three pieces of gum in his mouth. They stopped just outside the lieutenant's office. "You flew that ship like it was your own the other night."

"Yeah, hey, I'm sorry. I know you told me to catch some air but—"

Cooper stopped him. "No, listen. You did well. You saved all our asses. I just want to say—"

"Yeah, I know. You don't have to say it."

"Good."

"I'll take a hug, though," Paul said.

"What?"

"A hug. Look, this is a watershed moment in Phoenix Police history, Cooper Gardner saying 'thank you.' It's enough to make you tear up."

"I got your tears. Stop it or I'll go all *voodoo* on you."

"No, really, give me a hug." Paul reached out his arms.

"You touch me and I'll set you on fire."

"Okay, okay."

"Let's just go in and get this over with," Cooper said with a frown.

"That's fine. How about a kiss then."

"What the—"

"Come on, just a little peck. We're in a moment here," Paul was trying not to smile. He was sure Cooper was sweating.

"Fire. Big raging fire, I swear."

Both men talked to the chief and several assistant chiefs and commanders the night of the flight. That was common. The real interviews happened the next day by the shooting review team. Even if it was a bad shoot or some other event of high drama, the 'suits' would all show up, make sure their people were okay, then crawl back into the shadows, leaving the management of the event and its follow-up to the lower-rank supervisors. Paul and Cooper knew they weren't going to fly for awhile; they just didn't know what they were going to be doing pending the shooting review board.

Lieutenant Isaac Bridgewater was new to the district. He had transferred from the 500 area to the 200 hundred area three weeks ago. Not much was known about him. The rumors had started he was a real ball-buster, name-taker, snitch-hater. On the other hand, some said he was quiet and fair. Whether that was a good thing for Cooper and Paul remained to be seen, as far as they were concerned.

He wasn't well known, but his secretary was.

Maggie was the 'Gatekeeper.' She controlled access to the Lieutenant. She had been with the department for as long as anyone could remember; she actually started her career as part of the custodial staff when she was just out of high school. She had worked her way through two years of night school at Glendale Community College and got her Associate of Arts degree in Business Administration. Six months after she finished her program, a position opened in the police department and she got it. That was thirty-seven years ago. She worked for all the divisions including the assistant chiefs on the fourth floor. She knew more about the department than the department knew about itself and if one could look—where the skeletons were buried. She knew Cooper. She had done shots of tequila with Cooper and Moreno when she was a much younger woman, and single. Maggie and Cooper had toyed with each other, but both were involved with others and the timing was never right.

"Maggie, darling, how is my favorite Executive Assistant?" he said as he walked into her office and sat on the edge of her desk. She looked at him over the top of her glasses. Paul took two steps back and pretended to be looking at a picture on the wall.

"Cooper Harrison Gardner, what pooch did you screw this time?"

"Maggie, please—not in front of the kid. Kid, this is Maggie. There is no finer woman on the planet—this Maggie," Cooper said as he pointed to Paul and then back to her. He shielded his mouth as if he just let out a guarded secret. "She can drink you under any table from here to Manila."

"Officer Gardner, you're going to give this young officer a bad image of me. And frankly, no sweet talk will get me to tell you what the lieutenant wants to talk to you about. But, it wouldn't take a fortune-teller to predict it has something to do with you shooting up a neighborhood and almost crashing a very expensive piece of equipment the other night."

Paul moved from the picture to the conversation. "She's right. That shouldn't be too hard to figure out. He's our new lieutenant and he probably wants to know why we took a multimillion-dollar aircraft and turned it inside out while breaking about a dozen FAA flight rules. That's all—no big deal. My life is over." He went back to looking at the pictures on the wall.

Maggie and Cooper looked at Paul. "Coop, you've contaminated this boy already."

"You know, frankly, it wasn't me this time. This kid turned that ship inside out. I was just a spectator."

"Thanks for throwing me under the bus, partner."

"Not a problem, partner. So what do you think, Mag? What's this hard-britches like?"

As if on cue, a voice bellowed from the interior office. "Mrs. Turner, are those two officers here yet?"

She smiled. She squinted her eyes and the glasses rose up on her nose. "Looks like you're going to find out first hand. Good luck, boys." She turned and began typing again.

Paul and Cooper each took a breath and entered the lieutenant's office and came to attention in front of his desk. He was sitting with his hands folded on top of an open manila folder. He appeared to be reading it.

He had aged since the violence of his youth. Isaac Bridgewater was now a calm, white-shirted middle-aged man with silver hair across his temples and the sides of his closely cropped head. From the looks of him, anyone could tell he was a powerful man in his youth. Cooper and the lieutenant didn't recognize each other. There was no reason to. Now, in his fifties, there was a presence which Cooper had seen before. There was a presence he recognized, but he couldn't say from where. There, Cooper thought, sits a man who has experienced chaos. He had a look, a body presentation, one of quiet confidence. *We could be in trouble.*

His demeanor was such that nothing presented itself which couldn't be handled; things could always be worse. This man seemed to have dealt with chaos better than Cooper did; at least the crisp, white shirt and dark tie gave that impression. The lieutenant didn't look up when the two officers walked in. He continued reading the file, which Cooper assumed was the report on the night of the shootout.

"Gardner and Jackson reporting as ordered," Cooper said.

There was a pause, as if the man didn't hear him. He spoke without looking up. "Gentlemen, I have been reviewing the file regarding the actions from the other night. It appears, Officer Jackson, you had a busy night."

"Lieutenant, uh, Officer Jackson was obeying my orders," Cooper intervened.

"Yes, I noticed from your report," the lieutenant said, still not looking up.

"Lieutenant, although I was with and under Officer Gardner's tutelage, he did not order me to violate FAA air regs. I was responsible for those—"

"Tutelage?' Yes, I noticed that in your report as well. Well, tell me gentlemen. If both of you claim to be so 'in charge' of a multimillion dollar aircraft the citizens of this great city have entrusted you with, then who the hell is telling the truth? Hum? Can you tell me who was *flying* this aircraft?" He flipped back to a page in the file. "According to this report 'two to five feet off the ground at approximately 100 miles per hour'?"

Cooper turned his head to Paul. "Were you going that fast? That's pretty good."

Jackson just shook his head.

"Shut up, Cooper," the lieutenant said.

"Shutting up, sir."

"Officer Jackson. Son, your first few days in a new unit should not be followed by an ass-chewing by someone with bars on their collar. All I wanted to do this morning was enjoy a nice cup of coffee and read the god-damn paper. But no, I get a call from the Chief—*The Chief*—asking me if I knew two of my officers were playing 'Chicken' with one of our helicopters. I said, 'Why—no Chief, I did not know that.' I've been here for hours and I haven't read my paper. I'm tired, my feet are sore and I am terribly afraid you have given me the beginning of a three day onset of constipation. Do you know what that means? It really does mean the proverbial shit flows downhill—right on you two—a gift from me to you. I'm grumpy, gentlemen. You don't want to start your day with me when I'm grumpy. That's why my wife wants me to go to work, so I don't drip grumpiness on her new carpet, which I'm still making payments on. Do you hear the grumpiness in my voice, gentlemen?"

"You sound fine to me, Lieutenant," Cooper said.

"Shut up again, Cooper—rhetorical question." The lieutenant sat back in his chair. "Do you know how many bullet holes are in that ship?"

"Uh, no, uh, I didn't check, Lieutenant —we were, uh, I mean, they came and got the ship and flew it back before we had a chance to—"

"Eight. Eight bullet holes in a six-million-dollar aircraft that is two months old and doesn't belong to either of you."

"Eight?"

"Eight."

"That does seem a little—excessive," Cooper said, still at attention.

"You bet your ass that's excessive. Maintenance doesn't know when they'll get that ship back on line. We have a six-million-dollar paperweight sitting in the hangar out at Deer Valley Airport."

The lieutenant looked up at the two men standing in front of his desk. "Officer Jackson, that will be all. You are flying a desk for three additional days then patrol until this investigation is over and we determine your fitness for air service. Officer Gardner, you will stay for another minute." Paul acknowledged the order and did an about-face turn and out the door without looking at Cooper.

"Officer Gardner, you damn near got you and your partner killed. What were you thinking?"

"Lieutenant, the ground unit was getting overrun. If we didn't do something, they would have been killed as sure as you and I are here. You know that."

"No, I don't know that. I've checked your file, Officer. You've been here before, three times as well as for six general complaints about you flying too low and posing a threat to the citizenry of this city. It also says you won the city's Medal of Valor once, and you were nominated for it two other times." The Lieutenant paused as his eyes scanned the file. "It says here in one of the *dozens* of reports that you were playing music as you came over the officers on the ground. Neither you nor Jackson mentioned it in your reports. He somehow, conveniently, overlooked it. I'm assuming the music was your idea?"

"Yes, sir."

"Yes, sir, what?"

"Yes, sir, it was my idea. Steppenwolf."

"Steppenwolf?"

"Yes, sir."

Silence fell over the room before the Lieutenant spoke again. Cooper was looking at him, staring at the folder with the reports of the events of that night in it. It didn't appear to Cooper he was reading it.

"You were in Vietnam, Officer Gardner," he said as he came back from the day-dream. Cooper noticed a beading of sweat on the lieutenant's forehead.

Cooper frowned for a moment, confused by the change in direction. "Almost two complete tours with the Army, yes, sir."

"Where were you based?"

"Mostly in the north, out of Da Nang, and we spent a lot of time around Hue, near the border."

The lieutenant paused again. He walked around his desk and looked at two old photographs on the wall behind his desk.

He got back to the hole where his men, Tyrone, Victor, and Fitz were. He pulled the dead NVA soldier off the wounded marine and tossed him forward of the hole. Fitz was lying in the bottom, coughing. Blood mixed with the dirt to form a brown mud on his chest. He had lost control of his bowels and bladder and the scent filled the air in the base of the pit. Tyrone was tying a pressure dressing on the wound in his side, but it was just an attempt at delaying the inevitable. Fitz was dying. "How you doin' Marine?" Bridgewater asked as he crouched down next to him.

"I'm a little cold, Gunny," he said as he began to tremble. Bridgewater took out the med kit and pulled out an injector of morphine and shot it into Fitz's thigh. The trembling began to subside.

"There, that should make you feel better."

"Thanks. Is the sun comin' out?" Fitz said as he tried to look up. His head was wedged in such a way he couldn't move it.

Bridgewater heard the music at the same time as the others.

Fitz listened and smiled. "That's *Steppenwolf*. Air Calvary is here."

Bridgewater knew it, too. "Get your asses low in the hole. They're coming in and they're going to kill anything standing." Bridgewater turned back to the front of the shooting area and saw out the corner of his eye three shadows running up the slope toward their hole.

Cooper didn't know what the lieutenant was thinking. He couldn't make out the two pictures of Lieutenant's Isaac Bridgewater's company standing on a treeless hill. The lieutenant sat back down in his chair and pulled it up to the desk, his eyes back on the file. Cooper noticed there was a slight line of sweat on the Lieutenant's forehead. "You, also, will be on patrol until the investigation is done. I will let you know what your flight status is at that time. That is all."

Cooper felt he hadn't said enough. "Lieutenant, if it is any help, the, uh, the kid did a good job. I did all the rule-breaking stuff. He was —"

"I understand, Officer. That will be enough. You may go," the lieutenant said without looking up. "Officer Gardner," he called, just before Cooper got to the door.

"Sir."

"The next time you use police broadcast channels with non-sanctioned methods to intervene in a hostile action between other officers or citizens of this city, make sure it finds its way into your report. Do we understand each other? Your report is not complete. I expect a supplement on my desk by this time tomorrow."

Cooper smiled. He knew this would be the extent of the investigation as far as the Lieutenant was concerned. He and Paul would push a patrol car for awhile, but the rest of the events would either be validated or forgotten about. "Yes sir. And might I add the Lieutenant is a peach."

"Officer Gardner," Lieutenant Bridgewater started with a sigh. "I have spent too much time carrying these gold bars on my collar and days like today, dealing with your white ass, causes them to drag my black butt home, tired and wanting to drink myself into a stupor. I would, too, if I didn't have diverticulitis, a headache, and a wife with a list of honey-dos the length of my arm. You think I'm a peach? If you don't want this peach to fall from the stratosphere onto your balding-ass head, then quit getting my aircrafts shot up, and log the damn music!"

"Yes sir. The Lieutenant is not a fruit of any kind."

"Fuck you. Get your tail out of my office. You're tiring me."

Cooper turned and left the room. Lieutenant Isaac Bridgewater sat back in his chair and looked at the door. He stared at the door for a moment, then back to the file. As Cooper shut the door behind him, he looked right at Maggie, who was looking at him over the top of her glasses. He smiled at her as he approached her desk and walked around to her and kissed her on the cheek. "He loves me, Maggie."

"Yeah, I heard—clear out here. From the sounds of it, he loves you a lot."

"Damn right," he said to Maggie as he walked out with a little swagger in his step.

CHAPTER THIRTEEN
The chief obstacle to the progress of the human race is the human race.
—Don Marquis

———————————

After desk duty for three days, the partners spent the afternoon after their patrol shift in the workout center. Paul spent the time working with the weights and Cooper spent his time hitting the strike bags. He laid on the matt and practiced striking the fabric-covered bag with a scissor kick while lying on his side. It had been awhile since he had formally worked out. Paul prodded him into it. It felt good to get physical again, even though he knew he was going to be painfully sore in the morning.

"So what do you think is going to happen?" Paul asked Cooper after they had been working out for about twenty minutes.

"It's hard to say, but I think we're going to be fine," Cooper said. He lay on his side, and punched the bag propped on a stand from the side in a whip-kick motion with his legs.

"We're fine? That's it? That's all you've got to say?"

"Yeah, what did you expect?"

Paul walked over and picked up a strike bag, walked back over to Cooper who began striking it. "God, Cooper, we're hanging out here. At least I am. You can retire. I still have years to go before I punch out."

"Relax, we're all right. We got that officer to the hospital in the nick of time. We got a load of vermin off the street—some permanently. We got a lot going for us." He kept striking the bag.

"Tell me every night is not going to be like that one? Tell me you're getting too old to be doing that shit anymore and we're not going to get called into the LT's office on a weekly basis?" As Paul spoke, he kept moving closer to Cooper. Cooper's leg strikes were shortening, drawing Paul in nearer to him. As Paul waited for his answer, Cooper rolled his body and switched his kick to scissor Paul's legs, taking them out from under him. Paul fell forward to Cooper's side who caught him and quickly put him in a choke hold, still holding him with his legs. He spoke into Paul's ear as Paul lay on top of him. Paul grabbed Cooper's arm around his neck in a spontaneous reaction to the fall. "Like they say, partner, nothing is certain."

"All right, fair enough. You've been in the system longer than I have. But could you wait until I get more familiar with the aircraft? I've just started on this gig with an old man at the stick and I was feeling like I was back hopping rooftops and dropping LRP teams in downtown Iraq. Be gentle with me," he said as he lifted himself off Cooper who was still on the ground. "And show me that move you just did, will you? That wasn't bad."

The next day, the two found themselves back in the squad room, paired together to patrol the downtown area. Paul was disappointed there wasn't a resolution. He thought the delay, even one day, was not a good sign. Cooper knew the city had to cover themselves and make sure there was nothing wrong with what they did. It was dramatically unorthodox; their 'adventure' as the rest of the district officers were calling it. The city lawyers would be fielding calls from people who wanted to sue the city because the helicopter disturbed their sleep or made their cat run away. Someone was going to sue because that's what people did. Cooper knew the Lieutenant had made up his mind and was probably letting them cool their heels pushing a car. As the two walked into the briefing room, someone started, then the rest of the officers kicked in, with a chorus of the Air Force anthem. On the white board in front of the room, was written, 'Phoenix Police Strategic Air Command—we shoot anything.'

"Ha—ha—ha, very funny, very funny," Cooper said as he walked into the room with Paul right next to him. "Hey, speaking of shooting people, anybody hear how Tony and Julie are doing?"

One of the officers in the back piped up. "He came through the surgery just fine. They were more concerned about the blood loss than anything but apparently it all worked out in the operation. Julie's fine. Well, I guess as good as she can be after living through that. That was some good flying, Coop."

"Don't thank me; thank my little Ethiopian-looking partner here. I haven't seen flying like that since I crashed in Hanoi in 1969," Cooper said. Cooper turned to Paul and put his hand on his shoulder as the officers gave them both a round of applause.

"You didn't crash in Hanoi in 1969," Paul said out of the side of his mouth.

"I know, but it sounded good. Most of these young pukes couldn't find Hanoi on a map anyway."

The shift sergeant, Douglas O'Donnell, a grizzled old man with a thick chest and a flattop haircut, called the briefing to order.

"Okay, item first. There have been no new developments regarding the multiple explosions at Paradise Valley Mall. According to ATF, the explosives were homemade devices. ATF is keeping a lot of the information close to the vest, but we are to pay particular attention to anyone standing around fast food locations, food courts, trash cans, and holding shopping bags, which narrows our field to about fifty-million suspects. There were twelve victims at the mall; two did expire and another is close, but is believed to eventually pull through." The sergeant looked up and saw Paul and Cooper sitting off to the side. "Lucky for us, we have two of our grounded Blue Angels. Jackson and Gardner, you two will be on foot beat instead of a car today, from Central to Seventh Street and from Jackson to Van Buren, until you are reassigned or until further notice. Jacobs and Tommer, you'll drive the Sam Unit, and Toolie, you take the swing. Okay people, this individual has killed and critically injured several people. The FBI's profile on this guy isn't complete, but they're saying he will probably get bolder as time goes on."

Paul raised his hand. "Sergeant, has anyone laid claim to this thing yet?"

"Yeah, about a half-dozen different groups, including Al Qaida. That's why ATF isn't letting anyone in on what they found. When they find a suspect, they'll match 'em to the evidence. What we do know is the explosive used is common and homemade—that's not good. What *is* good is some of the other explosive devices with it were not. Those are traceable." The squad could tell the Sergeant knew more than he was saying.

"Those guys couldn't match their socks, let alone a bomber," Cooper whispered to Paul.

"Officer Gardner, did you have something to add to my briefing?"

"I was just telling him, Sergeant, that those fries match their locks left alone at Bob Stomer's," he said with a straight face.

The sergeant looked over the top of his reading glasses at Cooper. "I thought so. Okay, people, let's go earn our pay."

Paul was lost, perplexed; a frown on his face begged an answer as they walked out of the briefing room. "Who's Bob Stomer?"

Cooper smiled and shook his head.

An officer stepped out into the hall and called to Cooper. "Coop, your sister is on the phone, line three."

Cooper went into an interview room. Just before he shut the door he turned to Paul. "Go get our stuff. I'll meet you outside."

Paul turned to the officer as he walked by him. "Cooper has a sister?"

"Yeah, back in D.C. somewhere. She isn't doing so well, so she calls her big brother every so often and I guess he perks her up. She calls here because she knows he's here and he doesn't answer his cell during shift."

"What's wrong with her?"

"Cancer, I think, at least that's the rumor. He hasn't really told anyone."

Jodi's home was well kept, orderly, even as she was planning to blow up everything and anyone who had anything to do with her husband's and son's death. The mall was just an icebreaker.

She continued to work, even as her life was consumed with acting out her retribution. She was still able to function in both worlds: that of a professional engineer and now of a mass murderer. Even though her business was failing, she worked as if it wasn't. No one witnessed anything more than a struggling widow and a crumbling business she was still trying to keep afloat.

Jodi had bought a new couch and matching end tables just before her husband died. When she got home from work, she tossed her purse and bags down on the floor next to one of the tables, kicked off her shoes, and looked through the stack of mail. "Hi guys, I'm home," she called out loud to the empty home. She stopped for a moment, listening for a response. "You guys aren't here?" She stared for a minute, then back to the mail. Nothing of interest for her, a Macy's catalog, a few ads, nothing. She walked into the kitchen, retrieved a small bottle of water from the refrigerator and a frozen dinner of macaroni and cheese, and popped it in the microwave. She headed into the dining room where, spread out on her antique Dunkin-Phyfe table, were the separate parts of the next set of bombs, ready for assembly. She walked over to the CD player and pushed 'Play'. Vivaldi's Largo from Winter from *The Four Seasons*, began to play. She put the water down on a coaster, rolled up the sleeves on her blouse and started in as if it was just part of her workday.

On the corner of the table were old articles about an investigation into city workers submitting fraudulent paperwork getting paid off to accept it. She knew it. It validated her belief the city was corrupt. She believed the city was to blame for her family's demise, and these articles inflamed her and justified, in her mind, that what she was doing was good and pure and maybe even the work of God, if she believed in such a thing. She didn't. She took a sip of water and went to work.

Paul and Cooper walked the tight streets and alleys in downtown Phoenix. There were things they could only see on foot that they couldn't see in the front seat of a patrol car, tight, confined spaces, hidden from view from the street, tremendous places for people to hide.

"So, how long did you say you've been a cop?" Paul asked Cooper, who was looking in a trash dumpster.

Cooper didn't break stride or look up. "So, how long have you been alive?"

"Come on, you're not that old. Now, don't get me wrong; you are old. I mean, I just hope that when I'm your age and *if* I look like you do now, someone will suffocate me in the middle of the night. I mean really, partner, look in the mirror. Seriously, why haven't you left the street? Or the air? You could be flying some desk by now, or fishing on some abandoned atoll, cursing out the natives, collecting your retirement check. How come you're not?"

"Sometimes I feel real old." Cooper walked a little farther without saying anything, and then stopped. "Here's an answer to your question." He walked over to a set of stacked boxes laying next to a blue steel dumpster. Under the shelter of the boxes, sat a man who found life living off the waste of others. His clothes contained months of filth. The man was sleeping, or appeared to be sleeping. There was a slight twitch, a muscle constriction in his right hand, the index finger specifically.

"He's passed out," Paul said.

"No, he's sleeping," Cooper shook his head. "His name's Skinner."

"First or last?" Paul asked.

"Don't know. That's all I ever called him by. I also heard he was a lieutenant in the Corps in a prior life."

Neither knew what the man was dreaming about. Had they known, they would have awakened him to end the nightmare.

He was a Marine lieutenant in a burned out jungle a long way from where he slept now. It was the same dream, over and over with different parts showing themselves at different times. This time, it was the conversations and faces he overheard and saw as he walked the perimeter of a hill a firebase was on.

Skinner struggled with names, working to keep them in his fading memory, but he never forgot their faces. Their voices were still just as loud as the day he heard them. They filled every part of his life now, awake and asleep. They never left him—ever.

110

One of his soldiers, Skinner thought his name was Tyrone, was busy wiping down the individual components of his rifle as he sat against the reinforcing sandbags in his fighting hole. He was careful not to let any more dust than possible get into the machinery of his weapon. A bead of sweat ran down the center of his forehead and between his eyebrows, down his nose and eventually to the tip where it tumbled to his exposed chest, already soaked with sweat. Skinner was sitting a short distance away, looking at a recon map of the surrounding area..He remembered watching the bead of sweat and trying to guess when it was going to fall.

"Jesus it's hot, even for January," Tyrone said as he wiped the tip of his nose where the sweat bead jumped from. He took his thumb and squeegeed the sweat from his brow and forehead.

"Quit your bitchin'. It's no hotter here than where you're from. Your Daddy's farm along the Mississippi ain't any cooler in July than this here hole in January," Barnes Skomer said. Barnes was an 'odd fellow,' Skinner thought. Others in the company agreed.

"I ain't bitchin'. And even if I was, you're still the odd man out here. You like this shit too much. If we was back in the States and you was black, you is the type of guy I wouldn't want my sister to date unless I went along with a loaded carbine."

In Vietnam, Skomer was the guy, when the *Boogieman* came, people wanted to be near, even Skinner.

"Well, they can stay in that jungle the rest of their miserable little lives for all I care. They can even have Hue again. Just once I'd like a nice, quiet, night's sleep in my damn hole—without any rain if possible, but I ain't too picky. I'd settle for a night without someone trying to stick a bayonet up my ass," Victor said, chewing on the tip of his filter-less cigarette as he adjusted the sandbags around his fighting hole.

"Who would want that burned out wreck of a city anyway? There's nothin' left," Tyrone said.

"The NVA do," said a voice past Victor. It was Fitz, short for Corporal Jonathan Arnold Fitzpatrick, the ranking marine of the group. Skinner remembered Fitz was the smart one of that particular fire team. Skinner always remembered that Fitz was on one end of the spectrum and Barnes Skomer was at the other end.

"How many times are you going to read that damn book?" Skomer lit a cigarette, then tossed the pack to Tyrone who was looking through a pair of binoculars at the distant tree line. The air was still.

Skinner pictured in his mind seeing Fitz remove his glasses and rub his eyes. They were tired, along with the rest of his body. "First of all, this ain't no damn book; this, this here is *the* book. My uncle gave it to me, for my birthday. Secondly, I'm three weeks behind you for time in-country and we both are in our ninth month in this here paradise."

"I read that book once," Victor said, licking his fingers.

"You read?" Tyrone asked.

"Yeah."

"My grandma use to read it every day. She would call me over and have me sit down and read it with her," Victor said.

"I never did. My mom had one and wanted me to read it. I started, but the damn thing was boring," Skomer cut in.

"You want to read it?" Fitz said, holding it up. "I'll let you have it if you want—"

"No, Shit for Brains." Skomer turned around, slid down the pile of sandbags and lit the doused end of his cigarette. He took a deep draw and let it out while allowing his head to rest back on the sandbag behind him. His eyes were closed and the sun landed full on his face. Fitz just ignored him and returned to the contents of the book.

"Corporal Fitzpatrick," Skinner could see himself calling to the corporal as he walked over the hill toward the men. The company Gunny was with him. "Put that book away and make your hole deeper."

Back in his youth, Patrick Skinner was a lean marine; who had graduated from one of the California college ROTC programs, not one of the 'ninety-day wonders' as the troops liked to call the guys the Corps was turning out as fast as they could. He envisioned himself as a career Marine, skinny, as were most of the men in-country, on a thin five-foot, ten-inch frame. He had been in for four years and was on his second tour. The boys trusted him as well as 'Gunny', Gunnery Sergeant Isaac Bridgewater. Then the dreamed turned. It always did. This was the easy part of the dream. But, it never ended here. It always went beyond the conversations he overheard, just before he would wake up in a cold sweat and his heart beating through his shirt, the part that alcohol and drugs were the only thing to make it go away.

"L.T.?" Fitz whispered.

"Right here son," the Lieutenant said. There were only five years difference between the two but war had aged them both.

"In, my jacket, take it." Fitz tried to reach for it but couldn't. The lieutenant reached in and took out the book, looked at it, and without comment shoved it in his own shirt. "Got it, okay, let's get these people out of here."

He could watch himself, like a movie, an image of him jumping in a fighting hole next to these same men

early the next day and saying something flippant—
something about it being a good morning and eating pie.

"Mornin' boys," he said as he fired two quick
rounds down range. "All we need now is a slice of pie
and we can have us a party. Sergeant, we getting these
wounded out of here?"

He remembered even having a smile on his face
when he said it. He couldn't remember what exactly he
said but he remembered their faces after he said it.
Humor, in trauma, was weird. Their faces were blank; as
if the men, whose faces he was looking at, were dead
already. Many of them were. The faces on the living
were the same look on the dead. His smile appeared,
just before he began to shoot his weapon, fighting for
the last few seconds of his life, just before the
helicopters came and made everything louder. The
dream, where ever they started, always ended up here.

Skinner's beard was silver now, with streaks of
brown, stained from food or liquor or vomit or some
combination. His clothes were in tatters. His shoes were
old, black Converse All Star high-tops with no shoe
strings. The dirt around his ankles under the flapping
loose top of the shoe almost matched the color of his
sneakers. It was hard to see where the shoe stopped
and his skin started. The man was gaunt, probably in his
late fifties, but looked seventy. If the two had been in a
patrol car, they would have never seen him, which was
the man's goal. He woke with a start. He was breathing
hard and fast. His eyes rolled like they were on a
carousel. He looked up, focused on the images of the
two officers, then went back to doing what he appeared
to be doing before, digging through what looked like
three food bags from various fast-food restaurants that
dotted the downtown area. He was working on a Jack-
in-the-Box bag, checking the inside of a taco pouch. He

had torn it open and was licking the remnants off the inside of the pouch as if the two officers weren't there. Some he got in his mouth, some in his beard. Cooper moved an open box; the man froze, like a wild animal waiting to see if the predator was coming after him or going to move on.

"Hey Skinner, how you doin,' man?" Cooper said as he lifted the box off of the man and got a full view of him. He was filthy with a worn Hawaiian shirt and dirty slacks.

His eyes, deep in their sockets and bracketed by deep crow's feet around their corners, rolled up from looking in the bag to Cooper's face. He squinted as he focused on him. His brain ran the image of Cooper's face through what was left of the files of familiar faces in his brain. A smile came, a weak, soft smile. The crow's feet cut deep. The smile exposed empty holes where teeth used to live, long since gone, and others that were in the process of leaving. He reached up with his right hand after first wiping it off on his shirt. His green eyes were shaded in red. He smelled of stale liquor and filth. Cooper reached out and shook the man's hand. "Hey Coop, you ol' bastard. Where have you been?" Skinner said.

"Skinner, I thought the last time we met, you were going back to live with your niece in Detroit. Why are you back in my city?"

"I went to Detroit, Coop, just like you said. I took that ticket you bought for me and it got me back."

"What the hell are you doing here, then?"

The two let go of each other. Skinner wiped something away hanging from the corner of his mouth. It didn't appear to either officer to be anything related to what he found in the Jack-in-the-Box bag. "My niece died last month. I had no one back there to stay with. Her sons hated me being there, so I hopped a Big Red back out here. Coop, you got some coin I can borrow, just until my VA check comes in at the end of the month, huh? I just need a little, you know, *nudge* to get me through the night."

Cooper knew Thunderbird or Cobra 40 was Skinner's drink of choice. He pulled out his radio. "Two-Adam-seventeen."

"Two-Adam-seventeen," came the radio operator's voice.

"What are you doing?" Paul asked.

Cooper held up his finger as if to pause his answer to his partner before he spoke again into the radio. "What's the call sign for the wagon tonight?"

"Three Indian forty-three."

"Can you tell them to go to channel ten for me?" he said. Channel ten was the operating channel that allowed officers to talk to one another off the normal chase bands used for traffic. He turned back to Paul. "I'm having the wagon meet us down the street," he said as he switched to channel ten on his own radio.

"We don't wagon drunks. That's what LARC is for."

"They won't take him where this guy's going," he said, holding his radio up to his ear so he could hear the response.

"Where is this guy going?" Paul said.

Cooper looked at him and winked. "Where the ghosts won't get to him tonight."

The radio squelched to life. "Three Indian forty-three to two-Adam-seventeen."

He looked at Paul and smiled before he spoke into the radio. "Terry, you on tonight?"

Paul could hear the conversation. "Yeah, Coop, I heard you were down with us for a while. What's up?"

"I have some found property."

"Where do you want me to pick it up at?"

"Meet me at Beany's in about forty-five minutes." He turned to Skinner who was trying to stand. "Skinner, you know I won't give you any money, but let's you, me, and the kid here go get something to eat. The kid said he'll buy."

"What did I say?" Paul chirped over Cooper's shoulder.

"Thanks, kid." Skinner finally got to his feet leaning on the dumpster to stabilize himself. "Say, do I know him, Coop?" he said, gesturing with his thumb to the younger officer.

Cooper grabbed Skinner's arm to support him as he let go of the dumpster. Paul followed his lead and came around and got Skinner's other arm. "He's all right. He was a squid." Cooper got Paul's attention and pointed to Skinner's legs. Skinner had only one leg. He stuffed his pant leg back up into itself. "You lose your leg again?" Cooper asked. Paul started to look around on the ground with his flashlight to find the missing leg. It was early evening and the shadows were getting long and dark in the alley.

"No, it's over there," he said pointing under a pile of boxes. "Those young bastards tried to beat me with it the other night." Skinner's wheelchair was also buried under the boxes. Cooper helped him to his chair, retrieved the leg and gave it to Skinner. Skinner stuffed his stump, cut off just below the knee, back into the filthy artificial limb and pulled his pant leg over it.

Skinner was looking past Cooper to Paul. "He was a fish, huh?" he said out of the side of his mouth with a thumb gesture aimed at Paul.

"SEAL," Paul said.

Skinner just nodded. "Boy, don't even look like he shaves yet." Skinner paused before he spoke again. "You must have stepped in some bad crap again Coop if you and the boy are on foot patrol in the alleys."

Cooper smiled. "Yeah, never can seem to get out of that, can I?"

He looked at his partner with a smirk, and said to Skinner, "Come on, Lieutenant, you push this chair over to Beany's and we will be right behind you. If you get there, we'll buy you whatever you want to eat and some for the road, and then I got your ride for you. But you got to get between here and there. We aren't going to help you."

Skinner straightened his back and somehow managed to lift himself out of the wheelchair and lock his legs, his feet at a distinct forty-five degree angle. His right hand was covered in sores and old cuts. Skinner brought it up and touched his forehead, saluting Cooper. "Don't be too long," Skinner said. He turned the chair around and using the handrails to lean on, he pushed the chair in front of him down the street to Beany's, a small coffee shop with four tables and half-dozen counter seats one-hundred yards around the corner.

"What—" Paul stumbled on his words as Skinner moved out of earshot.

"They're everywhere. That one received the Silver Star in 1968 for some piece of real estate in Vietnam to support operations in Laos. I heard his group would go out and harass the NVA in Laos and other parts of south country. He was shot in the arm and in the ass, and most of his company, I heard, was killed in some gun fight during Tet. He spent the last two hours fighting with his bare hands. He was lucky then. He lost the leg sometime after that, I heard."

"1968 - we weren't in Laos in '68 ."

"Uh-huh," Cooper said. "Actually, his official citation did read South Vietnam, you're right." There was a sarcastic tone in his voice. "We were not in Laos in 1968. Anyway. He came home, but his mind stayed there. He blames himself for all the people he lost under his command; his friends, his wife who left him, his son who is god knows where. I'm sure on that little trip you made to the Middle East, you saw a few things you wish you hadn't."

Paul looked down the street. There was a man out for a jog. He was running with long, fast strides. He was a young man with a lean, fit body. He looked back at Skinner and the prosthetic leg. He knew some of his generation who had to wear the same thing and why. He had seen this movie before.

"Come on, run, run, run," Paul said as he watched the team he had just put down north of Kuwait City as they were running to the pickup point. They were drawing machine gun fire as they fled. The charges they set hadn't gone off yet and the Republican Guard spotted them and were giving chase. Paul's escort helicopters were giving cover fire and his door gunners were melting barrels. All he could do was sit and wait for the men to get loaded. Then the splatter hit the side of his face.

"What the—," he started to speak and then turned to his right. His co-pilot, Benny Rodriguez, had half his cheek explode with a lucky long shot from an Iraq AK-47, exposing his cheek, shredding his lower jaw, and scattering it all over the cockpit. The second co-pilot in less than two days and Paul, without a scratch. Benny was either real lucky or real unlucky, Paul thought. He lived.

"Did you hear me?" Cooper said.

"What? Oh, yeah, sorry. I did." Paul didn't say anything for a moment. "So, what's his full name?"

Cooper shook his head. "I don't know, don't really care." He watched him for another moment then Cooper continued. "He can go to this place tonight that isn't part of the homeless shelters. He can hang out there for a few days, get dried out and food in his belly."

"How come no one knows about this place?"

Cooper shrugged. "It's not on the charts. People would misuse it."

"What?"

"It's one of several safe places for people like him—" He turned and looked at Paul. "—and you, and me, if we ever turn out like that," he pointed in Skinner's direction. "They don't pay me enough to turn my back on them. They don't pay you enough, either. Remember that. There is a very thin line between him and us."

Paul looked at his partner's worn face. He could tell and knew enough about Cooper's war to take his words of advice to heart. Paul too, had seen carnage and violence to such a degree that he could not describe it to anyone with any accuracy. People had to see the movie first-hand to truly understand it, and he had seen it so he could relate to what his partner was saying. There was a thin line between sanity and insanity.

The two made it to Beany's right after Skinner arrived. Cooper ordered Skinner a breakfast sandwich to go. While Paul waited outside, the police van pulled up. He and Cooper helped Skinner into the back. After closing the door they stood and watched it pull away.

"So, where's he going?"

"There's an old converted house on the south side of the river a friend of mine runs as a veteran's shelter."

"You know how many vets are on—"

"The city would tie my friend up in all types of red tape—zoning, inspections, and any other B.S. thing they could find. This guy just has a thing for these people and he depends on a few of us to feed them to him. He patches them up and kicks them loose when they're ready," Cooper said.

Paul knew he was right. He had seen the services provided to the military by the V.A. They were good, the best in the world when compared to other countries' military support. But it wasn't good enough. Nobody thought it was good enough. "That was a good thing you did back there," Paul said.

"Yeah, I'm just a regular friggin' Florence Nightingale. Come on, we have to walk a foot beat." Cooper turned just as both their radios cracked with a three-second tone indicating emergency traffic.

"Assault in progress. Victim is being beaten by at least five males-sixteen to twenty-five years," the radio operator said, and then repeated the address of the assault.

"That's one block from here," Paul said.

"Tell them we'll respond." Cooper and Paul turned down the street in the direction of the call and broke into a trot.

It wasn't quite a full block for the two to get to the site where the call sent them. It was down a dark alley that turned back on itself behind one of the taller buildings downtown. As the two rounded the corner, they heard several voices. Paul led the way with Cooper huffing and puffing behind him.

A man was kneeling on the ground. He was surrounded by what Cooper and Paul could see to be six males in their late teens or early twenties. The man's hands were tied together. The teens were taunting him, laughing and spitting at him, throwing beer cans at him. The man on the ground looked older than Skinner and just as worn. He had what looked like to Cooper a piece of wood. He was holding it up in his bound hands in a poor attempt at protecting himself from the cans and spit being slung his way. The younger men were so focused on their victim, they didn't notice Cooper and Paul until they were on them with their Glocks drawn.

121

Paul commanded, "Police—everybody hold it right where you are." The alley was a dead-end. There was no way out except past them.

"Listen to the man, boys, and no one gets hurt," Cooper added. "We need to see everyone's hands right now," Cooper said slightly out of breath. He could see Paul had his gun trained on the men to the right, so Cooper put his sights on the ones closest to him on the left.

The biggest one of the group, and farthest away, looked at the two officers. He smiled. "There's only two of you. There's six of us. You can't shoot us. We ain't got no gun."

"Don't need you to have a gun," Paul said, never moving his gun or his eyes off the group he was watching. "Those sticks and cans are good enough to get your ass shot off. You boys need to drop them now."

The shortest of the group said, "You ain't gonna shoot us. We'll sue. Go ahead," he said as he looked at the bigger man for acceptance. Cooper figured the big one was the leader of the group.

There was a moment of quiet. Time froze. None of the men moved. The only movement came from the victim on the ground who took deep, labored, breaths. Cooper could see by the light, the streetlight on the corner, he was bleeding from his scalp.

"You know, Mouthy Ass there has a point, partner."

"That point being?" Paul said over the top of his gun.

If we shoot 'em, the paperwork would be downright chilling, especially on all that other paper we've been writing. Then our pictures will be all over the newspapers—aaagain. Frankly, if we kill them, we don't have to read them their rights. I hate reading people their rights." He spoke as he moved toward the man on the ground. Cooper holstered his gun and pulled a knife from his left boot. He flipped it open and cut the man's bindings in one stroke. "Then the press will want statements, and when they find out what these bastards did, they'll want to make a movie about us. They'll ask me to play a small cameo role. You, too, probably. I would have to memorize lines and then there's the makeup. I just hate makeup. That just doesn't fit into my lifestyle." Cooper pulled out his M-3 Taser, pointed it at the big guy and pulled the trigger. The two darts found their mark in his left shoulder. Fifty-four thousand volts coursed through the man's body as he dropped to the ground, flopping like a fish on a dry riverbank.

"Then they'll start talking about how we suppressed the creativity of the youth of America. But the paperwork—wow." After five seconds, the big man lay still, moaning and rolling from side to side. He had lost control of his bladder. He made a feeble attempt at getting up. "Nope, I would just lay still if I were you, or I'll have to pull the trigger again," Cooper said as he pulled the trigger again. "Oops, my bad." He reloaded a second dart and pointed it at the small mouthy one.

"Like I was saying, partner, I don't want to do the paperwork; do you?" he said, turning to Paul, who was still holding his gun trained on the others.

"Don't you think we should call for backup, *partner?*" Paul asked over the top of his gun.

"Nope, I think we got this." Cooper holstered the Taser and then pulled out his expandable baton and opened it. "I have to agree with Floppy and the boys here. We can't shoot them. At least not all of them, but I sure would like to beat them half to death."

Paul wasn't quite sure what his older partner was going to do. In his mind, it looked like an old fashioned ass-whooping. "Cooper, they have weapons."

One of the other bigger boys said, "Yeah, old man, we have 'weapons.' You think you can take this knife away from me, old ma—"

Paul pulled his taser again and shot him. The man arched his back and then fell face first to the asphalt.

"Apparently, someone didn't get the memo on concealed weapons and trying to use them on police officers," Cooper said.

"What about us? That's only two and there's still four of us," piped up the kid again. He had found his voice.

"Winston?" Cooper said to the smaller one. Cooper recognized him from the neighborhood. The boy's face indicated he was surprised Cooper knew his name. "Yep, I know your name, your real name—not that pussy name your *homies* gave you, but the one your dear mother gave you when you were born. You know, boy, I really like your mother. She works really hard to keep your sorry ass out of situations just like this one. Your mother made me promise to keep an eye out for you whenever I could. You were there when I promised her. You were about twelve then."

"I don't care what—" the boy interrupted, but Cooper didn't stop.

"I promised her I would. I would suggest you leave while we have a little discussion with Doofus and Water-on-the-Brain here," he said pointing at the others.

The boy looked at the remainder of his friends still standing. Cooper knew he couldn't leave, but he also knew he had to make him the offer.

"I ain't leavin'. You want a piece of us? Come and get it."

Cooper pulled and shot Winston with his last Taser dart and let him flop on the ground next to the other two. He disengaged the wires and holstered it, still holding the expanded baton. The sound of Winston's body hitting the ground eliminated smiles from faces. "You know, it really speaks volumes how manly you all are beating up this old guy. I'd be willing to bet in his day he could clean all your clocks—all at the same time. Now I get the honor of doing it in his place," Cooper said as he approached the group. Paul looked at his partner and didn't say a word. He didn't have time to debate the pros and cons of the two-on-three ratio. He just knew you never leave your partner—ever.

"You ain't got nothin' for us, old man," challenged one of the remaining hoodlums still standing.

"We'll see," Cooper said as he took two quick steps and swung his baton, landing it across the man's thigh just above the knee. The nerve bundle sitting just under the muscle sent out a massive electrical impulse on impact, and the leg collapsed. He was out of the fight, holding his leg in agony. One more step to his right and Cooper shattered the wrist of another who had pulled out a knife. As the knife flew to the ground and the man grabbed his wrist, Cooper came in with an elbow strike to the man's face. He fell backwards, his nose exploding with snot and blood. He didn't get up, just laid there holding his broken nose. The last one found himself in a choking fog of pepper spray. Cooper turned to see Paul approaching him as he was bent over, coughing and choking. Paul walked up like he was approaching the 18th green at Augusta. He holstered his spray and using his baton as a pointer, he tapped the side of the man's leg, just above the knee.

"Listen to the old man and don't give me any reason to treat you like a par three. Lie flat on the ground or you're going to get the same thing your buddy got." He repeated himself, while at the same time tapping the leg just to let him know he was ready to

125

send him screaming, if he could actually scream. He was still choking on the pepper spray. The fight was over.

"There it is," Cooper said to him.

"There what is?" Paul said over his shoulder as he kept his eyes on the men on the ground.

"Your accent. I guess when you get busy your southerner comes out," Cooper said with a grin. Paul looked at him and frowned.

They never made a radio call for backup. By the time the two men called radio and told them they were in need of a wagon to transport the six men, they had all been handcuffed and left lying pretty much where they fell. Paul requested paramedics to check out everyone. When Phoenix Fire arrived, the lead paramedic just looked at the six men, then the two officers, and shook his head. He called for another medic unit to respond to the scene to assist. Two other police units showed up about the same time, as well as Sergeant O'Donnell. The sergeant talked to each officer separately and was satisfied with what he heard. He reminded both of them to include the use-of-force sheet in their reports and to supplement it when they turned it in. Cooper's wish for less paperwork didn't come true. When the discussion with the others was over, Cooper found his partner and walked over to him.

"Well, that was fun," he said with a half-smirk on his face.

"Don't you ever do that to me again," Paul said, poking Cooper in his chest.

Cooper frowned. "What are you getting your panties all in a bunch about?"

"You know damn well what I'm pissed about. We could have gotten our asses kicked, or shot, or cut or—"

"Oh come on, you knew as well as I did they didn't have anything—"

"Oh, now you're a psychic. Or you have x-ray vision and can see up their butts where they keep their bazookas. You know, Coop, you have a rep in this department but I, I didn't believe it. 'No one could be as crazy as the rumors say,' I told myself. 'Nah, it's not as bad as I've heard,' I said. No—its worse. You're a friggin dinosaur with a death wish. Anyone around you is in the blast zone."

Cooper looked at Paul as if he was hearing the words for the first time. "You're upset because we did our job? Is that what you're upset about? Did you see what they were doing to that old man? He could have been your grandfather—or mine. What they did—"

"What they did was break the law. We're paid to enforce the law. Sometimes we win and sometimes we lose. And someday, if we're smart enough, we retire from this young man's profession and remember these days and smile at a job well done. I want to be able to look into my son's eyes, if you allow me to ever live long enough to have a son, and tell him how his old man did well. I want to finish this race strong and have those most important to me, those who love me the most, come up to me and say, 'Good job, I am so proud of you.' I don't want them to say 'Hey, remember the time you beat the hell out those guys in the dark alley?'"

"Those guys understand this justice. They know if they do A, B, or C—D, E and F will happen. If we don't do what we need to do, then all hell is going to break loose. It already has," Cooper said.

"You think you made an impression with those boys?"

"Yes, I do."

"The only thing you did was mark yourself. They will submit to your authority as long as you are the authority. As soon as you turn your back, they'll be right back at it. You didn't change anything with them except make them bitterer toward everyone wearing this uniform. Now I, we, every other cop in this city, have to deal with the seed you planted."

"What are you talking about? These guys have been like this—"

"Since when? Since the last time they got thumped? Look, these guys were bad, no doubt about it. But Coop, there's a right way and a wrong way. One way makes them our enemy forever."

Cooper looked at Paul before he spoke. "What would you college boys say we need to do? Breast-feed these people? Life is hard. Life is long and hard. Some days are easier than others and some days are downright shitty. No one is going to give these people anything that isn't labeled as a government handout."

"You can't change the person until you change the heart. You can't change the heart with the point of a gun or a swing of the big ugly stick. If you change the heart, you change the head," Paul said.

Cooper snickered. "You're so full of shit. You expect me to hug these—people? These people have got to learn. Someone has got to teach them."

Paul pointed at Cooper's chest again, "And I suppose you're the one to teach them?"

Paul saw Cooper's teeth clench and he rolled his eyes. Paul continued. "I do expect you to do your job, at least as long as I'm your partner. What you do on your own time is your business. When you're with me, I expect to be able to trust you're not going to get us into a blender with the switch on 'puree.'" Paul was angry. He moved in close to Cooper before he spoke again. "And if you ever get me into another situation like this again, I'll take that stick from you and make it so you have to squat to piss. You want to see my southern drawl, I'll go Cajun on your ass." Paul turned and walked over to one of the patrol cars.

Cooper stood and watched Paul. He looked at his hands and rubbed them together, then shook his head. He knew his partner was right. He always knew; he just hated the answer.

CHAPTER FOURTEEN
Evil is obvious only in retrospect.
—Gloria Steinem

Two days after Thanksgiving, 2003

Jodi's silver Pontiac pulled into the dark, empty, parking slot around the corner from the front entrance of the building that housed the city's human resources department. She turned the engine off and sat for a minute. She was anxious; she had made up her mind to fulfill the plan to purge the wrong done to her family. There was excitement in this for her. Life, somehow, returned. She could breathe again. The thought of what was about to happen thrilled her beyond anything in her life. After the mall bombing, she was a trendsetter of sorts. There were reports of copycats. Jodi loved that.

When she was sure no one was around, she got out of the car. She was carrying a brown paper sack while holding her oversized purse. She pulled the sweatshirt hood over her head. It was an unusually chilly night this early in the fall. She didn't want to make it easy and show her face on the surveillance cameras surrounding the building. She walked toward the double-front doors that led into a small lobby. Without waiting, Jodi reached inside the bag and started the timer. In four hours it would be eight o'clock in the morning. A good portion of the employees would be entering through these doors, scrambling through the lobby on their way to cheat more citizens. She adjusted the volume on the small police scanner clipped to her belt and made sure the earpiece was secure, then set the bag down and reached into it for the hammer. Without hesitation, she swung at the glass, shattering it,

130

then stepped through the steel frame and into the lobby. Jodi calculated the police could get a call within ninety-seconds and since this building was only four blocks from police headquarters at Six-Twenty, police response could be quick, assuming someone heard the call. She would need to move quickly. This added to the excitement. She found herself smiling. Police in the explosion would be a bonus, a long-shot seeing it was so long before it was set to go off. It was the innocent she wanted to be targets, just like her family.

Her movement was deliberate. "There's no rush boys," she said to her always present husband and son. "We just can't dawdle." She had watched the building at night and knew it had no posted security. She was right about the alarms. When Jodi entered, she heard nothing. There didn't appear to be any activated motion sensors in the lobby, not with the possibility of an employee working late. An employee could enter the door and with the proper pass code, deactivate the alarm that was on a time delay. If the door was never opened, the alarm never went off.

She walked over to the corner of the lobby, next to the closed doors of the city's human resources department. Two pay phones and a trash can stood outside their closed doors. She knelt down and opened the paper bag. She had modified the timer with two petal strips. One of the strips was connected to a terminal and a small battery. The other part of the wiring ran to a small primer and then to the five pounds of AMPHO held in a galvanized pipe with screwed-on caps. She had drilled a hole in one end to insert the primer and lead wires. When the timer ran down to zero, the circuit would complete, detonating the explosive. She made sure the timer was set for the peak time, when most of the employees would be arriving, and closed the brown paper bag. She lifted the lid on the trash can next to the doors, and placed the bag inside the can and replaced the lid, making sure it was on tight. Building maintenance had already emptied the container so there was a fresh plastic liner in the can. *Oh good, nice and clean*, she thought. She still hadn't heard of a call out for the front door on the scanner so she walked over to the phone and dialed 911. She let the phone receiver hang by its cord after she heard the operator answer "Nine-one-one, what is your emergency?" She walked out over the shattered glass, straight to her car, and drove to a spot where she could observe the events she had put into motion. It had taken her less than two minutes. By the time she had gotten to her car, she heard the now-familiar tone in her ear indicating a priority call. It was her call. The police were on their way. They would respond to the hang up call, and find the door. They would look and find nothing; then, hours later, the explosion. "They'll be blaming each other. 'Why didn't you look in the can, officer?' they'll ask." There would be no reason to look in the can; at least that was her plan.

She pulled her car to the curb and turned out the lights. She was about three blocks away and could clearly see the front doors to the building she wanted to watch. She knew there was a chance they wouldn't find the bomb, a good chance. It was just a break-in, an anonymous nine-one-one call. They would clear it quickly. But later, when chaos hit, she would be pleased with the response of the panic instilled to her newest bomb creation. She kept checking her watch. The police should be along any moment. But they didn't show. It frustrated her and she grew even angrier. *Where's a cop when you need one?* she thought. She didn't know most of the units were south of the main downtown area.

The first officers were on their way, having finished on their last call. Officers hated responding to anonymous nine-one-one calls. Jodi waited another hour. Two officers finally responded, found the door shattered and the phone off the hook. They waited for a sergeant and eventually someone from the city's maintenance department to come plank the front door. Nothing else was done. No one looked in the trash can; no one looked outside. The officers cleared radio once they hung up the phone and maintenance personnel was on scene, less than an hour. Jodi was livid. 'Typical,' she thought, even though it was the way she thought it would go, she seethed through clenched teeth as she watched. Even though she didn't want them to find the device, *would it hurt for them to at least look?* She thought as she drove away.

Her anger at the police was quickly replaced with excitement of the morning news. She would not be disappointed. As she was watching the day's weather forecast, the news team broke in with the announcement of the explosion. There were no reported deaths, but the female newscaster reported there had been injuries and showed an aerial shot of the city building from the news helicopter. The front of the building was smoldering. Jodi smiled and took another sip of tea.

"Okay, settle down," O'Donnell said to the room full of officers, waiting for the afternoon briefing. "There's only one real item on this afternoon's list. As most of you have already heard, the city's human resources building was broken into and an explosion occurred. Our people have ruled out accidental issues, considering the explosion was in a trash can. Officer Carter Boyce and several others are working the angles on this thing and will brief us on what the status is today. Officer Boyce."

Carter Boyce was in his mid forties. He had been with the department since he was twenty-two and moved his way up. He had been with the General Investigations Bureau for the last seven years. He worked everything from fraud to homicides, and recently had been assigned to work crimes related to Homeland Security with a joint task force stationed out of the state attorney general's office. "ATF, as you know, has been called in," Carter started. "Bomb parts have been found and they're doing their laboratory magic with what's left. Video cameras recorded what appeared to be a white or Hispanic female, although the perpetrator was hooded, entering the building with a hammer through the front door on the west side at about 0400 last night and leaving just a few minutes later. She parked right outside the window, later leaving in a four-door sedan, no plate. You have a copy of her photo there in front of you."

The officers shuffled through the pile of paperwork on their desks and found a grainy photo taken from an outside camera.

"There's another issue here. A nine-one-one call was placed from the lobby phone at about the same time as the break-in. The theory is the perpetrator wanted us to be there when the bomb went off, although it didn't go off until much later. From now on, any unanswered or hang-up nine-one-one calls will be a multiple-unit response with a supervisor. We think the person or persons responsible for this could be targeting cops. Questions?"

"Any prints on anything?" came a question from the side of the room.

"On what? That entire floor is in postage-stamp pieces scattered across the street. I know initial press reports said there were injuries only, but that is going to change. As you know, the bomb went off right as people were getting to work. The mayor and city council have authorized overtime for off-shift security of nine city buildings. Those of you wishing to get a head start on Christmas can sign up at the watch commander's office as always, and we will go by seniority. By the way, if you do not sign up, you *will* be signed up. This is a big deal to the council. This person is getting bolder and bolder and the powers-that-be think this person is the same one who hit the mall and will not stop until they get whatever they want, which might just be more bodies."

"Any ransom demands or communications?" came another question.

"None," Carter said. "That's the scary part. This person is not asking for a thing as far as we are aware of."

"We've heard rumors they think it's a fired employee?" came another question.

"That's just a rumor, but nothing to say otherwise," the sergeant interjected. "Okay, let's saddle up." The room broke up like any other day; men and women talking about a bomber whom they would hopefully find. The days were never routine but from the atmosphere in the room one couldn't tell; their minds, their actions, all calm and professional. But there was nothing routine with this job. Paul and Cooper gathered their paperwork and gear and headed for their patrol car. They weren't walking today.

It was quiet between the two officers for the first part of the shift. They had been assigned a car, a nice change from walking. Paul could tell it was more than just the start-of-shift silence. He thought Cooper was still peeved about the day before. He waited awhile and then started.

"So, what do you think about this bomber? You think it's a former employee like they said."

"Could be," Cooper responded, shrugging his shoulders.

"You think they're right?"

"Nope, I didn't say that, now did I? I just said it could be."

Paul paused at the tone. "You still mad at me for yesterday? Look man, I'm—"

Cooper stopped him by holding up his hand. "No, no, don't apologize. You were right. I was out of line. You do this stuff long enough and you start to try to cut corners. You want to eliminate all the crap you've tried a thousand times before and get to the fix, 'cause you know that crap you tried a thousand times before isn't going to work. You were right. I can't go around stirring up hate and discontent just because I'm right."

"You're kidding me. You still think you were right after all that?" Paul said.

Cooper just looked at him and smiled. Paul was starting to understand his partner. He could see, in that grin, Cooper knew he had stepped over the line, even if he thought it was just a toe over the line. He also knew some of what Cooper said was true. The radio broke their conversation.

"Two-Adam seventeen."

Paul reported back into the microphone.

"Two-Adam seventeen, assist fire with a man down in the alley north side of twenty-three five West Buchanan, 400 south."

"Twenty-three five West Buchanan, ten-four," Paul repeated back. "Suppose it's another one of your boys?" Paul said to Cooper as he replaced the microphone back into the cradle.

Cooper shrugged.

Jodi was smiling. Lately, she always had a smile on her face, especially when she was fighting for justice for Joe and Anthony. She smiled when she thought of joining her husband and child in heaven. She was doing God's work; she just knew she was. All those responsible for their pain and suffering were going to feel their own pain.

It was time for her to leave. By now, the investigators would have found at least one of her fingerprints either at the mall or at the city building, something would lead to her; she knew it. She sorted the one-gallon bottles of bleach and made sure they were in a straight line. Jodi *always* liked lines. She liked things in order. She couldn't depend on anyone else to keep order now, just her. She arranged them next to the kiddy pool she bought at the store for ten dollars, a decent buy for this time of year, she thought. She had set it up in the middle of the living room. She placed one of the dining room chairs in the middle of it. She picked up the heavy, orange Igloo cooler and placed it on the edge of the chair. The ammonia liquid in it sloshed from side to side. She tied one end of a rope to the handle of the cooler and the other end to the front doorknob after threading it through a small pulley she had screwed into the wall. Then she emptied the containers of bleach into the kiddy pool. The room quickly filled with the smell of "mountain fresh" bleach. She liked the smell. She was then very careful with the clumps of aluminum foil. They were filled with the dried ammonia and match heads, making them shock sensitive. When they fell or were kicked on the ground they would spark. She gently placed them on a section of newspaper lying on the ground. She attached some tape from the newspaper to the top of the cooler. When the door opened—she smiled at her creativeness.

She checked her makeup in the hall mirror and made sure she had her keys and the SIG semi-automatic pistol in her purse. She left through the back door after setting the timer to turn on two house lights and the radio at eight o'clock and then turn them off at midnight. If anyone was looking, they would think someone was home. Then, just as she was leaving, she disconnected the line to her gas stove and turned the flow valve to half. The gas fumes would fill the house over the time she figured she had, creeping their way down from the roof to the floor, filling the house with gas, right where the sparks would be. She smiled again. "Okay, boys, we need to leave our home now. Say goodbye." She left out the back door, down the street to the bus stand and away from her home. An hour later, the SAU team set up on the empty home

"All right, we have some good news for a change," said Ben Sargelli, the morning's briefing sergeant, starting the next day's morning briefing. He was reading the briefing summary from the detectives working the bomber case.

"ATF did find an identifiable thumb print. They found three prints actually, but one came back to a Jodi Campbell in AFIS. What is interesting about Mrs. Campbell is she is, or was, an independent civil engineer, along with her husband. Her contract with the city was terminated about three weeks before the bombings started. She also had numerous contracts with small mines around the state. According to city staff, who were dealing with the Campbell's company on projects, Mr. Campbell died in a car accident which eventually took the life of their son. Within the last month, Jodi Campbell started not answering calls. From what ATF can tell in checking with the Campbell's former clients, one of the mines finally let her go and hired someone else a few weeks ago. A day or two after that, the site supervisor at the mine noticed his explosive inventory for the project was short. ATF said some of the material used in the mall and the city building has the same composition, detonators, as the stuff from the mine. Only she's making AMPHO, diesel fuel and fertilizer. Nasty stuff."

"Were her prints on the building where they stored the explosives, Ben?" Cooper asked.

The sergeant answered Cooper's question to the room. "The dicks pulled the print records when the company filed the initial report on the theft. They sent them to the Feds and should hear back today. The standing bet is they will be the same. You have a picture of Mrs. Campbell in front of you. Our squad is going to assist the Special Assignments Unit in the execution of a search warrant on her house today as soon as they get back from the judge. A scout team went out this morning to keep an eye on the place. Go ahead and get on the street, but do your best to stay available. We will be used for traffic and securing the perimeter of the house while the tactical team enters. Okay, that's it. Let's hit the streets. Cooper, you and Jackson need to see me."

He waited until the room was clear before speaking. "A complaint has been filed with the fourth floor about the flight the other night, and the chief has been told by the city council's office to look into the events of that night and make it go away."

Cooper snickered. "Make it go away? What the hell does that mean, Ben? The LT has already talked to us about this."

"It means the I.A. boys are going to be looking into whether you're flying endangered the civilian population. You had to know Internal Affairs would dig into this."

"The only civilians we were endangering were the ones who were trying to kill us, Sarge," Paul said.

"Again, what the hell does 'make it go away' mean?"

"Coop, you got a crapload of comp time built up. I want you to use it. The word is the boy here is fine," he said gesturing to Paul. "I want you to go on vacation for a while."

"I don't want to use it. I don't need to take any time."

"I know, but this would be a good time to get away and forget about this place for a while," Ben said. "Come on, Coop, you know how these things go. The city council gets a little sideways when one of their constituents threatens a lawsuit because we kind of shot up their neighborhood."

"I don't want to forget about this place for a while, Sergeant."

"What about me, Sarge?" Paul asked. "I was flying better than he was."

Cooper looked at his partner.

"Well, I was," Paul said. "I should be getting a Notice of Investigation too. I haven't heard anything about an NOI."

"Yeah, what about the kid? If I have to leave, he has to leave, too. Maybe he could take some flying lessons or something,"

"Thank you, asshole."

"Anytime, crap for brai—"

"I don't know anything about you. I just heard about Cooper and I want him to take two weeks— starting today. As of now, you are officially on vacation. Have a nice time," Ben said as he turned to leave.

Cooper and Paul stood for a minute and watched their sergeant walk down the hall. "What do you think?" Paul asked.

"I think you'll be fine. You were following my instructions as the senior pilot. Remember that when they come and talk to you."

"Hey, Coop, that crap I did on my own. I don't need to tell them you told me—"

"I know, I know," he held up his hand. "You did great, really. But I have a pension. All I have to do is quit and I'm set, sort of. You still have miles to go for yours. Just do what I tell you and you'll be fine. The reports of the events speak for themselves. If we didn't do what we did, cops would be dead." Cooper smiled and winked at Paul. There was a kindness in his eyes Paul hadn't seen before.

CHAPTER FIFTEEN
In a mad world, only the mad are sane.
—Akira Kurosawa

That same night, Cooper had his seat at Moreno's. He had finished the plate of spaghetti three scotches ago. Now, it was him, a few others, and the old George Burns and Gracie Allen Show. It was crowded for a Thursday night. Almost like a weekend night. Cooper sat on the short 'L' leg of the bar and had his back to the side room where the pool table and some additional high-top tables and bars stools surrounded the table. "Good drink, this scotch," he muttered as he worked on the second half of the bottle of single malt. He told Moreno he could charge him for each drink, even though he bought the bottle in the first place so the bar would have it when he came in. It was against the liquor laws, but it was just Moreno and Cooper who knew and Moreno never charged him.

The crowd around Cooper was loud and having a good time. On Thursday, Friday, and Saturday nights, Bob Ryan and the Catfish Hunters played music on the short, squatty stage at the far end. The band was a two-piece group of middle-aged white guys, Bob and long time friend Terry, who was a magician with the mandolin. Both worked day jobs. Bob, an advertising professional for a major hospital, couldn't leave music. If he could make a living at it, he would, even if it meant living on freeze-dried soup. He had a family now and his dreams submitted to their care and his middle-aged comfort. His blend of ballads was hard to describe, somewhere between traditional, country, Dylan, and Cooper thought, a smattering of reggae. He heard someone describe the Catfish Hunters music as

'Americana'. It was good enough of a description for Cooper.

Bob played guitar with a short stool next to him. Two drinks were perched on it, one water, the other, some of Cooper's scotch. Four couples shuffled on the dance floor to the tune of the Catfish Hunters.

'... you are out there, thinking of me ...'

Two of the couples were just trying to hold themselves up. The third couple wasn't dancing so much as trying to check each other's tonsils, and the fourth couple was actually country dancing around the other three. It was sometimes a bar of desperates. They sailed the seas of the day and for whatever reason, docked here, at Moreno's. It was a safe port for most of the ships that sailed that night. Like Cooper had said and heard, the bar was *sacred.*

The band's music made it hard to hear the television. It didn't bother Cooper. He found it soothing just watching George and Gracie. He sensed sincerity in how Burns looked at his wife. He wished he had that look to give. He found comfort in seeing someone, even someone long dead, give that look. It was out there, a love of someone else. He looked deep into his glass. He felt himself fall into it. He had no love to give. His was tainted. His would be rejected. He knew it. He had tried and he could never get it right.

'... nobody to answer to or criticize me ...'

The sign-off by Burns marked the end of the night for Cooper. It was almost midnight. He'd had enough. He had dinner at Moreno's more than he did dinner at home. He wanted the company, but it still wasn't enough to cause all the dreams and thoughts of failures to leave him. It was like they loitered into the next room and waited until he was home in bed trying to sleep; then they'd crawl out of his closet and taunted him again. They ambushed him. Sleep wasn't a relief to

143

Cooper; it was a chore. His failed marriages, his job, the kids he never had—he determined the latter a divine blessing; he'd take credit for that. Allison didn't want any kids and he definitely didn't need them. He looked into the low ball glass still holding a half inch of amber-colored liquor. He swirled it. That's what he was doing when three of the men behind him stumbled into his back, spilling his drink.

"Hey, asshole," Cooper said over his shoulder.

The three caught themselves and the younger of the three turned to Cooper. "Excuse me?"

"You heard me. Watch what you're doing. You and your buddies spilled my drink."

"Oops, too bad, sorry," the shorter of the three said.

"You're not sorry." Cooper felt the heat rising up the back of his neck.

"You got an unfriendly attitude there, old man," the big one said. He was six feet tall and solid. Cooper could tell the man could hurt him if he tumbled with him. The heat grew.

Cooper turned on his bar stool. "Who the hell are you talking to?" Cooper said to him.

Moreno walked up. "My friend, you are too old and too drunk to be getting into a bar fight. No trouble in here, boys. Cooper, I'll get you another drink," he said, hoping to disarm the situation.

The big one snickered. "Yeah, old man, the bartender will give your soggy ass another drink. That's all you barflies want anyway. What happened? The old lady kick you out because you got fired from another job? Or did you spend your crappy little savings on the ponies? I bet yo—" Cooper's fist fit quickly and neatly into the man's mouth. He fell back into his buddy's arms, breaking his fall on the way to the floor.

"That's it, boys. You guys need to leave," Moreno said. He pulled a Louisville Slugger out from under the bar and pointed it at the two men holding their buddy.

"Yeah, settle down. We were just playing with you. Ya didn't have to go get all bent on us like that," one of the two catchers said.

"Don't do it, Coop, you're too old," Moreno said. "You've done enough now. Leave it alone."

"You boys didn't apologize for my drink."

"Look man, we're sorry. Just back off," The younger one said.

"I think you boys need to go—now," Moreno said. "Take your friend and leave."

Without a word, the two shuffled their friend out through the front door. The shorter one found his friend's tooth on the floor. He put it in his shirt pocket.

Moreno and Cooper watched the men leave before Moreno spoke. "Are you out of your mind?"

"They spilled my drink and didn't apologize."

"What do you think you're doing? In my bar? You're too old for this Cooper. We're both too old. If you're gonna act like that, you need to find yourself another waterin' hole, amigo."

"He spilled my drink."

"Finish that one and get yer ass home. You've played on the swing set long enough for one night."

Forty-five minutes passed before Cooper left the bar. Most of the other patrons had already left as he walked out the door. There was an alley a half block down the street. It entered the street at a forty-five degree angle and boxes of wet cardboard lay against both walls next to steel trash dumpsters and puddles of mud and trash. As he crossed he never saw the two-by-four that hit him across the shoulders and corner of his head. Once he was on the ground, all he could do was curl into a ball and protect his already bloody head and face from the blows of feet and fists finding their mark. There was a combination he remembered later, a shot to the rib cage that made his arm drop, then a solid soccer kick to the forehead. The last thing he heard was someone far off, yelling as if in pain. He realized one of the men was hurt, apparently as he was hit, one of the men broke his fist. Ironically, his face was as hard on a fist as it was to look at. He came to that conclusion just before he passed out.

CHAPTER SIXTEEN
*Eat a third and drink a third and leave the remaining
third of your stomach empty. Then, when you get angry,
there will be sufficient room for your rage.*
—Babylonian Talmud

———————————

Two days later

Cooper's mind was a rush of sounds and images. He felt his mind spin. Pictures of his childhood, his ex-wives, his ill sister, a tree he would jog by in a park when he was a cadet, a wall of black granite, music with the beat of a drum, sun shining on a hill; random photographs broken apart by individual flashes of light. Even part of the same, reoccurring dreams were back, in between the lights and sounds.

"Roger, Tango. Tell your people to get in their holes. We will be coming northwest to southeast inside the wire and on the deck. ETA forty seconds," Cooper said, and pushed the control stick forward and the nose of the copter down. The rest of the flight heard the transmission and followed.

"I don't like this, Coop. It makes me have to pee," Joe said.

"I never did like this," Cooper said to Joe, with a slight grin and a glance before he focused his attention back out of the windscreen. "This thing doesn't have any wings. How do you suppose it stays in the air?" The rotor pitch began to whine as Cooper continued. "It could be worse. We could be one of those poor bastards putting our bayonets on the end of our Matty Mattel's. Wouldn't that be a world of fun?" Cooper pulled the stick back to level off their flight.

"The day is still young," Joe said without taking his eyes off the lights in front of them.

Cooper looked at his watch. "An hour before sun up; put the tape in."

"Roger that," Joe said, and then reached under the front of his seat and pulled a cassette tape. He checked which side was the right side and then pushed it into an improvised cassette player tied to the side of the center console by his feet while Cooper talked to the flight.

"Okay, flight, you see it. Marines are getting their pee-pees wacked. It's time we do some whacking ourselves. Follow me in by the flight numbers. We'll go between their outer holes and their interior fences and on the deck. Rake anything that's standing. Try to keep your muzzles out of the holes and bunkers." He turned to Joe. "On my mark, start the tape."

"Roger."

Cooper turned the ship in the direction he wanted it to go. There weren't any trees to worry about. The ground had been shorn to the dirt. They were at less than fifty feet and coming in fast. Cooper nodded to Joe; he pushed the play button on the side of the player. The tape started. *Born to be Wild* by Steppenwolf blasted over the landscape.

On the ground the fighting was now a wash of shadows and muted shades of brown and black. Those watching from the sidelines would have been bored because there were not as many pretty lights streaming through the sky as there were earlier, just sounds, sounds rarely heard and only in whispers among those who experienced them later, in nightmares of sleep. The sharp cracking of rifle fire took over the sound of large mortars and cannon. Cooper could see from his copter The *Boogieman* was inside the house and he had to be dealt with, up close and personal.

The Hueys were in their final approach. Cooper made a final instrument check and flipped the arming switch off the rocket pod on the center of the control stick. He spoke into the microphone to the rest of the crew. "Randall—Tailgate, if it's standing or moving, cut it in half.

"Roger, Sir," came the voice over his headset.

"Flight, this is Lead. Follow me in. We'll take a left-hand orbit and hit them again when we come back around."

Cooper made the lead pass with the others right behind him. He made a left-hand turn and raked the other forward areas. Both door gunners were shooting, meaning many of the NVA were already up the hill and working their way into the heart of the base. Cooper continued to circle and came back to the first position, flying over the central command post in the heart of the base. It seemed to still be secure. He flew straight down the hill and headed toward the woods. They launched rockets into the woods ahead of them as the door gunners raked the dirt around the fighting holes. Anyone on the open ground was going to die. Dozens of men fell in the second pass as the airships made their way past the perimeter, right over the heads of the marines huddled in their holes.

Cooper saw a large group of NVA coming directly at a group of fighting holes from the woods. They were at a dead run, attempting to overrun the post and the base behind it. "Hold on boys," he said to the crew. He pulled back on the stick and looped the aircraft, bringing it back in a tight loop right over the marines in their hole. The manufacturer said pilots weren't supposed to be able to loop a Huey helicopter. No one told the pilots. The gunners in the back found it 'sporty.' Holding on to anything in the ship in spite of the safety strap that was holding them in, they rode out the orbit.

"Crap, crap, crap," Joe said as the ship climbed to the top of the arch and then back down. "I hate it when you do this."

Cooper brought the ship down to within five feet above the fighting holes. The prop wash from the craft seemed to push the men farther down into the bottom of the holes. He held the hover with the front of the craft, pointing toward the woods and the approaching army. There must have been two hundred NVA running at the base. They could smell victory. Just another charge and the *Boogieman* would be able to overrun the base and kill everything in it. Those thoughts ended when the gunship opened up. Yawing the nose left and right, Cooper controlled the twist of the craft and used it to launch the rockets into the advancing troops and the woods beyond. The door gunners were able to cut anything down on their side of the craft. He stood the craft just a few feet above some American troops in their fighting holes. There weren't many left.

As Cooper kept his copter on the deck and laid down wilting fire, the rest of the helicopters orbited or took up similar attacks on the rest of the advancing forces, pouring thousands of rounds into the shadow-filled jungle and now-decimated advancing troops.

Cooper pulled the craft up and made a looping right turn to get altitude. The other gunship on his right followed.

Deep in the background, behind the images and flashes of colorful light, was a sound that was almost palatable. It would fade and then come back. Each time it got louder. There was a taste to it. He thought, in his dream, the idea of sound having a taste was common. He wasn't dreaming of the war anymore. He was focused on the sounds and smells. More sounds and flashes of light and images of random things. Each image was broken by a flash of light and then the sound came again. It was almost as if it was a song; an image, another flash and then the sound. After a while, he felt a breeze and then it went away. There was an odor to the breeze. He couldn't place it. He felt the breeze again and then it went away—then the odor—then the sound—then the flash of light. It was getting closer; he sensed it.

It went away for a moment when he was back in the cockpit.

The ground in front of the marines burst with fountains of dirt. One NVA soldier ran straight to the side door of the helicopter where Cooper sat after he landed near the marine fighting holes. The bayonet on the end of his gun was pointed at Cooper, but the soldier didn't pull the trigger. Cooper was surprised he had gotten so far before he noticed him. The soldier held his rifle in one hand and tried to open the door with the other. Cooper didn't know why the man didn't just shoot him; maybe he was out of bullets. Cooper yelled at his co-pilot without taking his eyes off the man outside his door. "Joe, take the stick," he said, and without waiting for an answer, he reached up and pulled the 45 from his shoulder holster under his left arm and pointed it at the Plexiglas and pulled the trigger. "Keep your grimy little hands off my ship," he said, as the glass ruptured, leaving a clean hole in it as well as the soldier's forehead. He shoved the gun between his left thigh and seat and took control of the ship again. "I have the ship," Cooper said as he took the controls again.

The NVA began to withdraw into the woods— what was left of them. Some stopped and tried to drag a wounded comrade as they passed them on the field, only to be cut down by the hovering helicopter's machine guns. The woods were on fire, but the troops withdrew into them regardless; it was the only path of escape.

The gunfight was over for now. The area surrounding the base was full of smoke and fire and haze. An occasional single soldier ran out to the edge of the jungle, but was quickly dispatched by the circulating copters or the rifle fire from the troops still in the base. "Firebase Tango, enemy is pulling back. Requesting permission to land and extract your wounded," Cooper said into his radio. The responding voice was clearly relieved and out of breath. Cooper wondered if the *Boogieman* got as far as the Command bunker.

"Roger, Mud Pounder. Thanks for your help. You are cleared at your discretion."

"Remind me to get this window fixed when we get back," Cooper said to Joe with a wink and a slight grin. Joe smiled back weakly then looked out the side window. Cooper thought Joe might want to throw up.

"Roger, Tango. Kellogg—you, Hermit, and Stanton, stay high cover. Gonzo, you and I will pick up first. Let us know if you see any movement." The radio transmissions came back from each ship, acknowledging their orders as Cooper negotiated an approach back to Point Guard Four, or what was left of it. He wasn't sure anyone was still alive, but thought he saw some movement. Once he landed, a sergeant asked him to take a seriously wounded man out. He looked passed him. There was a lieutenant with him and a couple of others. No one else was around. He remembered looking back towards the gun bay and making eye contact with the young marine as he lay on the floor of the helicopter.

"Consider him out of here," Cooper finally said to the sergeant. As the sergeant nodded and turned to walk away, he remembered calling to him again.

Cooper opened his eyes. The comfort of the
dream was gone. Feelings he had not felt, like the pain
in his ribs and face, were now in the room, or wherever
he was, right there with him. He was lying on a floor of
cardboard, the side of his face pressed against it. A
rainbow sheen of light covered his eyes. There was
movement in the light. He tried to open his eyes as he
brought up his arms to lift himself up. He wasn't quite
sure he had arms anymore. He couldn't really feel them.
Then the vision of light was replaced with a dark object
blocking the light; then came the breeze, then the odor.

Cooper worked to clear his vision. He blinked
several times, eventually clearing the rainbow. There,
about six inches from his face, was another face looking
back at him. The bearded, pock-marked face in a well
worn Hawaiian shirt was lying in the same position,
mirroring him. The face smiled a blackened-tooth smile,
then blew air into Cooper's face. Now Cooper knew
what that smell was— day-old bourbon breath. The
stale air was saturated with the smell of whiskey that
hadn't seen light for a long time. The face wrinkled into
a smile. "Awake, oh knight of these valiant deeds and
will your arms to their great feats once again!" the man
said as he noticed the light behind Cooper's eyes
appeared at least partially lit. "Well, hot damn, you're
still alive," the man said with a laugh. "Ya like my
Shakespeare? Henry V, or maybe it was Bob Dylan.
Don't remember," he rolled his head back in laughter.

Cooper's vision was still blurry. The man's shape
turned away from him towards, what looked like to
Cooper, a wall. "I told you boys he'd make it." He turned
back to Cooper as Cooper started to move. "No, don't try
to talk or sit up too quick. You got the crap kicked out of
you pretty good. You were buried under a bunch of
boxes, left for dead it looked like. The boys and I figured

you stepped on someone's dick at Moreno's. Don't worry about Moreno. I flagged him you were okay. I told him you took a few hits but you were all right."

Cooper heard the noise again. It was a phone, his cell phone. The face in his line of sight looked surprised. "Gosh, you're a popular fella." The face moved out of Cooper's view; he could hear him answer the phone. "Free Masons Union Local fifty-one, Judd Yokie speaking. Oh, no problem, good-bye." The face came back into view. "Sorry, your phone keeps ringing. What were we talking about before you became conscious? Oh yeah, the movies."

"Who are you?" Cooper slurred out of his swollen mouth. He blinked hard and looked again, trying to focus on the face. The face and voice looked and sounded familiar. It was Skinner.

"Me? You know me, Coop. You just can't see me clearly yet. Skinner's my name—Sandlot's my game. I drive a mule all day, and dance the Macarena all night. I leap tall buildings with a single bound; set up crackers all around. Wanna get up?"

"I'm not sure I ca—" Cooper said as he tried the arms again.

"Oh, sure ya can. Come on, I'll help."

Cooper felt Skinner reach under his armpits and begin to lift. All the pain that was not in the dream, now became a reality.

I don't think—holy shit, man!"

"Come on, it's like my momma always said, 'no pain, no need for recess,'" Skinner said as he pulled Cooper into a sitting position. He leaned him up against an old sofa. "See? Don't you feel much better since I got ya off that cold, tile floor?"

Cooper looked down to where he was just lying, just in case he had truly imagined what he was laying on. He confirmed it was cardboard boxes the man called 'tile'. His phone rang again. Cooper watched as the man in the room moved towards it. He recognized him from before when he and Paul found him in the alley. He was wearing another Hawaiian shirt, not as dirty as the last one. Skinner walked over to a small box that doubled as a table and picked up the phone, flipped it open and answered "Good day, Tucson Gas and Electric customer service, this is Fran DeStephano, how may I help you? Oh, certainly, happens all the time. No problem."

Cooper watched the man put the phone back down on the box. Skinner's clothes were worn. His face was cut deep with lines of age and sun, but he looked better then the last time he saw him in the alley. He looked around the room. Cooper was sitting on his legs; a chair was stuffed on the other side of the box-table where the phone was.

There was the couch he was leaning against, and around the area he was in were various other containers, milk crates, boxes, shoe boxes, small buckets, an old beanbag chair, and a small ironing board with a hotplate on it; two five-gallon bottles were behind it half filled with water. On the hotplate was a teapot. An orange extension cord snaked across the floor and over to the hotplate area. The only light came from a small lamp next to the hotplate and beanbag chair. There were no windows, just four walls which didn't rise to a standard ceiling height with random photographs on them. Cooper couldn't focus that far. Some looked like individuals and some looked like group pictures. He was still having trouble focusing.

"I think you need some tea," Skinner said. He turned and crawled across the room to the teapot.

"Don't do anything special on my account," Cooper said, as his mind cleared and was now

155

thinking he was finding himself in a Stephen King movie.

"Nope, you're my guest. I'll set you up with a fresh cup." Skinner moved over to the teapot and reached into a small box next to the hotplate. He turned to one of the photos on the wall and stared at it. Cooper watched from his place on the floor and held his ribs. Maybe cracked, maybe just bruised. He wasn't sure. "I will. You don't have to remind me. He's our guest. Of course I'll give him the good stuff," Skinner said to the photograph.

Cooper looked at him. At first he thought Skinner was talking to him. "Who are you talking to there, Chief?"

Skinner went back to his work, placed a tea bag in a cup and then poured water over it. "Just one of my nosy roommates. Sometimes they have no faith I have any social graces or that *I know what I'm doing!* He raised his voice as he looked back at the picture. "Here ya go. This will fix you right up," he said as he handed Cooper his tea.

Cooper wasn't sure if he should drink it. He didn't see Skinner put anything into the cup. The water looked like water and the tea seemed to be in a tea bag. He figured if Skinner had wanted him dead he'd be dead already. He took a pensive sip. He was in no shape to upset this man and hold off a possible axe attack.

Skinner watched him in anticipation. Cooper nodded his thanks. "See, I told ya I know what I'm doing," he said over his shoulder to the photograph again. "Your ribs seem okay. I didn't feel anything that appeared like they're broke. You'll be sore as hell for a while though. Those boys whipped on you pretty good with that board. That cut on your head needed a stitch. Actually, I put in about four there. There were a couple of other spots you needed the gaps closed on."

Cooper felt his head and found the tails of the suture. "You sewed me up?"

"I had to. You were bleeding all over my new carpeting. Now, don't go worrying about that. I played a doctor on TV once. I know all about sewing stuff together. Skinner reached up and handed Cooper a small compact mirror. "Take a look. I think I did a pretty good job if I say so myself. The fellas think so, too," he said, thumbing to the pictures on the wall. "It helped that you were passed out and couldn't feel a thing."

Cooper looked in the mirror and what he saw surprised him. His face was swollen and puffy. It was covered with cuts and deep bruises. He had dried blood in his hair and it had streaked down the front of his forehead. There were stitches in his ear, looking like he might have had part of his ear torn off, and Skinner sewed it back on as well. He touched it lightly with his finger.

"Oh, yeah, about that one. Sorry. I—forgot. Tied them together with some number four-pound test line I use for fishing in the lake at the park. Thought for a minute about making soup out of it and giving it to you if you woke up. Geez, now that would be funny, but then I thought you wouldn't see my unique sense of humor in it so I just put it back on," Skinner said with a cockeyed grin.

"How long have—"

"I found you yesterday morning about five. Had you drug back here—I'm just around the corner— patched you up and you've been lying there ever since. You think you can swallow some more tea? Might help that headache and, if I got it figured right, your stomach is cramping from the DTs."

157

"No thanks, I don't think I could drink any—"

The phone rang again, and before Cooper could respond, Skinner answered. "Tails and Whiskers Pet Cemetery—who? Oh yeah, he just got here. May I say who's calling? Just one moment." He spoke like a professional receptionist who had worked at the location for years. He turned to Cooper. "It's someone named Paul," he said, handing Cooper his cell phone. Cooper reached for the phone and Skinner handed it to him then went back to the hotplate and began to set up some more tea.

"Hello," Cooper said into the phone. "Yeah, no; it was just someone pretending—what's up, Paul?" Cooper asked as he rubbed his eyes and the back of his neck. "No, I think I'll be gone for the full two weeks. Yeah, I'll give you a call in a couple of days— no, that's fine. All right—nope—everything is just fine. I'm just feeling a little under the weather. Okay, bye." He finished and Skinner had already snatched his mug and was serving some more tea. Cooper didn't want anymore. He just wanted to get going. "No, really I don't think I could—"

"Come on," Skinner said as he came over with a pot of hot water and a fresh tea bag. "Do me a favor, will ya? The only thing worse than your smell is your breath." Skinner moved close as if to whisper, looking first over his left shoulder and then his right as if to see who was there. He gestured with his thumb to the pictures on the wall. "The guys think you can tell a lot about someone from their breath. You know–hygiene issues–like white socks. Nothin' like a good pair of white socks to set the tone for the day. Makes your feet happy. Happy feet, happy day. That, and a good bowel movement. Day don't get no better. Go on, take it." He stopped talking. His ground-down black teeth were shown to Cooper like a proud man waving a flag.

Cooper looked over Skinner's shoulder to the wall across the little room.

He reached for the cup and took it out of Skinner's hands. "Thanks."

Skinner's smile grew even bigger. "That's it. Now, I don't get a lot of company, so, in hopes you were going to live, I went out shopping this morning at a real store. I love doing that. Usually right after a bloodletting at the blood bank or my V.A. check comes in. I take the money and go stock up. This last week I was a little ahead so I made a McDonald's run. Got us each the ninety-nine-cent specials *and* a cup of joe for me and their hot apple pie, *God* I love pie, can't get 'nough of it! Sorry, I didn't want to waste a good cup on you in case—you know—you croaked. Boys over there told me it was a wise decision," he said, pointing again at the pictures on the wall. "I didn't know what you would like, you know, like the bacon or ham or sausage, and whether you liked a biscuit or muffin. Then I thought it really didn't make any difference, because whatever comes with the ninety-nine cent meal is what we get." He held out the bag to Cooper.

"Thanks." Cooper took the bag and looked in it. There were two wrapped sandwiches in what appeared to be a clean new bag. The smell of the food triggered an appetite he didn't know he had. He reached in and grabbed a sandwich and handed the bag back to Skinner while he felt his side.

Skinner took the bag and noticed Cooper feeling his ribs. "It's got a pretty good bruise going. I don't think you broke any; maybe cracked a couple, but ya didn't break any."

Cooper kept feeling his side. He set the sandwich in his lap. "They feel like they're wrapped."

Skinner took the bag and reached for the other sandwich. "Yup, three pairs of ladies' stockings. Two taupe and a midnight blue. When you get home, you can wrap an Ace bandage around it instead. I prefer the nylons because they're not as stretchy and you can knot 'em. Plus, at my age and condition, it's the closest thing I'll ever have a woman's legs wrapped around anything of mine—get it?" he laughed. "I crack myself up sometimes. How's your sandwich? Want some more tea?"

Cooper shook his head no. He was hungry. When his mouth was empty he asked, "Where are we?"

"You're at Skinner Manor. Ya wanna tour?" he asked, gesturing with his hands in a sweep of the room as he wiped a crumb away from his cheek.

"What?"

"A tour. Oh, come on; let me give you a tour."

"No, I don't feel—"

"Oh, come on, you pussy," Skinner said as he licked the paper, which held the now-eaten sandwich, and slugged down his share of the coffee and dunked the pie in the cup. "You're not hurt that bad. I don't get to give a lot of tours, and turning one down is downright rude. It won't take long."

Cooper looked into the man's eyes. He was serious. "All right." He began to get up.

"Whoa, where are you going there cowboy?"

"You said you wanted to take me on a tour of your place."

"Yeah, but what the hell do you think this place is? The Hearst friggin' Castle? You can stay right there. Just pretend you're on one of those trams at Universal Studios." He turned to one of the pictures on the wall. "I know—I heard you. He did get up too soon." He turned back to Cooper. "Now, starting where you're at is the bedroom and sitting area. You noticed you were sleeping and now you're sitting. See how that works?

160

Over to your right," he continued gesturing with his right hand, "is the formal dining. Here obviously, is the kitchen, and there's the bathroom, and then we're back to where you're sitting," he said as his hand movements and statements had been obviously rehearsed a dozen times to unseen guests.

"Wow," Cooper said, nodding his head as he had done so many times before with nine-eighteens, the code for 'crazy.'

"Yeah, it takes your breath away doesn't it?" Skinner asked.

Cooper paused for a minute before he asked his host, "You happy here? You seem better than the last time I saw you."

Skinner took so long to respond Cooper thought he didn't hear the question. "I am what I am." A moment of lucidity washed over Skinner's face. "You know, it's not bad. All those places I lived while I was in the Corps then right afterward, when I got out. After I got, well, sick, my wife checked me into the first hospital. I knew I couldn't stay. I knew I would never be the same again and I would lose her. I read about all the problems I was going to have and knew I was going to drown." He took a deep breath. "So, I told her to move on and when she didn't, I did. I think that was one of my better moments. The boys and I bounced around a little and then we landed here and you and I met. I left on that bus you paid for and then came back after the time with my niece," he said, gesturing to the pictures on the wall. You know, I haven't told you, but a couple of days after you pulled my ass out of that alley, I got a job."

Cooper's head picked up. "A job, what kind of job?"

"I'm working on the loading dock at the city building on Adams. I escort the delivery people up to the floor they're delivering loads to. Ever since 9/11, they want everyone to be escorted. The V.A. helped me get it."

"How's the drinking? That getting in the way?"

"Hell, Coop, I'll always have a problem with that. But you know when you saw me the other night, I wasn't lit up. I had done some drinking but you and I go back a ways. You've seen me drunk. I've been in this daze and I finally just got tired of living the way I've been living. Too many ghosts, too much sadness, much of it I caused. I just got tired of looking at it and not owning it." Skinner paused. "Just like you."

Cooper looked up. He was startled. Skinner saw something in him. Cooper always thought someone would see through him one day. Maybe not from a transient living in whatever he was living in, but he expected it from someone. Still, there was no admission of his owning anything. "What are you saying? Don't put me in with you, my friend."

"You and I chewed some of the same ground. It took me a long time to look at what I did. I always thought it was someone else's fault, for what I was doing. You and I, we ain't much different than a lot of people. People walking around wounded and torn from crap in their lives. Some do better than others. We're all the same. This, all this," he said as he gestured with his hands to the surroundings, "this is crap, but it's mine and it's a start. You don't have to get *here* before you get well." His eyes locked on Cooper's.

"I'm not sick."

Skinner snorted. "You're not, huh? You got the stuffing kicked out of you because you pissed someone off, is my guess. You're at least one wife down–if you were smart, three if you weren't. I heard about the time off." Cooper looked up at him in surprise. "Yeah, word travels quickly around here. You keep going the way you're going and you'll get your wish." "What wish?"

Skinner picked up a saltine cracker from its package next to the hotplate and put it in his mouth, then turned to look at Cooper. "The wish you've wanted for years. You want to be dead."

"You're out of your skull."

"I've been told that. The boys tell me that every day," he pointed to the pictures on the wall again.

"I've got to go," Cooper said as he tried to roll over and stand up.

"Sit your little white ass down and listen for a minute. You haven't finished your tea yet anyway. Listen to me. You don't have much time," Skinner said as he pointed to him.

"What are you talking about?"

Skinner just smiled, then his eyes glazed over for a moment as he looked at the pictures on the wall.

"There was a beauty to the violence," Skinner started. "No one ever wanted to admit it, but a night firefight in the jungle was a light show of spectacular order. There was a part of me that loved it. Colors and patterns unlike any Fourth of July show in small-town America. Streamers of color came from the dark recesses of shadows and shapes moving unlike anything human. The darkness swallowed the colored streaks of light and then ricocheted them back, bouncing them off of things in the darkness." He looked back at Cooper. "You were there. You know what I'm talking about. On some nights, when the *Boogieman* showed up and things got real sporty it was like watching dancers in the open field, running, falling, running again, and lights—like lasers, streaming from their own shadows as they moved across the dark ground. Rockets of light flashed overhead; as they fell, each dancer lit up the small area of earth around them with secondary lights of colored phosphorous and magnesium. I remember things, like shadows, fell in contorted forms and lay still on the ground. It would be a beautiful sight if you could sit in grandstands on the sideline with a bag of popcorn, a soda, and earplugs."

There was a look on his face that Cooper saw. It didn't appear to him that Skinner was in the room anymore. "You wouldn't want to listen to the show with the soundtrack. The violent sounds of screams and terror would bring you back to what it truly was—men at war. Nothing had changed in thousands of years. Men still fought for causes and beliefs, sometimes just because they could."

"Eventually, however, it still came down to having boots on the ground to finish the dance. Man, despite all his abilities, still had to look his opponent in the eye and take his life. We owned a hill one night and the *Boss* said we were suppose to keep it. My little platoon was part of a company that was being overrun. I can still see my gunnery sergeant, who I had just promoted, running in front of me, a corporal and others, many others. His face went blank.

"'You have a hot one?'" Skinner said. "I heard my sergeant, he was just across a few yards of trench from me with two others. One of them, Tyrone, popped two quick rounds to the head of a dark figure standing over him on the edge of the trench. The guy crumpled and rolled into the side of the dirt berm. Then, he reached up to his shirt and pulled a grenade off of it and underhanded it to another guy, Skomer, who caught it with one hand, lifted it to his other hand holding his rifle, pulled the pin with his loose index finger, waited to a count of two while it cooked, and threw it sidearm like a shortstop to second base. It hit another figure in the chest, bounced off the person's foot, and then exploded, sending four bodies into the air in various directions. Like I said, it was sweet to watch."

Cooper just sat and listened. He knew what Skinner was talking about.

"'Gotta go, gotta go, move faster, move faster!' Fitz kept saying as he pushed and pulled the boys farther down the line. I was just ahead of them. 'Come on, the hole down here is deeper.' I said. We crawled into our fighting holes; somehow they didn't stray far from each other or their original location even as the NVA ran past them. Gunney saw that Tyrone and Skomer still had not been able to move far from their bunker. They had been stopped on two attempts to leave it. Somehow, the place hadn't been rocketed. The two took turns shooting in their two halves of the field, single, selected shots at specific targets. Some of the bad guys fell in front of their trench, providing the slit in the dirt with more protection, the dead bodies absorbing the incoming rounds. God, I can still smell it," Skinner said. "I can still feel chunks of meat splattering in my face." Skinner reached up and stoked his face. "Just about dawn, a flight of Hueys showed up and burned those bastards back to hell. I remember that sergeant, Jeezus he was someone you wanted to be around in a fight! I can still hear his voice. 'Shut your ass and get away from that damn bunker, Marine! Move it! Move it! Move it!" he said, and then he reached down and jerked the small marine out of the hole by his shirt collar and threw him towards what was left of my platoon. With him following. We formed a box and I said 'kill anything in front of you'. We just found the hole when a bright light shined from the woods, followed by a *whoosh* sound. We could see the stream of white and we fell into the hole just as the rocket hit the front side of the bunker. God that was pretty! Sergeant saved those boys. Most of them anyway."

"Then what? Cooper asked, shifting his weight from one side to the other.

"It got personal. They moved into the trench and one of the last things I remember was that sergeant pulling out this shotgun, you know the kind, with the pistol grip, for those 'up close and personal moments'."

Cooper nodded.

"Yeah, then more of the pretty lights and loud music."

"'Music'?" Cooper asked.

"Yeah, you can't have lights and dancing without music—rock music." Skinner smiled. "The following week, I wrote or helped write forty-nine letters home to parents and family who would never see their child again. I was responsible for their deaths, their violent deaths."

He blinked a few times and was back. "Wow, I need my lithium," he said with a crazy burst of laughter. "Time, I'm talking about time. Time is running out for you, for all of us. You have got to come to the answer you're worth something." Skinner's eyes softened. Cooper could tell something Skinner said, or maybe it was the way he said it, caused Cooper to feel like he needed to listen. "Look, I know your thoughts. I've been in your brain. The only difference between you and me is I made a few choices that took me here, a couple of simple forks in the road. I'm telling you, it takes only a couple to get this bad. I was so angry at myself that anyone or anything that was good, I hated." He pushed his thumb at his chest. "I hated this guy so much, anyone who loved him I had to hate, too. I was not worthy of love. Then the sick part was when people didn't like me or love me, I hated them even more. 'How could you not love me?' I asked myself. I couldn't win."

Cooper started to shake his head. "Look man, I appreciate the free counseling but—"

"Look, I'm telling you the truth. You don't have much time, maybe ten years, maybe ten minutes. The guys think it's closer to ten weeks, but they're just friggin' pictures on the wall; what do they know? You got two things to do." He shuffled over to a short bookshelf and pulled a book from it. Cooper couldn't see what it was. "First, you got to start reading. Start with this. I marked a couple of pages for you—then go back and start at the beginning." Skinner opened Cooper's sports coat and tucked the small book inside his breast pocket.

"Look, Skinner, I don't know about this. I'm sure you mean well. I really appreciate your concern but I'm all right—"

Skinner grabbed Cooper's shirt and was shaking him. His eyes were aflame and he was close to Cooper's face. "I was given this book years ago. I've had it since then. I didn't even look at it for decades. You got a bunch of stuff in a box you put up on a shelf in a dark closet in your melon you call a brain. When you get to those pages I cropped, find a sunny place outside somewhere, have a friend you trust with you, if you got any left, and open that box. Look hard at each item you wrapped up and stuffed away in it and take ownership of *all* of it. Then read the pages."

"What are you talking about? 'A box in a dark closet in my brain?' What is that? Is it supposed to be full of all my memories? Is that what you're trying to tell me in your pathetic way? Let's play along. Suppose I've got some stuff from the past I can remember; who the fuck doesn't? So I'm supposed to dig up all this crap I did or was done to me and look at it again? Then what? What do I do with that crap I now have dumped all over me again?"

Skinner just smiled and said nothing.

"When you get to the sunny place and open the box, do the second thing I told you—read the pages. Now, your time is done. Get your ass out of my condo."

The two looked at each other for a second and then Cooper slowly and painfully rose to leave. He ducked on his way out; the ceiling was low and slanted up. He found the opening and just before he walked through the makeshift doorway, Skinner called his name.

"Cooper."

Cooper looked back.

"It's going to be okay. You're going to have to trust me."

Cooper frowned. He didn't know what Skinner was talking about. Or—and this just breezed through his still cloudy brain—he didn't want to know what Skinner was talking about. He didn't even know Skinner's full name. He turned and headed down the alley. After a few steps, he turned back to look. Skinner was living in a steel room behind a small commercial building. It looked like it had been a storage room added on years ago. It was never meant to house anyone; it had no windows and walls made of corrugated steel.

Just down the street from Skinner's, Jodi Campbell walked through the security checkpoint in the city building. She placed her purse and laptop case in a bin as it went through the x-ray machine. She also had a bag of toys that she placed on the conveyor belt. The security officer watching the screen pointed to the outline of an image inside her laptop case. Another officer pulled it aside and asked Jodi if he could open it. "Sure," she said as she followed with her purse. The officer opened the case and looked inside. The only thing inside were the laptop and miscellaneous papers.

He looked in the bag of toys then he looked at the woman. Jodi smiled, "I'm taking them up to the nursery to donate to the kids—if that's okay?"

"Absolutely," he said as he secured the lid to the briefcase.

Within a few minutes she was standing outside the door of the seventh-floor nursery. She walked up to the young receptionist at the front desk and told her she had just bought some toys and would like to donate them. The receptionist smiled and took the bag. Jodi Campbell had just tested the system. The plan to kill all the children was on schedule.

CHAPTER SEVENTEEN
*Nurture your mind with great thoughts; to believe in the
heroic makes heroes.*
—Benjamin Disraeli

Early December 2003

Cooper needed to go see his sister Peggy. After he left Skinner's hovel and delicately walked back to his home, he stood in the shower until all the hot water was gone and just tepid water fell on his body. He went over and opened the medicine cabinet and took four-Ibuprofen. Cooper stood for a moment, naked, and looked at himself in the mirror. He was beaten up. But it was beyond that; he was worn out. His mind felt like his body looked. It ached. Cooper drew his hand over his face and stubble chin. The lines of age had cut deep into his face; signs of life's battles were everywhere; eyes and hair, the edge of his neck and shoulders, all showing the scars of living life hard. He needed to get out of town for awhile. He leaned on the edge of the sink, looking down into the bowl and watched the water as it gathered in small reflective blobs near the drain.

He got dressed and walked into the kitchen and picked up the phone. He could go see his sister and brother-in-law and hang out with his nephew. Cooper didn't really consider whether his nephew would want to hang out with him. Peggy picked up on the third ring.

After catching up with each other, Cooper asked if he could come out and see them. "Why?" Peggy asked. She was right. He had never made that gesture before, although she had invited him numerous times. He told her he had been thinking about coming out to see her and the gang and just needed a little vacation from work. She wasn't buying it; he could tell. But she sounded excited her big brother wanted to spend time with her; she said Luke and Lindy would love to see him. Cooper told her he would call back with the flight as soon as he booked it.

He went on line and searched for flights, finding one leaving the next morning. He booked it with a return in ten days, leaving him a day on either end for travel and decompression from the travel as well as for the day he spent beat up in the alley. He then called his sergeant and confirmed his leave. He called Peggy back and gave her the flight number. She had called her husband at work and he too, was happy about him coming out.

After Cooper hung up, he went into his closet, pulled down a suitcase, and laid it on the bed. He always packed light but this time he threw in a suit, sweats, a swim suit, a heavy jacket, and sweaters. He thought he would take them out to a nice dinner, in celebration of Luke's belated birthday, sweats for exercise or if the day was unusually warm and pleasant, you could never tell about D.C.

In less than twenty-four hours, Cooper was at his sister's house near Colonial Village and North Bryan Street on the south side of the Potomac.

It hadn't been that long since he had been in Washington. He had been in town three times in the last five years for conferences; he just never told his sister. He didn't want to have to explain why he didn't come by and see her; he didn't want to see his sister dealing with her cancer. He didn't want to see the bald head and the sunken cheeks and he didn't want to be down the hall from the noise of her vomiting, all those things he thought she was walking through. Cooper was anxious about the trip. He had to deal with enough suffering at his job; he didn't want to deal with his only sister's inevitable death. But, he knew he needed to see her and the more he thought about it, the worse he felt. But when Cooper got off the plane and made his way through security, he was pleasantly surprised when he almost didn't recognize her.

Peggy was tan and had a full head of curly hair and laughed when he crossed through the checkpoint and into her arms. He could see in her eyes she was looking at his beating wounds. He was able to clean himself up before he left and changed out the women's nylons for an ACE bandage, just like Skinner recommended. When she asked about the cuts and stitches on his face, he made up a story about an arrest that went bad. "Yep, don't like arrests like this," he started. "Makes you old before your time. But hey, I thought after a couple of days, I'll let the boy take out the stitches."

"That's gross, Cooper."

"Well, that's why my nephew loves his Uncle Cooper. I let him do gross stuff."

They hugged and kissed each other on the cheek. She had put on about thirty pounds, he guessed, and she looked good. On the drive home she brought him up to speed on the cancer.

It had started in her breast and had spread to her bones and pancreas. After going through chemotherapy and radiation, the cancer went into remission. She was still doing well even though she was at stage four and had been so for the last three years. To look at her, she didn't look like anything was wrong although she wore an elastic sleeve on her arm to help with the circulation. But for right now, right this very moment, on that very day, driving with her big brother, she was fine. She told him, she hadn't felt this good in a long time. She was happy to be with her brother. He made her laugh.

After two days with Peggy and the family, Cooper began to relax. He sat on the couch in the family room and read some of the magazines they had in a basket next to it. He pulled the book out of his jacket Skinner gave him, but then put it back in his pocket without opening it.

When Luke came home from school, Cooper took his nephew out and threw passes with the football or played catch with a set of baseball mitts Luke had. He napped. He hadn't taken a nap in years, he thought, if ever. They went out to eat and laughed. He, Peggy, and Lindy would stay up and talk. Eventually, Lindy went to bed and it was just the brother and sister. She talked about life with a death cloud hanging over all their heads and Cooper talked about anything else.

The eighth day was like the rest. Coop was splayed out on the couch once again. He had fallen sleep in the late afternoon reading Cosmo. It was the only magazine left in the house he hadn't read. He heard the front door open and the familiar foot falls of the teenager enter the home.

"Hey, boy," Cooper mustered. "How was school?"

"It was all right," Luke muffled. His head was in the refrigerator looking for the leftover pizza from the night before.

"Wanna go throw the ball around?"

Luke shut the refrigerator and walked into the family room. "Nah, not really." He plopped down on the end of the couch by his uncle's feet and popped open a can of soda he got out of the fridge. There was sadness to him.

"What do you want to do?" Cooper asked.

"Nothing —I think I'll just go play some video games in my room."

"What's wrong?" Cooper asked. He poked Luke in the ribs with his sock-covered foot. Cooper knew something was up.

"Mom said she thinks the cancer is coming back."

"When did she tell you this?" Cooper sat up and scrambled through his memory to see if he could recollect his sister ever saying anything to him about it. They had only talked about how well she was doing, he thought.

"She said it a couple of days before you got here. I haven't thought too much about it until today. Sometimes it just shows up, but I haven't been able to shake it, the thoughts and the 'what-would-happen' stuff."

Cooper nodded. Apparently, he and his sister had both been acting.

"You ever think about stuff and just can't get it out of your head, Uncle Coop?"

Cooper snorted. "Hell kid, all the time."

"What? Like when you were in Vietnam and stuff?"

Cooper nodded.

"That was pretty bad, huh? Mom and Dad said you saw some pretty gross stuff."

Cooper nodded.

"You ever think about it?"

Cooper paused for a long second and then he nodded. "Every day."

Luke thought for a minute, nodding his head as if he understood. "Do you have bad dreams about that?"

Cooper nodded again.

"Every night?"

Cooper thought for a minute before he answered. "No, not every night."

Luke thought again. Cooper could tell something from Luke's face, like he felt better hearing his uncle's calm response. "What was it like, over there? Like, did you have any fun?"

Cooper snickered and shook his head. Then he thought about it. "Yeah, there were times that were kind of fun."

"Like what?"

"I liked the people I was with. They were nice. I really liked to fly, especially in the early morning." He hadn't thought about that in a long time. In the middle of a terrible war, there was fun to be had. Despite the violence, there were things about war which were absolutely wonderful—if you could find them.

"Is that why you became a police officer? So you could fly some more?"

Cooper had to think again before he answered. "No, they didn't have helicopters when I started. It just seemed like the right job at the time. I felt I would be pretty good at it."

There was silence for a minute while Luke took a drag on his soda. "You ever been to the Vietnam Memorial?"

Cooper shook his head.

"You wanna go there today? We can take the football and toss it around down there. There's a big grassy area—we could do that."

"I don't know, boy, I don't think it would be such a good idea," he said. "It's kind of cold outside," he added.

"Then we could stop for some ice cream before we come home. Mom won't care. She always said you should go. This would be good," Luke said innocently.

Cooper stared at his nephew. He had avoided this event since the Wall was created. There was always a reason not to go. He knew it was partly why he didn't call his sister when he came into town. Not just the cancer, but *The Wall*. Now those excuses seemed indefensible. "I, I don't know boy."

Luke's voice raised. "Come on, I'll teach you how to play Frisbee golf."

"Is that something a man my age needs to know?"

"Everyone needs to know how to play Frisbee golf. Come on." Luke's eyes were wide and playful. He didn't know what he was asking of his uncle. Cooper couldn't think of a place he would rather not be. He also knew it was a trip long overdue. "Crap, all right. Let me get my shoes and jacket on and we'll go."

They hopped in Cooper's rental car and drove down the street and in about ten minutes they were on the Interstate heading south to the Arlington Memorial Bridge and over the Potomac River, past the Lincoln Memorial, and finally parking. Cooper found a slot quickly and pulled in. Even when he had come to town before, he stayed on the north side of town, avoiding his sister but even more so, the Wall itself. He could feel it as he parked. It was there, just on the other side of the trees, to the north of the Korean Memorial. There was a part of him wanting to leave. He wanted to tell Luke this wasn't good; he didn't feel well, anything, just so he didn't have to walk down to the black granite wall that bore so many names. He wanted to leave, but he didn't.

Another part of him wanted to run to it and cry he was sorry, sorry for everything; sorry for the fact that some of the names on the wall he was surely responsible for placing there. As he and Luke walked, Luke seemed oblivious of the sheer terror building inside his uncle's mind. Cooper, on the other hand, was acutely aware that everyone around him knew him. They knew what he had done. They knew he was responsible for the death of those soldiers whose names were etched into the black wall. He avoided moving his head and making eye contact with anyone. They knew; they had to know. In his mind, they would point at him and yelling out he was responsible. He was the one who broke the one promise he made that really counted. He began to sweat, even though the day was crisp.

As they walked down the path under the oak tree canopy, his eyes strained to see the Wall before it saw him. In his mind, he felt over 58,000 pairs of eyes were waiting for him to come down the walkway and talk to them, to explain to them what he had done—or worse, what he didn't do. The man and boy walked down the path and as the black monolith came into site, the man reached over to the boy and stopped him.

Luke looked up at him. Without taking his eyes off the wall, Cooper spoke to him. "Our hats—take your hat off. We're on holy ground."

"Oh, yeah, sorry," the boy said as he pulled off his Diamondbacks cap, a birthday gift his uncle gave him when he first arrived.

Cooper kept his hand on his nephew's shoulder as they walked down the path. He took a deep breath and let it out. The Wall was in full view. A few people, maybe two dozen, stood at various parts of it. Up on the amphitheater to the east, there was another half dozen, some sitting and reading; a couple was having a late picnic lunch. Even in December, if the sun was out, people gathered. It had been unusually warm, making the scene feel almost like spring. As Cooper and Luke walked downhill to the center of the memorial, the wall grew taller. At its base, mementos and gifts were left— flowers, boots, notes of all sizes, candles, and photographs.

Cooper was so focused on The Wall as it grew, he didn't hear Luke's question the first time. "Huh?"

"I asked, when were you there?"

Cooper looked at the years etched into the stone. "Right here," he said pointing to the area marked "1968." He approached it and laid his hand on the cold granite. He felt the names etched into it. He rubbed his hand lightly over it.

"Do you recognize any of the names?"

Cooper didn't respond. His eyes were scrambling back and forth, looking for any familiar name while his mind scrambled for the names long ago buried in a file in the back of his brain. He realized many of the men he knew were known by nicknames, or their first or last name, never their whole name. He found a few names that looked familiar but he didn't link the names to the images of the faces in his mind. He couldn't. He had never really known first and last names together. 'Johnson' was always known as 'Johnson'. If he had another name, the two often didn't go together. If they did, it had been a long time ago. "No, my memory," he paused, "we used to all go by nicknames or just first or last, it's hard to remember their names." Guilt washed over him. He couldn't even afford these soldiers the honor of remembering who they were, he thought. His eyes moved from line to line. His lips moved as he glanced at each name, comparing it to those left in the file in his brain.

"They didn't get out—none of them got out," he whispered. After a moment, he continued his walk to the apex of the wall then continuing up the other side until he got to the far end. He turned around and looked back down the walk. Luke was a few yards back, reading one of the letters left at the foot of the wall.

Cooper looked back. The sun was getting low and he was looking right into it. The names called to him. He could hear the sounds of the days in 1968 and before, the laughter and moans, the shouts and screams. He squinted in the sun; he could feel his eyes fill with tears. He turned and walked up the hill of the amphitheater, pulling his coat around him. He found an open spot and sat down. He waved at Luke to come sit with him. He came at a trot and plopped down next to his uncle. "Uncle Coop, can I run over to the ball field and see if any of my friends are over there?"

He remembered what Skinner said. "It's a beautiful day, isn't it?" Cooper said and paused. "It was a beautiful night for flying," he said, looking at the trees and the surroundings, nothing in particular.

"What?" Luke said.

"The night some of those men died, it was a beautiful night. Actually, it was a beautiful early morning. I remember looking up at the sky and there was no moon, just a sky full of stars before the sun rose." He paused looking, as if waking from a dream. "You want to hear about it?"

Luke shuffled his feet and then shrugged. "Sure, if you want to tell it."

He took a deep breath, and then opened the box.

"It was one night in the middle of January in 1968 and Tet was coming undone. Tet was like their New Year. The North Vietnamese Army was everywhere. I was leading a flight of Hueys into a firebase to supply air cover. They were getting pounded real hard. The NVA were inside the wire and really creating a tough job of sorting who was who. We were able to push them back out of the base and into the trees. Then we set the trees on fire. Set the whole forest around one side of that base on fire. It was like daylight. We came in and landed the copters and started to evacuate the marine dead and wounded inside the base. It was almost daylight and I thought—I thought it would be all right to take some of the dead out instead of the ones who were still alive. I remember a sergeant forcing me to take this one guy. Cooper's mind was there again.

Cooper could see a sergeant and another marine carrying a young marine as carefully as they could and hoisted him out of the hole. He could see a lieutenant

179

take up a position in the hole and sent rounds down range.

They carried the marine by his feet and shoulders to Cooper's copter and with the help of the door gunner, pulled him inside. The marine rested near the bulkhead between the gunner's station and where the two pilots were. His head was facing the front, looking with glazed eyes out the front window, right across Cooper's face, their eyes met for a moment.

Other men were making their way to the ship from where they were fighting up by the edge of the main firebase. Some were helping other wounded marines into the waiting copters while others who could still fight took up cover positions to protect the copter while it sat so vulnerable on the hard ground.

The gunnery sergeant then moved around to what was left of the pilot's window after he got the dying marine on board. He knocked on its frame around the broken Plexiglas. Cooper slid the small vent window open.

"We have to leave now. No telling if or when those people are coming back. You have to get your people out of here now," Cooper told him.

"His name is Fitzpatrick—Take him out of here!" He yelled over the roar of the blade.

"Is he still alive?"

The sergeant looked at Fitz before he spoke. "Not for long."

"I'm only taking out the ones who are still—"

"He is one of mine. I don't want this marine here if they come back. He earned this trip. I want you to take care of him."

The two men looked at each other for a moment. The images all went by in an instant.

Cooper turned back to his nephew when he returned from the dream. "It was obvious he was dying once you looked at him, but this sergeant made me promise to take him and a couple of others. I told him— I told him to stay alive for an hour and I would come back and get the rest of them. There were only three or four of them left from what I could see. I probably could have gotten them on the first trip, even with the bodies I was carrying. Anyway, daylight came. The North Vietnamese Army hated to work that crap in the daylight. They always preferred the night." He paused to gather himself. The memories were flooding back now. "I never made it back to them. I promised I'd come back, but never did. I was sent somewhere else. I think the NVA ended up making another run at the base, right at the same holes we were just at."

He could hear the conversation—over and over again. His promise to the sergeant which he never was able to keep. "Gunny, you keep your ass alive for an hour and I'll be back. I'll get you out if you can buy me an hour. I'll drop him off, get more ammo and I'll be back. You hear me? You keep yourself and these people alive until I come back." He saw him step back, nodding his head. As the copter's blade began to whine, the sergeant saluted him. Cooper returned the salute.

"I pulled the copter up and into the air and flew the wounded back to the base."

Three weeks later, I received a promotion and the Silver Star." The thoughts made him feel sick to his stomach.

"What happened?"

Cooper stared at The Wall. "I'm not sure. I heard they got overrun. I heard when the air units came back, there were just bodies. It's weird." He looked at his nephew, now totally engrossed in the story. "When you flew into those things, it was like you couldn't tell who was American and who was the enemy, except as you got closer, their size gave them up. The Americans were bigger, and when they were lying on the ground they stretched out longer. I was told they must have hit the base right when we left, because it looked like they had been fighting hand to hand for a while. There were still some guys wiggling around on the ground. I heard they reached up with their hands as our pilots flew over. The copters couldn't set down. They had to hover and drop the two gunners so they could move some of the bodies before the pilots could set the helicopters down."

He stopped for a minute. He was remembering more as he talked. He could see the images again that had only come at night in his dreams. Now, here, during the day, they ran the field in his mind. "I could have saved some of them if I could have made it back."

"Did you ever find the guy you told you would come back for?"

Cooper looked at Luke. "No, I never did. I heard later when they got back to the base, all the ships had landed in about the same area at about the same time. We were the first ones back from our assigned mission. I got out and looked for him through the other helicopter loads." He thought about the picture in his mind. "You know, it wasn't just about him. I thought it was for years. It was about all of them. There were so many and it wasn't just that day, but all the days we flew."

"So did you find him?" Luke asked as he stretched out his legs.

"I couldn't tell. The men I had seen barely had on any clothes. They had all been burned so badly during the fight. I found out later they got rocketed right before we got there. We could have been picking up the enemy for all we could tell. They were all black—until you grabbed hold of them to lift them out of the helicopter. Then their skin came off and you could kind of tell what color they were."

Neither of them spoke for a few minutes.

"God, it was a beautiful night." Cooper said to the trees on the far side of The Wall. Another minute went by in silence. "Luke, if you want to run over to the ball field and see if your friends are there, you can. I'll be fine here for a bit; then I'll come find you."

"You sure?"

Cooper smiled gently. "You don't want to be hanging out with a doddering old man. Go. I'll come find you in a bit. It's getting cold anyway."

Luke leaned over and kissed his uncle on the cheek.

"What was that for?"

"I'm glad we came here today."

Cooper sat for a second. "Yeah, I guess I am, too. Go on, I'll be over in a bit. Then we gotta get home. Your mother is going to wonder where we wandered off to."

He watched the boy get up and jog toward the south where the ball fields were. He watched him until he entered the trees and disappeared. Then he turned back to The Wall. He tilted his face back and closed his eyes until the setting sun fully lit his face with warmth. Then, quickly, as if he remembered a forgotten thought, he sat up and felt his pocket and reached in and pulled out the book Skinner gave him. There was some faded writing on the inside front cover. The book was well worn with some dark brown stains on the cover and some of the pages—

Fitz,
Dare to believe,
Your loving uncle

He sat up and crossed his legs; he thumbed the stained pages until he got to the one Skinner had marked with a worn post-it note. There was writing on it. Cooper figured it was Skinner's shaky hand and took a deep breath before he read it.

'My dear friend, read these pages and dare to believe like it says.'

Cooper removed the tab to expose the words. He looked in the margin where Skinner had put a star next to the chapter and lines he wanted Cooper to read. It was the beginning of the chapter.

'Therefore, there is now no condemnation for those who are...'

He kept reading, there on the grass, for the next half hour, his face in the sun, the cold breeze across him, in view of the beauty of The Wall and the names who spoke to him.

'... the law of the Spirit of life set me free from the law of sin and death ...'

In the short time he was there, the fear and grief began to melt. The items in the box of memories, as Skinner described them, stored for so long on the top shelf of a dark closet, began to lose their power in the sunlight. He was no longer afraid of those names on the wall. He knew what they would have said, if they could. He was not at fault, and anything he was to blame for was long since paid for and forgiven. All it required of him was that he'd dare believe it to be true. He pulled his knees up and, with his hands over his face, he began to cry. At moments, he would hold the little book to his chest and sob.

When the two got home, they washed up and helped Peggy in the kitchen, who was already in the middle of fixing dinner. She was all smiles when the two boys came in. They would eat in an hour—steak, baked potatoes, and fresh salad. Peggy had felt extra domestic that afternoon and put the finishing touches on a fresh peach and blackberry pie with a lattice crust. They would top the warm pie with ice cream after dinner. It caused Cooper to smile.

CHAPTER EIGHTTEEN
Nothing is easier than to denounce the evildoer; nothing is more difficult than to understand him.
—Fyodor Dostoevsky

I t was a sunny and warm winter. Jodi Campbell wore a business suit and a blue blouse under the slate gray, tailored jacket. The red wig looked surprisingly natural. She also wore a large pair of sunglasses and a broad, silver Concho belt. She carried a large briefcase in one hand and her black leather purse slung over her shoulder. She parked her rental car in the garage across from the city building and crossed at the light, then made the walk up the Palo Verde-lined walkway to the large glass doors of the building that housed most of the city's government and operations. The same one she had gone through with her toy donation. She was going to test the system again.

Just inside the door, three security lines with metal detectors and x-ray scanners to check bags were busy working all the people coming into the building. Jodi placed her purse and briefcase on the conveyor belt and stepped through herself. The detector was set off as she walked through. The guard asked her if she had any other metal on her and she slipped off her watch and told the guard that the belt was attached to the skirt and couldn't be removed so the guard used a wand over her. She noticed a black-and-white picture of her driver's license picture taped on the side of the scanner. It was her but the picture was grainy and she had changed her looks so much, no one recognized her. She smiled when she saw it.

At that moment, the guard watching the x-ray scanner signaled to his supervisor and pointed to an item on the monitor in her briefcase. The supervisor picked up the case and asked whose it was. Jodi casually walked over. "It's mine."

"Do you give me permission to open it?" he asked.

"Of course," she calmly responded.

They walked over to a side table. Inside were three file folders and three cans of Playdough. "What's this?" he asked, holding up one of the cans.

"Oh, I was just dropping off more toys to the nursery. See, you can open them if you want." She took a can and opened it, exposing the neon green clay material inside. "The kids love this stuff. They can never keep enough of it up there," she said with a smile as she pulled her purse and material together. The officer smiled and replaced it. "Looks like fun," he said with a grin. He looked under some files and pushed aside some masking tape. There was an electric pencil sharpener in the case. He picked it up and moved it in the case.

"Oh, you won't believe the fun they'll have," she said with a sweet smile.

The officer snapped the case closed and wished her a nice day. Jodi thanked him, took her belongings and walked over to the elevator. She cheerfully greeted people on her way to the seventh floor and walked into the nursery and dropped off the toys. She laughed and was animated. Jodi, overall, was very happy.

She went into the restroom on the same floor. It was clean and quiet. She could tell not a lot of traffic on that floor saw the inside of this room. She entered one of the three stalls and took off her belt. The underside of the belt, attached to the metal, contained two detonators and spooled wire. In her briefcase was some masking tape. She removed the items from the underside of the belt and then reattached the belt around her waist. She left the stall and walked over to the sink, placing her briefcase on the counter. She took the tape and attached a length of tape to the wire spool and the detonators and taped them inside of the front lip, under the counter. She made sure there was sufficient tape and the items were not going to fall. She opened the briefcase and removed the electric pencil sharpener. She pulled out the pencil shaving tray. In it was a small toggle switch and button. She taped them to the underside of the counter as well. She closed the briefcase, checked her makeup and smiled at herself in the mirror.

On the other side of town, two officers still had Jodi Campbell's house under surveillance since early the night before. The indoor lights went off late and the car hadn't moved. For all the two officers knew, she was still home. The two kept an eye on the house while the rest of the entry team met six blocks away in a vacant grocery store parking lot. The plan was simple: As soon as it was daylight, they would knock and announce, key the door, enter and arrest the woman they were seeking—straight forward, simple.

As the sun began to light the day, the entry team drove to the house in a white panel van while two marked police cars sealed off both ends of the street with another two units watching the alley. The two surveillance officers watching the house were parked just down the street. The van pulled up and five officers in black tactical gear trotted to Jodi's front door. The lights were still out. She was, hopefully, still asleep.

"All units stand by for entry," the tactical sergeant said as his team prepared to enter the Campbell home. They were going to take her before she hit again. The sun was just coming up; there was enough daylight to give the team the ability to see without using their flashlights attached to their guns until they got inside. With any luck, they would get her while she was still in bed. They had the house staked out for the last twelve hours. The surveillance team reported no one had left; the lights came on about eight o'clock the night before and turned off about midnight.

As one of the officers began to swing 'the key,' a forty-pound steel ram, aimed at the front door, another officer yelled, "Police, search warrant!"

The entry team had passed well into the depths of the house before the gas hit them. In the semi-darkness they didn't see the kiddy-pool and liquid falling into it. They were looking for Jodi. The image of the two liquids coming together didn't register until it was too late and the mixture of the two chemicals was burning their lungs. The gas choked them, cutting off their ability to inhale. The ammonia and sodium hypochlorite in the bleach mixed, generating acid. The paper Jodi had placed on the ground moved with the igloo, which in turn moved the shock sensitive pieces of aluminum foil, causing them to spark.

The natural gas that had leaked out of the pipe and filled the house with the explosive gas ignited. The men stumbled and fought their way out the door. The acidic gas was cooking their lungs just before the entire house exploded. The flame erupted and ignited the gas in the room, setting off a fireball explosion.

Cooper stood with Peggy, Lindy, and Luke just outside the security checkpoint at Reagan International Airport. He was taking the last flight back to Phoenix with a connection in Chicago. It meant he would be flying all night but he would get in early in the morning and go straight to work. He changed his mind about taking a day off when he returned. The sergeant approved the early return. He wanted to get back to work. He told Peggy they could drop him at the curb, but she wanted to walk him inside.

Cooper replayed the tape in his head of the past week. It had been hard to come out to see them, but how it worked out was not what he expected. There was a part of him dramatically relieved and a part of him who felt cleansed. As long as he could remember, Cooper had never cried. It felt good to do what he did on the hill at the Mall. It felt good to come spend time with his family. There was a feeling of freshness in his heart, like a warm summer rain on a dry lawn. He almost didn't want to leave for fear the feeling would go away. But he knew he had to go. There was a change in him. He could feel it.

"Do you have everything?" Peggy asked with her arms folded across her chest.

Cooper took the shoulder strap of his bag off his shoulder and allowed the bag to gently slip to the ground. "Yeah, I think so. If you find that other sock, you can keep it. It had a hole in it anyway." He looked at his sister. She looked radiant. There was peacefulness in her face. She was smiling. "What are you grinning at?" she asked. "You look like a big, old Cheshire cat. I haven't seen you this happy since— well, for a long time. I think this was a good trip for you, Coop. It was for us. Luke won't stop talking about you for months. You've spoiled him."

Cooper smiled at his sister and stroked her face and kissed her forehead. "That's what crazy uncles are supposed to do. Ruin kids for their parents."

"I hate to tell you, my friend, but you better scoot or they'll give your seat away. You'd have to stay here with us," Lindy said as he looked over at the flight schedule board.

"Now that wouldn't be such a bad idea," Cooper said.

"You sure you can't stay through Christmas? We'd love to have you," Peggy asked, already knowing the answer.

"You think you'll be all right with the outcome of the internal investigation?" Lindy asked.

Cooper snickered. "I'll get an oral reprimand and have it documented in my file. That's about as low as you can go. I can live with that. They'll put it right next to the others," he said with a wink at Lindy. He looked over at his sister. "You did a good thing these last few days. You'll never know," he said as he hugged her. He turned to Luke. "Remember about your stance. Don't let that defensive tackle read your stance.

"I won't, Uncle Coop."

Cooper turned and hugged Lindy after hugging his nephew. "Take care of my sister." He drew close to him and whispered in his ear. "Love her with all your heart."

"I will," he said.

He turned and walked through the security checkpoint, cleared his bag, and quickly disappeared as he walked with an energetic stride to the gate. He had a long flight ahead of him; he wasn't quite sure what he was going back to other than the reprimand; he didn't care, but there was air in his lungs which hadn't been there for as long as he could remember. He thought he might even drink some of that blended swill they call scotch on the plane. It was better than nothing.

Cooper got to the gate and checked in. He walked down to the Starbucks and got a large coffee and returned to a seat where he got comfortable. It would be just a few minutes before they would announce the boarding. That was fine by him. His mind was relaxed and after a moment, he looked at his watch then he pulled out his cell phone and dialed.

"Allison? Hi, it's me. No, no I don't want anything. Well, yeah, I guess I do." He paused for a moment. This was usually the early point in their phone conversations when the argument started. There were no buttons pushed for an argument this time. "I'm back here visiting Peggy and I—she's good." He lied. The words of his nephew were still fresh in his mind. "The chemo might have worked. Listen I ah, ah, just wanted to tell you how sorry I am for all these years. I know it's too late and probably too little, but I wanted you to know it wasn't your fault we didn't make it. It was mine." He smiled a little. "No, honey, I haven't been drinking; good question, though. I am going to have one or two on the plane ride home. How's Tom treating you? Good. You know if he isn't, I know this cop." He laughed in response to what she said. "Listen, I gotta go, my flight is boarding. Yeah, thanks." He slowly hung up the phone, and then he lightly ran his hand over it and smiled.

Jodi rubbed her hands over the soft, cool, putty-like explosive. She divided the one pound of material into three equal amounts and placed them evenly on the bottom of the red, yellow, and blue cans of Playdough, topping the contents of each can with the corresponding color of clay. She placed the containers in the briefcase followed by a couple of boxes each of marbles and tacks. When the explosives were detonated, they would be additional shrapnel.

Holy Ground

When she abandoned her house, she moved into an old motel just down the street from the capital, about a half mile from the city building. She had moved all of her newspaper clippings and correspondence she had amassed over time, and papered the walls to the small motel room with them. In a corner by the small desk lay a cluster of newspaper clippings about the opening of the city's children's nursery on the seventh floor of the city building for city workers. Government employees and parents contributed to it and even helped with its design. Jodi Campbell was about to bring them the same pain they had brought to her. The news was on. "Early this morning, a police search warrant at a home in central Phoenix went terribly wrong...." She smiled.

Cooper had called Paul and asked him if he would pick him up at the curb. They arranged to meet on the north side of the huge Terminal Four arrival level. Cooper called him when he touched down. It took some time for him to get from the gate to where he was meeting Paul because of all the holiday traffic, people with packages, bags, whole families working their way through the airport. By the time Cooper got to the curb, Paul arrived three minutes later.

"You look good," Paul said, smiling.

"You ain't going to kiss me with those big old lips of yours, are you?" Cooper said, snickering.

"First of all, you wish you had lips like these and second, you do look, you know, relaxed, especially for someone as old as you and just getting off the red-eye. Your sister is doing better?" Paul said as they both went to their prospective sides of the car and got in.

"Yeah, yeah she is. I thought for sure you'd show up in a Santa costume," Cooper said, changing the subject. "What's new here? We any closer to popping that bomber?"

193

Paul pulled out into traffic before he spoke. "Word is we are either close to catching her or she's real close to blowing something else up. You heard about the search of her house turning sideways, didn't you?"

Cooper nodded.

"She's getting more and more aggressive." Paul paused for a moment. "Lieutenant said we can go back to the aircraft at the end of the week."

"Well then, let's go to work. I haven't gotten written up in a few days. I actually missed it."

"Yeah, I always knew you were a sick bastard. You are a sight for sore eyes though. I've been teamed up with Manley while you were gone."

"Turner Manley? Does he still pick wax out of his ear and wipe it on—"

"Sniffs it first. Yeah, that's the gross bastard. He left some on the friggin' steering wheel one time when we changed drivers. I almost shot him."

"I'm sorry for my race, man."

"Yeah, well, that doesn't help much. I've been washing my hands like I have OCD."

They both laughed.

CHAPTER NINETEEN
Courage is fear that has said its prayers.
—Dorothy Bernard

———————

It was hard to see the parked vehicle, let alone Jodi sitting in it. The sun rose late in winter. The way the alley faced, behind the city building and with all the tall buildings around it, Jodi noticed from inside her car that darkness lingered for a long time early in the winter morning. With the exception of the two streetlights at either end of the alley, halfway down the narrow road was still soaked in inky blackness. The car was next to the main city structure loading dock.

Jodi watched the platform and took a few notes. She wanted to make a final check to see if the dock entrance was a possible escape route for her, if she got the opportunity. She reached into her purse and placed the paper and pen deep within it. She put it right next to the chrome-plated Sig pistol. She closed her purse and lit a cigarette. *Now is as good a time as any to start smoking,* she thought.

She looked away, then back at the loading dock, emotionless. She watched the back door for awhile, bundled up in her coat. She was looking at the lights and the setting of the entrance. *Could she leave the building and get to her car through these doors? Yes,* this was her exit, she decided. She would escape from here in all the confusion, and work her way around to the public garage across the street where she had her mind made up she would park.

She heard a noise behind her. She used her side mirror and moved it remotely to see what was causing the sound. There was a figure of a man coming out of another dock door. He stepped down to the alley and walked over to the dumpsters. It looked like he was going through the trash. He was coming her way.

Cooper and Paul arrived at the Six-Twenty Station and after changing into their uniforms, they reported to the basement briefing room for the day's notices and assignments. They were working day shift until they returned to the helicopter. It added new life into the day, knowing the two were going back to flying at the end of the week. Paul walked a few steps ahead of his partner into the briefing room, then got everyone's attention. "Ladies and gentlemen, boys and girls! First of all, Merry Christmas or to be politically correct, *Happy Holidays*. Secondly, returning from an engagement on the East Coast where he has spent the last few days relaxing and parasiting off of his beloved family, I bring you the King of Flight Rule Violations, the Sheik of Bullsheek, give it up for our very own Cooper Harrison Gardner!"

The room broke into a rousing round of applause and paper and trash throwing all aimed at Cooper.

Tom Hyple, the shift sergeant for that day, who was up front, ready to start the roll call and briefing, had a big smile on his face. "Welcome back, Coop. How's your sister?"

"Good, thanks, Tom," Cooper said as he sat down. The room settled and everyone found a seat.

"On a more serious note, you'll see in front of you the Feds and our own guys have identified the bomber as Jodi Campbell. To review, her husband died in a car accident with their only son a few months ago. Mrs. Campbell was quoted by one of the social service workers interviewed in this case as blaming the city for her husband's and eventually, her child's death. They executed a search warrant on her house and as you know, it went very badly. It appears she knew we were coming and booby-trapped the house. Somehow, none of the officers died, but several have extensive burns. Her car was at the house and we believe she is driving a rental or maybe even using public transportation. She has knowledge of explosives, having used them in her engineering work. It is believed Mrs. Campbell was responsible for a break-in at a construction site and the removal of bomb-making material."

The room was silent. A copy of her driver's license photo was being passed out to everyone in the room. "We can assume Mrs. Campbell is armed because records show a small semi-auto, a Sig, was registered to her deceased husband about five years ago."

The man in the alley moved closer to Jodi's car. He was hunched over, carrying or pushing something. He had a stick in his hand and appeared to be using it to rake piles of trash aside to see what lay underneath it. He was wearing a City of Phoenix t-shirt. She noticed he had on another shirt under it, a collared shirt; it looked like a Hawaiian shirt. She didn't know him. She had only been here once and had never seen him. She didn't know he checked the dumpsters before his shift every morning, before they were emptied. Morning was the best time to look in them. He was within ten feet of the rear bumper of Jodi's car, but on the opposite side of the alley. He turned once to look over his shoulder, then back to his foraging. She didn't know who it was. She didn't care.

The sergeant continued. "She may have colored her hair, cut it or performed some other kind of change or disguise such as a wig. This picture you have of her is going out today on all the news channels. Just keep your eyes open. Cooper and Jackson will be pushing patrol car four-Bravo twenty-three and twenty-four today, down by the courthouse and downtown area. Everyone,

Jodi silently got out of her car and took a step toward the man looking in the dumpster. She knew no one was in the alley; she had been there long enough to notice any movement. She could take a city representative personally. She could see a face that would represent all the faces she wanted to exact revenge on. That was the one thing she missed about her plan, the personal satisfaction of seeing the faces of the dead and dying. He was too busy with his foraging to hear her get out of her car.

Skinner dug for gold, rare gems from others who didn't see the value in what they had so they threw their garbage away. Before he started his shift each day, with the city the VA was able to line up for him after a new course of anti-psychotic drugs began to make the ghosts and dreams subside in his head, he went into the alley. He felt comfortable there. For the first time in a long time, he felt like a man. He still liked to search the dumpsters for thrown away treasure; old habits were hard to break.

He loved the mornings. It made him feel safe. The *Boogieman* can't live in the light. It was a lesson he had learned a long time ago, in another life.

"Hey," a voice behind him called. His attention was drawn to the voice of a woman. All he saw was a silhouette close to him cast by the street light some eighty yards away. He squinted.

"Hello?" he said, just as he saw a flash of light. His mind recorded it and then there was nothing.

CHAPTER TWENTY
I'd rather get my brains blown out in the wild than wait in terror at the slaughterhouse.
—Craig Volk, *Northern Exposure*

Paul and Cooper were the second unit to roll up on the shots-fired call just as they were pulling out of the station parking garage. The city building, where the victim lay, was only three blocks from the main station. "Hey, Petey," Cooper said to Pete Turley, a fifteen-year training officer. His rookie partner, fresh out of the academy two weeks, was taping off a perimeter to his first homicide. "What did you find?"

"Someone shot this guy at close range, it looks like. Probably another gang initiation," Turley said as he looked past Cooper and Paul to watch what his rookie was doing.

Cooper walked toward the body. He recognized Skinner as he lay on his side, the hair, the shirt. Cooper stood over him for a moment. From this angle, he couldn't see the head wound. The blood was dark and blended with the asphalt of the alley and still dark shadows of the early morning. There wasn't enough light yet to distinguish color. It just looked like Skinner was sleeping on a dark blanket. The blanket was his own blood.

There was something in Cooper's mind—the melody of a song. They were bagpipes. Why they arrived at that time he couldn't tell. He actually looked around trying for a moment to see where they were coming from. He couldn't shake it, then, he didn't want to. It bathed him in soft warmth. For some reason they played. He hadn't heard those sounds, truly heard them, since his youth. His grandfather, James, was said to have played them. He heard the pipes at funerals, but this was different. This was deep within him.

Paul came up alongside of him. "Welcome home partner," Paul said as he looked down at the body, not recognizing the man they rescued a few weeks before. Cooper said nothing. He just looked down at the man lying in the alley. Cooper and Skinner had saved each other's lives over the course of the last few weeks. It was the end of Skinner's run. *Now, it's my turn,* he thought; wherever that took him. There was something new in his step. He got it at the amphitheater. He got it from this man, now lying at his feet.

The military honor guard carried the casket from the hearse to the burial plot. Only Cooper, Moreno, the minister, and fourteen members of the honor guard were at the service. Skinner, for all his adult life, struggled with mental illness, but it didn't take away the service he gave to his country. Cooper hired a piper to stand at a distance and play. It was as much for him as for Skinner. He wanted to hear the pipes again. There as a shadow in his mind, a memory.

He had an image of being on the porch of his grandparent's house. He remembered playing in the dirt of the old dairy his grandparents had, his father, Jacob, had returned from the war and they would sit on the porch while he and his sister played in the yard. At night, he remembered his grandfather would get out the pipes and play. Cooper's father would sit and listen and his grandmother and his own mother would come out and listen as well. He remembered he and his sister would cover their ears, not liking the sound. It would take years until he appreciated it. At this point in his life, he wished he was back on the porch.

Holy Ground

Skinner had no family that Cooper could find. He promised himself he would not allow Skinner to go out with no one standing watch. He made sure of that.

The pipes played. There were three volleys of seven rifles as the casket was lowered by six, crisp marines. Then, as the casket came to its rest at the bottom, the music stopped. There was silence except for a slight rustle in the trees and the ever slight sound of people walking away from the grave. There was a memory from his past. Something deeply imbedded in his mind. He smiled. Cooper thought of an ancient story of warriors coming home and the pipes were the welcoming. An ancient story of ancient times, words from a long time ago, *today looks like a good day to die.*

Later that day, Cooper walked down the street and turned into the alley that led to Skinner's shed, tucked away down an old service entrance to an abandoned garage. A custodian was servicing the air-conditioning units for the other side of the building. Cooper showed him his police identification, pulling his identification badge case from his jacket pocket. He told the custodian it was police business; that a man had died. The custodian didn't flinch but simply opened the access door that Cooper told him to open, down a short side alley. The man appeared surprised there was anyone living in this part of the building. Cooper thanked him and assured him he would secure the door before he left. He remembered to duck when he walked in and began to look around. He had a small flashlight and used it to light up the space. He propped the door open, letting fresh air and the light outside to filter in. The small room smelled of stagnant air. It was worse than he remembered, probably because the time he was there before was clouded in a fog of scotch and the pummeling he took. It did seem larger when he was lying on its floor. But it was clean. There was order to it.

201

Someone had lived here and while their accommodations were less than choice by other's standards, it was still someone's home.

He found the photos on the wall. Cooper looked at each one and in each one found the man who, at one time, occupied this place. In some he was smiling, but in most he gave a warrior face, one of seriousness and focus. That's what boys did when they went to war, Cooper remembered. They had to look hard, even when they weren't. Cooper removed one frame from the wall and took the picture out of it. He carefully placed it in his jacket pocket and returned the frame to the box-table next to the kitchen area. When he left, he found the custodian just inside another door and told him he was leaving and thanked him for letting him in.

He walked out to the alley and turned right when he got to the street. He walked into Moreno's and sat on his usual barstool. The day bartender was on and didn't recognize Cooper since he was never in during the day. He ordered his usual scotch, but only drank half of it before he left. He walked down the street with no clear destination, his hands tucked into his pockets.

Cooper found himself in the retail district and walked along, looking in windows. He sought nothing in particular and found nothing. He just walked. His mind rolled from one image of his life to another, stopping for a moment in Skinner's home. He pushed the thoughts away and tried to think about anything else. He focused on his sister and her family. He even thought about his retirement, something benign. But it didn't work. He kept coming back to Skinner and what he said to him when he lay busted up on his floor. This man's life was bleak, and yet, there was contentment in his eyes. It was the same contentment he saw in Peggy's eyes.

He kept walking and crossed the street and into the city's light rail terminal park on the other side.

There he found a bench and sat. He was just another businessman from the looks of him, sitting quietly, observing the world as it passed. He reached into his jacket and took out the picture he removed from Skinner's wall. "This could have been me," he whispered to himself, as his fingers stroked the photograph. The man lived like a sewer rat and yet he seemed more at peace than Cooper. His sister was dying, although she'd never admit it, and she was more at home with her heart than he was.

He lifted his eyes to the buildings around him. The sun was between the courthouse and the Bank of America building. The world around him took on colors and hues which seemed soft and calling. He could hear a piano of an old instrumental he recognized coming from a corner restaurant. Music was occupying space in his consciousness, it seemed. It never did before. *Weird*, he thought. It was there, playing, soft yet firm. It made him smile. He began to play along with it, drumming his fingers on the bench next to him like he was playing the piano. The song just kept playing. It blocked the darkness he had been walking in and enabled him to run in his mind with happiness again, weird, free, happiness, the feelings at The Mall. He looked at his watch. He had been sitting there for almost an hour.

Cooper Gardner found himself joyful for the first time in maybe his entire life.

CHAPTER TWENTY-ONE
*You're not to be so blind with
patriotism that you can't face reality.
Wrong is wrong, no matter who does
it or says it.*
—Malcolm X

Christmas Eve Day

Jodi woke up, showered, and brushed her hair and teeth. She had checked into another small efficiency motel room in the northern part of the city just off Interstate-17 and Dunlap Avenue. She kept moving, performing her daily routine. It was as if she was going to work, just another day at work. She put lipstick on and checked her makeup before she finished packing the clay containers with the explosive in each of the three smaller containers and fit them snuggly into her briefcase. She washed the dishes before she left. She hated dirty dishes in the sink. The firing fuse was already in the building. She had run this scenario and knew it would work. Today, the city would pay for all it had done. Today, Christmas Eve Day, would be the celebration of her dear son's birthday, and this was her birthday gift to him.

Jodi put on her wig, finished her makeup and packing her briefcase. She put her clothes back into the small travel bag she had with her, then called the front desk and asked for her bill to be totaled. She walked down to the motel office and paid cash, leaving no credit card trace and then returned to the room, wiping down the counter in the bathroom and shut out the lights before she walked out of her hotel room and got into her rental car. She had left a large cash deposit for the car, keeping it off the credit card radar as well. "They're going to find us, boys," she said when she got in the car.

"It's just a matter of time, but then we'll all be together."
Her time was coming to an end. She was almost done,
her life, almost complete.

The last day on patrol for Paul and Cooper
began with the briefing. It was far from routine. The
report on the failed search warrant for the Campbell
woman was telecast nationwide; news hit the Internet
like a virus. The talk was centered around terrorism
and terrorists. That was all people talked about.

The briefing sergeant walked over and turned
the sound down on the television before he began. "I
don't need to tell you what our priority is today. Jodi
Campbell is the suspect allegedly blowing up property
and killing people. Ladies and gentlemen, once again,
on your desk, is her picture and bio. We have a delay
in reports on her credit card usage. We believe she
rented a car and instead of using her card, she used a
large, cash down payment. ATF and the detectives are
checking with the car companies. Stay focused on
your patrol areas and answer to all calls for service.
But, if you get any hint of something that might lead to
this woman's apprehension, make sure the detectives
and radio are aware of it quickly. We don't think she's
done yet."

"Sergeant, any leads as to where she might
be?" one officer in the front row asked.

"Not a clue. She could be anywhere." He looked
down the list of notes in front of him. "That is all for
this morning. Let's be careful out there today people."
No one spoke. The blue uniforms worked their way
out the door and down the hall.

It was almost eight in the morning when Jodi
Campbell pulled into the parking garage directly
south of the city building on Washington Avenue. She

Mark Williams

placed an envelope with a letter inside she had
drafted the night before and left it on the seat,
knowing they would find it, eventually. In case she
didn't make it out of the building that morning, she
wanted the last word to be hers. It was three pages,
both sides, of rambling hate. Jodi pulled the visor
down and checked her lipstick and gave herself one
last look over. "I look good, don't you think, boys?" she
said to the empty car.

Jodi felt a flash of anxiety as she grabbed her
briefcase, but then it was gone. She got out of the car
and locked it as she proceeded to the corner of the
garage and down one flight of stairs to the ground
level. The parking lot was pretty empty for a workday;
it was Christmas Eve after all. Many people had taken
the day off. The light was green and she crossed. In
two minutes, she was at the front doors of the city
building.

Jodi had done this enough times it was
becoming routine. She made sure she made eye
contact with the same male security guard she had
met before. She smiled and said "good morning" as
she placed her briefcase on the scanner. He greeted
her, smiling and appearing to recognize her. "How are
you today?" he asked.

"Just fine, thank you."

As she passed through the metal detector, it
went off, just as planned. She again moved to a side
table where the briefcase was searched. She brought
in more of the Playdough as another donation she told
the guard. The guard opened the container. Jodi
expected that. But then the guard sniffed the dough
and frowned. Jodi didn't expect that.

She needed to break the guard's concentration.
"Those kids upstairs, I think they eat the stuff. They
can't get enough of it, making animals and—" the

206

guard moved away carrying the container. He walked over to another guard, his apparent supervisor and held it out to him and was talking, gesturing back to Jodi.

She hadn't planned for this. Someone was actually doing their job. She hadn't thought what to do if she was stopped here. It wasn't part of her plan.

The supervisor sniffed the container and shrugged and then shook his head as if saying he didn't smell anything. The guard returned put it back in the container.

"Something wrong, officer?" Jodi asked.

"It just smelled funny to me. It's been a while since I got to play with this stuff," he said with a partial smile.

Jodi gave a fake laugh. "Oh, wait until you get some on your hands, it never leaves. You smell it all day." There was a small hand-held radio/scanner in the case. One of the guards picked it up and turned it on, then looked at Jodi.

"My nephew is a new police officer and is working his first shift today. I thought I would bring that and listen for him." The guard nodded and placed it back in the case after he turned it on to make sure it worked.

She relaxed again as she walked through the scanner. It was the same Concho belt again causing the alarm. The guard took a wand and scanned her by hand after securing the briefcase. It beeped but it was supposed to. "Have a good day," he said.

"Oh, thank you, I will," she said with a sincere smile. She retrieved her briefcase. She thanked him and walked across the vast space which made up the lobby of the building. She entered the main floor woman's restroom and went directly into one of the stalls. She reached up under her dress and at the metal buckle of her belt, retrieved the Sig she had duct-taped to her abdomen. Jodi felt a quiet moment of contentment.

She sat down on the toilet and set the briefcase on her lap. Opening it, she placed the gun inside, next to the new containers of clay explosives. The timer and detonator was all that was needed to be attached, still—hopefully—taped under the sink upstairs.

Paul drove. Cooper was attentive, but quiet. "You thinking about your sister?"

Cooper nodded. "Yeah, it was a good trip. I'm glad I went. I'm not sure when or if I'm going to see her again."

Paul looked over at him as he drove. "You said she looked good though."

"Yeah, for a cancer patient. I don't know, Paul. I think that might have been the last trip. Something about it; I don't know. She was peaceful. They all were peaceful. It was good," he said as he looked out the window.

A moment passed. Paul thought he would change the topic. "So, you ready to get back in the air this week? I can't friggin wait."

Cooper looked back at his partner and smiled. "Are you kidding me? This pushing a car is not for me. I don't know how I did it for so long before I got selected for the air wing. Me as pilot and you as the observer."

"Wait, observer? I, as you may recall, am a fairly decent pilot myself. I think I get a little stick time."

Cooper looked at him and smiled then back out the window. "Yeah, you'll get some stick time." Paul pulled the car to the curb on the south side of the city's parking garage at Third and Jefferson. "What are you doing?" Cooper asked.

"I just need to stop at the ATM. Doris took my last five dollars and I need some money for lunch," he said as he put the car into park and got out.

"Take your time, honey," Cooper said through the open driver's window. "I know who's buying lunch today."

The elevator doors opened on the seventh floor. Jodi stepped out and walked down the short hall toward the nursery. She passed it and walked into the restroom. She was anxious to see if the things she planted were still there. They were. She reached up under the sink counter, retrieved the items she had taped in place, and placed them in the briefcase. She breathed a deep sigh of relief. She quickly assembled the parts while the case was open, in case she needed to close it quickly if someone came in the restroom. She pushed the detonator into the first container of green explosive and the second into the blue one. The case was filled with bags of tacks, marbles, anything that could serve as a projectile in the explosion. The last thing she did was run the wire in the briefcase and hooked it to the transmitter for the dead man switch in the sharpener, which she taped to the side of the case. When it was time, she could grab the switch and push the button. She extended the short antenna from the receiver. It allowed her to move away from the briefcase and still be able to set it off. Once Jodi activated it, and then pushed the button down for the first time, she would have to continue to hold the switch down or it would detonate. If anything happened to her, her finger could easily come off the switch, activating the circuit and setting off the explosives. She took the gun from the case and placed it in the pocket of her skirt.

The walls on the outside of the nursery were painted with murals of animal cartoon characters. They were covered in cheerful, primary colors. Jodi could hear the giggling of young children at play as she approached, children, whose parents had to work that day. She entered and was greeted by two adult women who recognized her from the time before. Seven children were in the main playroom; three other staffers and one father were chatting. They smiled at Jodi and kept talking. Jodi stepped over to a nearby counter and set the briefcase down. She reached into her dress pocket and pulled out the Sig. "All right everyone, just sit back and relax and no one gets hurt."

One of the staffers, a young Hispanic girl, gasped when she saw the gun. "Oh my god, what are you doing?"

"Again, do as I say and no one gets hurt," Jodi repeated.

The sound of the elevator opening about thirty feet down the hall drew her attention. A young woman stepped out and their eyes met. The woman saw the gun, taking a few steps for it to register that something was terribly wrong. She turned to get back in the elevator but the door was already shut. She frantically pushed the elevator button. Jodi stepped back through the outer room, aimed, and fired three quick shots through the glass which made up the upper half of the exterior room's wall. As the bullets passed through the glass, they caused the windows to explode with shattered glass flying like dust in the wind. The first two rounds ricocheted off the door of the elevator and the door frame. It caused the woman to flinch to her right. The third round pierced her shoulder and tore through it. She found herself grabbing for the door handle to the emergency stairwell and pushing herself through it. The woman made it into the temporary safety of the well and then ran and stumbled down the stairs, not stopping until she got to the ground floor.

Jodi turned back into the main playroom, and pointed the gun at the oldest attendant. A small curl of smoke rose from the barrel. She smiled as she spoke.

"All right everyone, as I said—just sit back and relax. The police will be here in a few minutes and all this will be over soon after that." She opened the briefcase and made the final connections while pulling out the police scanner. She closed it and held the remote switch in her non-gun hand. Jodi put an earpiece in her ear and plugged the other end into the scanner. She pushed down the button on the dead man switch and a small red light came on; the circuit was complete.

Paul got back into the car after counting the bills and stuffed them in his wallet.

"So, where are you taking me for lunch?"

"Why do I have to take you to lunch? You're the one who just came back from vacation. You should be taking me to lunch, telling me how much you missed me and all that crap. Why is it every time we stop at an ATM and I get money, you expect me to pay for whatever meal we're eating? Why is that?"

"We've been partners for a short time. You've never stopped at an ATM. So, I just assumed you would be nice. I don't have you buy my lunches a lot."

"Yeah, you do."

"No, I don't."

"Yeah, you really do."

"Do I really?"

"Yeah, you really do."

"Geez, I didn't know I did that."

"You have a reputation."

"Again, with the reputation."

"Yeah, and that's not good. Just once I wish you would wait for an invitation. That's all."

"I can do that." Cooper paused. "So where are you going to invite me to have lunch with you?"

"Geez. You piece of shit."

"Thank you. I did miss you. And, it is because I just came back from vacation that you need to take—" the radio broke in with a hot tone.

"All units, shots fired seventh floor, city building nursery, Washington and Third Avenue."

"We're a block away," Paul said.

"I'll put us there," Cooper said. "Four-Bravo twenty-three and twenty-four responding. We're a block away," he said into the microphone.

The radio kicked back the units responding to the call. The female voice was calm and steady, as if she was reading a grocery list. "Four-Bravo twenty-three and twenty-four; four-Bravo ten; four-Adam twenty-five, ten-four. What we have is a woman in the childcare center on the seventh floor who shot at our victim as she got off the elevator. The woman doesn't know if the shooter was alone—no description. Special Assignments is responding."

"I bet we'll know who they are by the guns they're holding," Cooper said as he grinned to Paul.

Paul pulled the car around two corners and parked right in front of the main entrance. People were running out of the building. Cooper and Paul were the first two officers to arrive.

"Four-Bravo twenty-three and twenty-four are twenty-three," Cooper said into his radio on his shirt. "Let's take the stairs," he said to Paul as they entered the lobby.

"Want to wait for SAU?"

"We gotta get to the threat. We don't have time to wait for those special assignment units to show up. If it's who we think it is, by the time the lieutenant and Tactical set up, everyone will be dead. This could be our gal, and if it is, she's not going to stop until there's dead bodies—small bodies, from the sound of it."

They entered the front doors and passed security as they trotted to the stairwell. Cooper stopped Paul just before they entered. "Listen, seven flights. We'll take them one at a time, and when we get to the landing, we'll catch our breath."

"We're not taking the elevator because?" Paul asked.

"Because we can't control what happens when the doors open. The shooter could be standing there waiting and we can't stop those elevator doors from opening. We would be sitting ducks."

Cooper paused before he spoke again. "We gotta buy time for Tactical. This is going to be bad."

"I know."

"You ready to do what you have to do?"

Paul nodded. "You?"

Cooper nodded. "Don't think you're getting out of buying lunch for this."

"Shit."

"Right, let's get this done."

"Okay, but I'll lead," Paul said.

"No, the oldest goes first. I got more experience."

"Listen old man, you are no Jack-Be-Nimble okay. Some crazy comes around a corner up there we can't wait for you to get your friggin cane out."

"You got a wife."

"That's exactly why I'm leading. I want to see her again sometime today."

"Bastard."

"Bite me, come on," Paul said and turned.

The two men turned their ball caps backwards then entered the stairwell with their guns drawn. There were two flights of stairs for every floor. After the first flight, Cooper got on the radio and told dispatch they were in the stairwell, moving up to the seventh floor. They would hold at the door to the seventh floor.

"Radio, this is Patrol fifty-one," said the responding lieutenant for the area.

"Relay to those units to hold on the ground floor." By the time Paul and Cooper heard it, they were on the third-floor landing, moving to the fourth. Paul was in the lead. He looked back over his shoulder at Cooper as if asking with his eyes what they were going to do. Cooper looked at him and stopped. "I can't hear him in this damn stairwell can you? I think he said he copied our plan. Is that what you heard?" Cooper said with a deep breath.

Paul smiled, "ten-four partner." He turned and continued the climb.

Jodi heard the transmissions, all of them. Her little belt-clipped police scanner she purchased at Radio Shack worked just fine. She knew they were coming, just what she wanted. This was going to be big, and even though she had hoped on being able to leave to do more on another day, it was fine for it to end this way. It would be a fitting birthday present for her boy. She moved out of the nursery toward the elevator and stairwell door. She could see the door to the stairwell and noticed the elevator was on the ground floor. She could still watch the nursery with the children and adults. All the children were crying. She moved toward the stairwell door. The gun was up and ready. She had a smile on her face.

CHAPTER TWENTY-TWO
A hero is no braver than an ordinary man.
But, he is brave five minutes longer.
　　　　　—Ralph Waldo Emerson

The two men reached the sixth floor landing and stopped. They moved as if the threat of the world waited for them on the next landing— carefully, slowly, one quiet step at a time, their guns focused on the stairwell area above them as they pressed their backs to the wall. They were slicing a pie; each step exposed a couple more degrees of vision of the seventh floor into view. Soon, they were standing on the seventh-floor stairwell landing. They quickly cleared the eighth floor landing making sure no one was above them. They could hear on the radio other units were arriving. Cooper and Paul were clearly alone, at least for awhile.

The two men heard the radios broadcasting the traffic in their ear-pieces. They could only hear the base radio and not much of the units they were talking to. The dispatcher was talking to several units and relaying information to Patrol fifty-one. "Four-Bravo ten, you still a minute off? Roger. Patrol fifty-one, they're still in the stairwell is the last communication I have from them. The stairwell might be blocking their transmission. I will try to reach them again. Four-Bravo twenty-three and twenty-four, Patrol fifty-one said to hold your position at the bottom of the stairs. He will be coming twenty-three in about three minutes."

Cooper turned to Paul and shook his head. "This shit will be a real mess in three minutes."

"I think we should wait for the SAU units now," Paul whispered. They got bigger guns and negotiators and shit. We just have, well, you."

"Thanks for the vote of confidence."

"Hell partner, *you* wouldn't vote for you."

"Yeah, you're probably right. All right, I'll call." Cooper dropped to one knee and spoke softly into the microphone. "Four-Bravo twenty-three."

"Four -Bravo twenty-three," came the radio response.

"Four Bravo twenty-three and twenty-four, we are on the seventh floor landing. We are holding at this location," Cooper said. He turned to Paul. "Who's pushing Patrol fifty-one today?"

Paul thought for minute as he wiped the sweat from his forehead. "I think it's Jacobs."

"Shit," Cooper said.

"Yeah, those little kids will be cold and buried by the time he acts. The guy can't take a crap without asking permission from the chief," Paul said.

A minute passed. They could hear children crying down the hall from the stairwell. The two sat for a moment. "Four-Bravo twenty-three," Cooper called quietly.

"Four-Bravo twenty-three."

"We can hear children in distress. We request permission to engage." They waited while the radio operator relayed to Patrol fifty-one. Cooper and Paul couldn't hear the lieutenant's response. They could only hear the radio operator repeat back what was relayed. The walls of the stairwell were blocking the lieutenant's transmission. "Four-Bravo twenty-three."

"Go," Cooper responded.

"Patrol fifty-one said you are to hold position where you are. You are not to engage until he is twenty-three, about two minutes."

Cooper looked at his partner. "We're not going to be flying tomorrow, are we?" Paul asked.

"What do you think?" Cooper said. "Only if you're on board with this."

Paul snickered. "You know what I think. Make the call."

Cooper's eyes smiled. "I find myself strangely attracted to you right now."

"Eat shit and die," Paul said with a grin.

"Probably," Cooper said. He then keyed the radio. "Four-Bravo twenty-three, roger, we are clear to engage. Advise SAU we are engaging on the seventh floor." He looked back at his partner. "Us flying tomorrow all depends on how we write this report."

"Yeah, well, I'm leaving that to you," Paul said as he looked at his gun, pulling the magazine and reinserting it, then tapping the butt of it to make sure it was all the way in. Their radios were transmitting in both their ears the repeated instruction of the Patrol unit not to engage.

Paul keyed his mic. "Four-Bravo twenty-four, Radio, you're breaking up. Again, advise arriving units we are on the floor." He looked at Cooper. "Damn low-bid radios. Let's go."

Cooper led. Paul was right behind him against the wall that separated them from the seventh floor. Cooper opened the door, bringing his gun up and into the crack of the door. Jodi was there, gun drawn, pointed right at Cooper's face. Instinctively, he pushed back from the door and pulled the trigger to his own gun at the same time. He fired three quick rounds, all three shots going low into the floor on the other side of the door. The explosion of sound included two rounds from Jodi. Her first shot was muffled as it creased Cooper's shoulder, just inside the strap of his body armor. The second was much lower, as if Jodi was firing as she fell back, away from the door opening seeking her own cover. The round caught Paul's knee as Cooper

217

spun back and away. It was a freak shot, a one in a million shot. But it caught him right at the knee joint. Both rounds bounced off the concrete wall behind them as the bullets traveled through their bodies.

Jodi walked back to the daycare room. The bullets from Cooper's gun had missed her and drilled themselves into the wall behind her. She still had a smile on her face, but it was smeared with the complexion of a woman gone mad. She was sweating profusely and her heavy makeup was now starting to run down her face. Her wig had tipped and was not sitting straight on her head any longer. She was in a place where everything happening was by her design. She was feeling the revenge she had so long sought. It was a feeling Jodi didn't want to end but knew it would, probably with her life. It would all be worth it if she took all these children and adults with her, and she was going to do just that.

"Okay, the secret's out," she announced. "The police are here to save you. Everyone just needs to stay where you are. It will all be over in just a few minutes."

"Shit, shit, shit where did that come from?" Paul said as he flopped on to the floor in the corner, holding his thigh just above the knee. His ears were ringing from the concussion in the stairwell. He looked over at Cooper. "You're shot too?" He said as he saw the blood oozing from Cooper's shoulder as he slid down next to him.

"She stuck her gun almost through the door, right at my head. She was there waiting for us. It looked like she had an earpiece. She's probably listening to every damn word we're saying." He keyed his microphone with his left hand. "Four-Bravo twenty-three, nine-nine-nine, shots fired. We have an officer down. Four-Bravo twenty-four is down. We are holding on the landing of

218

the seventh floor. She's monitoring our radio traffic. Where is that SAU team?"

"Four-Bravo twenty-three, SAU is about 10 minutes out."

Cooper looked at his shoulder while trying to keep an eye on the door. The bullet must have gone through his shoulder and glanced off his arm, he thought. It tore his shirt and took out a piece of shoulder meat.

Jodi smiled when she got back to the now hysterical children. "Hush now children, we have about ten more minutes. Then it will all be over."

"What are you doing?" the father said. "What do you want?"

Jodi pointed the gun at him and smiled.

"Four-Adam thirty-one, I'm on the seventh-floor landing on the east side," Cooper heard in his earpiece. It was another officer, Packard Thornton; 'Bull' was his nickname. He had made his way up through all the commotion and finally cleared his position. He was a good friend of Cooper's, cut of the same cloth. Cooper could tell by the radio transmissions that Bull knew about the hold on the bottom floor. He knew Bull wouldn't let Cooper be in the gunfight alone.

"All units, Patrol fifty-one instructs all units to hold their positions. No further engagement of the suspects are to be attempted," the radio operator repeated. Patrol fifty-one had heard Bull's broadcast in the other stairwell. He repeated his order.

"Four-Adam thirty-one, Central, you're breaking up. We are unable to copy at our location," Bull's transmission came back. Cooper smiled. He knew Bull. He would have done the same thing. It was his way of telling him and Paul where he was and they were free to act if needed. His transmission was clear as a bell. It would all be suspect later, but no one would question it, not much anyway.

"Those kids can't wait ten minutes," Paul said as he glanced down at his leg. He closed his eyes and tried to control his breathing. If he wasn't careful, he would hyperventilate.

Cooper looked back at him. "In case you haven't noticed, partner, we just got our pee pee slapped pretty good. I'm not leaving you for them."

Paul was breathing hard, his face glistening with sweat. "You know you have to. I'll be all right. It didn't hit an artery or I'd be dead by now. I can still shoot. Bitch ain't gonna get a piece of this black ass without a fight!" Paul said, clenching his teeth.

"Shoot at what? You can't walk," Cooper said. He glanced over to the side by where the wall and stairs met. "I think that's part of your kneecap over there."

Paul leaned his head against the wall and calmed himself and his breathing. "No, that's not it; it's still in my pants. Look, I can't go down the stairs either. And your sorry ass can't carry me down and I can't follow you in. But I can cover you from here." He stopped for a minute and grimaced in pain. The initial shock was wearing off and the body started to feel its pain. "Prop me in the door jamb and that way, as you go down the hall, I can give you cover and secure the exit for anyone coming out."

"Sounds like you thought this out. I'm not leaving you."

"Shit, I haven't thought of anything! You aren't leaving me, you gay old piece of shit. You're going for a walk down a friggin' hallway. God, you're the only one left for those kids! You know as well as I do she's going to kill herself and all of them. There is no negotiating here. We have got to get to her. You can't leave those workers in there. By the time Jacobs gets here and finishes kissing the chief's ass, we're all dead."

Cooper hadn't taken his eye off the door. His right arm was beginning to spasm. He transferred his gun to his left hand. The pain from the wound was more of a burn, a hot screaming burn. "You sure?"

"No, you creamy piece of bird crap! Does it say 'daycare madman super planner' on my big black forehead? Do you have a better idea?"

Cooper made his way to the door and slowly opened it, his gun up and ready. No one was in view. He walked back to Paul. "You ready? This is going to hurt— a lot."

Paul nodded and took a deep breath. Sweat was running down his face. Cooper dragged him by his left hand after he holstered his gun, to the door while Paul stifled a scream of pain by biting down on the rubber handle of his expandable baton. Cooper took his gun out and squatted down before he slowly opened the door again. He crawled into the hallway after looking in both directions. She could have stayed there and probably zapped them both, he thought. All the more reason she was going to do something real bad and real big. Paul scooted on his bottom and wedged himself into the door jamb. He propped himself up with his back to the door frame and, with his good leg, held the door open. His gun rested in his lap. Once he was set, he armed himself. "Go," he whispered to Cooper.

Cooper looked down the hall toward the nursery. He turned back to his partner. "She's down there. Listen to me. I'll be back for you. You keep your ass alive until I come back and get you out of here. Do you hear me?"

Paul's eyes stayed focused on the end of the hall. He never looked up at his partner when he spoke. "Remember I said my kneecap is in my pants? Don't let them lose it when the medics come and get me. Now go, and keep your big ass down. My dead mother could hit it without even trying." He grimaced out a smile. "I know you ain't coming back."

They looked at each other. "Well, don't count me out too early partner," Cooper said.

"Look, she's going to kill them if you don't stop her."

"I know."

"It's going to cost you."

Cooper looked at his friend and touched his shoulder. "Take care of my ship."

Paul nodded, still looking down the hall. As Cooper turned to move, Paul spoke again. "Remember partner, you won't have to read her any rights." He smiled at his friend as he continued pointing his gun down the hall.

Cooper smiled back and turned to the hall.

Jodi walked to the window and looked out to the west. The sun was on the other side of the building, but she could tell it was going to be another beautiful day. She removed a roll of duct tape from her case, tore off a piece and began to tape the switch to her hand so it couldn't accidently fall out prematurely. The only finger free was the one on the switch. All she had to do was keep her finger on the button. "Soon, it will all be over," she said to the group of hostages as if to comfort them. She wiped the sweat from her brow, smearing her makeup even more. "Okay, we're all set. When they come in, this will all be over, as I promised. There's going to be a lot of police up here and a lot of loud noise but it won't last long—I promise." She smiled at her hostages, but it was a face reflecting horror.

Cooper began to move. He was going to where the *Boogieman* lived. His shoulder hurt, but the adrenaline in his system overloaded everything else. He transferred the gun back to his shooting hand. He willed his right hand to work and hold and aim his weapon as he moved in a crouched position down the hall. Behind any post, the three chairs in the lobby waiting area, the desk in the far corner, all were hiding spaces for her. But he knew where she was, just on the other side of the shattered windows. That's where she would be. This was her show. She was going to kill as many innocent people as she could to make her point stick. She was going to kill the children and their caretakers and as a bonus, a few cops. He could see the outer room through the shattered windows of the stub wall. Several of the windows were shattered with the glass blown out.

The main entrance to the children's area was on the east side of that same room. When entered, parents and staff would walk through it and into at least two other rooms consisting of an office and another large multipurpose room, the nursery. The outer room stub wall was merely dry wall hung on steel two by fours. Cooper knew the wall offered no protection from gunfire. However, if he kept the angle of his advance low, he thought Jodi couldn't see him from inside unless she got high up in the glass or stepped out into the hall from the front door. If she did, he could kill her. He could see both of those sight lines from his advance.

Jodi could see Cooper enter the floor from where she stood at the interior door looking through the edge of the window she fired through, just inside the main playroom. She had been watching him from the time the door opened in the stairwell.

She stepped back into the nursery with her captives and turned to her group of adults and children. Jodi moved across the room to the office area, just an open space to the main play room. She began to motion the adults into the room. She kept the children with her. She wanted some distance between herself and the adults in case they tried to rescue themselves. She pressed her finger to her lips to indicate silence. The father in the group, was the only man. As they began to move, he gave a look as if he was going to do something—anything. He needed, in her mind, to do something now, before he went away from his daughter. Jodi raised the Sig and with a grin, pointed it at him. "Let me explain something to you, Hero," she said in a low voice. "If you even think about jumping me, if my finger comes off this button I'm holding, we all go up in a big pile of flames and screams. Do you want the last thought of your life to be that you killed your child? Or worse, burned and maimed her so badly she wished she was dead? Or do you want me to blow your head off right now and have your child think it was her fault her daddy died? Hmm? Now move!"

He kissed his crying daughter and told her everything was going to be all right; he would be back for her in just a minute. Then he went into the room as Jodi directed. As the last adult was stuffed into the office, Jodi shut the door behind them. The door didn't lock but she didn't need it to. She didn't want it locked.

The phone rang. She knew it would eventually. It would be them. The police wanted to talk to her about releasing everyone. *They're so predictable*. It was almost time. She picked up the phone and hung it up.

Cooper low-crawled toward the nursery door. He had to remind himself to breathe. He always had a tendency to hold his breath when he got excited; now would not be a good time to pass out from lack of air. He knew Bull Thorton and others would be coming, but there was something different to this situation, he and

Holy Ground

Paul knew. She wasn't coming out. Jodi was going to end it right here. She was making a statement, a big one, punctuated with the deaths of the children, not to mention any parents or cops.

Jodi could see Cooper's shadow coming down the hall and then in front of the door. The officer she saw was low to the ground. He came up to the wall next to the door. He had about four feet to go. The light was streaming from inside the room and Jodi knew he would be near the entrance in just a few seconds.

SAU was moving up the stairwell on both the east and west side. The commander split the squad and sent them up both stairwells. They moved in silence.

Cooper knelt down just to the side of the front door. He quietly caught his breath, keeping his gun up in case Jodi Campbell came blowing around the corner trying to get a quick shot at him. He could hear the children clearly. They were whimpering.

Jodi looked at her hand holding the trigger. She edged over to her briefcase, opened it and took out the roll of duct tape. She quickly pulled off a piece and added it to her hand already taped to the trigger. It was a simple device really, a toggle switch and a button. She smiled again at her work. When they killed her, her finger would come off the button and kill everything in the area. She stepped back from the door and closed it slowly. They were coming to her now, right where she wanted them. "Come on, let's celebrate my baby's birthday," she whispered to herself. As she moved back, she stepped on a little girl's foot. The small girl in the pretty dress screamed, not so much from pain, but from the surprise and the fear she already felt. The scream was rocketing. It startled Jodi and caused Cooper, to spin quickly into the outer room just as Jodi shut the interior door.

225

He moved quickly across the room, almost twenty five feet, to the door Jodi had just closed. He could hear the muffled sounds of the crying children through the walls and door. His shoulder hit the wall next to the interior door. Then his radio cleared.

"Four-Bravo twenty-three." It sounded like it was on a loud speaker. His earpiece had fallen out of his ear. Cooper quickly reached behind his back and turned down the radio.

Jodi stood on the exact opposite side of the wall from Cooper, waiting, listening; she could feel the pressure of his body against the wall and heard the garbled transmission through the wall as well as from her scanner. Jodi smiled. She pivoted with the gun in her hand and pointed it at the children. "Who wants to go first?" she asked with a wide, wild look and a maniacal grin. "Huh? Who wants to lead the way? I know, I think the police are on the other side of this wall, too." She stepped away from the wall and turned to it. "Let's find out." She fired three quick rounds at the spot on the wall where she was previously standing and where she felt the pressure.

There was no time to react. The wall exploded three times. The first round found Cooper's inner thigh and pierced the femoral artery. The second bullet felt to Cooper like getting punched in the side with a sledgehammer. It hit his vest, and came to a stop in its fabric. The third traveled downward, puncturing the gap between the front of the vest and his neck, just under the collarbone into his left lung and out through his web gear. The three rounds knocked him almost into the middle of the outer room.

Paul heard the explosions of gunfire. They weren't the sounds of a Glock. "Four-Bravo twenty-four, shots fired. What is the status of the SAU units?"

226

"Four-Bravo twenty-four, this is SAM twenty-four, we're on the fourth floor landing.

"Cooper! Cooper?" Paul yelled franticly, as he adjusted his seat and continued to point his gun toward the noise.

"Four-Bravo twenty-four, we can hear you. We'll be there in a moment," the SAU commander radioed.

"Four-Adam thirty-one engaging," Bull said.

"Four-Adam thirty-one negative, hold for SAU," the lieutenant instructed.

Jodi opened the door and looked into the room. A fog of dust and powder from the three rounds filled the room. In the center of the room lay a single officer, on his back. A dark pool of crimson oozed from under his waist and legs. She glanced around the room and frowned. She was surprised he was alone. She thought she would have more to kill. She would fall and the button would come loose in her hand and the lights in the little lives would go out. That was Jodi's plan. But it was just him. One, lone cop bleeding to death on the floor; his legs splayed out and his gun out of reach.

Cooper watched her. His was barely conscious. She approached him, still smiling. She looked over her shoulder back to the playroom where she left her hostages. Jodi looked out into the hall and found it empty. She came back and stood at Cooper's feet, pointing the Sig at his head. "You're all alone, huh? Too bad for you, but I can wait for your friends." She held up the switch so Cooper could see it. "When they come and the end is here, my poor little finger will fall off this little switch and we'll all go away, together." She looked out the door again; the crooked smile drained from her face. "That's it? They send me a couple of cops? That's all they think of me? They'll wish they had this day over by lunchtime when I let this thing go. They'll wish they'd never heard of my family by the time I'm through with them." She heard the crack of the radio again.

Cooper could hear Paul's voice, "Four-Bravo twenty-four, four-Bravo twenty-three is engaging the subject at this location. We need multiple nine-oh-sevens here right now."

The radio cracked again. "SAM-two, the SAU units are right under you. Stay put and we'll be right there."

Jodi walked over to the hallway door and looked toward the elevator. Cooper was able to follow her with his eyes. He heard the crying from the inner room and his eyes rolled back in that direction. He could see into the office and see shadows moving. He was surprised at the lack of any pain, with the exception of an inability to grab a full breath.

Cooper was dying. He knew it. He knew the wound and could feel the amount of blood he was now laying in. There were only a couple minutes he would still be conscious, if she didn't finish him first. She walked over to the interior door and pointed the gun into the room at whoever was crying. Cooper couldn't see that far. "Stop your belly-aching, right now!" she screamed. Her emotions now began to swing wildly. She finished it with what looked like a smile on her face. Cooper thought the sound from inside the office subsided, or maybe it was his hearing fading.

He lay there. Time dragged. The lights in the room were starting to fade and warmth came over him.

Cooper wanted to close his eyes and fall asleep. But there was something inside of him pushing him to get up. He couldn't. But there was something—something keeping him conscious. It was a voice, something. His own voice told him to fight, for just a few seconds, he needed to fight.

Cooper knew where he was going. He wanted to run to it. But there was something deep inside him, deep in the back of his brain, wanting him to hang on for just a few more seconds. He could see the light of the day come through one of the windows. It was strangely odd to him, but the light streaked into the room and fell on the floor near him. There was a simplistic beauty to the way it looked. He had never noticed something so plain before. Then there was a calm thought in his fading mind. A voice from the past came to his mind. *Yep, it looks like a good day for a fight,* he thought. He smiled. *Grandfather?*

Pictures ran through his brain. They seemed to be on a reel and moved quickly. Images flashed through, yet he recognized all of them. He smiled at each one. His childhood, his ex-wives, playing cards with his sister and brother-in-law, the time at The Wall, his nephew, flying—they were all there.

He watched as Jodi looked into the playroom. She was still pointing the gun at the children. Was she going to shoot? He didn't know. He had to distract her back to where he was laying. "You're going to die you know," he said. *Yeah, that should get her attention,* he thought.

She closed the door to the playroom and turned and looked at him with that same grin, the gun in one hand and the dead-man switch in the other. "What? I thought you died already," she turned and walked toward him.

That's it, come here, he thought to himself.

"Yeah, you're right. I am going to die. But so will they," she said pointing back to the room with the children. "And many of your buddies. They shoot me, they die. Perfect-don't you think?"

"Why such a hard-on for cops?" Cooper said. He could feel the left side of his chest begin to fall. He knew he was either going to bleed to death or drown.

"Oh, no, don't get me wrong. I like police. You just represent the city that killed my family!" she yelled into the air over Cooper's head. You killed us. Now, it's your turn."

Half of the SAU team reached the seventh-floor landing where Paul was. One officer took up a position at the stairwell door while two others tended to Paul's wounds.

"Why are you so upset?" Cooper almost whispered.

"Because you ask too many questions!" She was standing over him at his feet, and pointed the gun at his head. He couldn't see it clearly. It was blurred.

"So you kill a bunch of kids?" He began to cough. *Closer, get closer.*

"That's right, after I kill you." She sighted down the barrel.

"Hell, I'm already dead. Let me ask you something. Are you supposed to be on meds? You seem a little high-strung to me." *What the hell kind of thing is that to say with a woman pointing a gun at your head? Closer, get her pissed and get her closer.*

"Shut up! Shut up!" She said as she took two steps up. She was standing between his open legs.

There, right there. "Mighty big talk for a sociopath with a big gun and no fashion sense. Come here and fight like a man, you bitch," he said. Jodi took another half step.

"I'll make you wish I killed you quick. There's still time to have your friends hear you screaming for me to stop."

"Not today," Cooper uttered. He had no strength left. It had all leaked out on the floor. But somewhere inside, he found the reserve to move. Maybe it was the sound of the crying children. Maybe the thoughts of the parents who would never see their children again, or his partner down the hall. It could have been for his sister, his nephew; it could have even been for Allison and her husband. What Cooper did next was nothing short of Herculean. He kicked her.

His left leg was useless other than as an anchor. The femoral artery had been nicked and a good portion of the muscle had been destroyed by the bullet that drilled the leg. He used it as a base and swung his right leg up and caught the nerve bundle in Jodi's upper thigh and sent a shockwave through her, collapsing the leg. She fell like a tree—right on top of him.

They were face to face. He reached up with both hands and grabbed her hand taped to the dead-man switch. He folded his striking leg over hers and clamped down. For the next ninety seconds-the rest of his life, Cooper Gardner was focused on holding on.

From around the corner of the door, the father stuck his head out. He began to move toward Cooper, as if he was going to pull the woman off when Cooper shook his head. "She has a bomb. Get everyone out—quickly," Cooper said to him looking up into his eyes.

The man hesitated then nodded and turned back to the door where the children were. He waived to the people inside and in a stream, they came out and started to run by Cooper and Jodi, lying in the middle of the floor. "We're just going to lay here for a bit. Move quickly," Cooper said to the man as he ran by. "Hurry."

Jodi tried to get up. She was small but strong. She was draining the last of his energy quickly. She tried to knee him in the groin, but his leg kept her too close for her to pull back to strike. Soon she would be able to get up because Cooper would be dead. He figured he only had a minute of strength left. The SAU team, which surely was close, would walk right into an explosion.

The children and adults moved quickly by him. He couldn't see them except for their shadows and dark outlines of the hostages as they passed by. His eyes were shutting down. Somewhere deep in the back of his brain he heard the voice of Paul, calling, calling.

Paul could see the first of the children and then an adult. He began to wave to them "Down here, down here quickly!" He waived to them again and they ran toward him. An SAU officer took up a position in the hall and directed them into the stairwell while telling the adults to put their hands on their heads as they stepped over Paul. As the father approached, Paul asked him, "How many are there?"

"I think only one woman. She shot a cop but he has her. She has a bomb she's trying to detonate." Then the man moved on. Paul turned to the SAU sergeant standing over him. "We gotta move."

Cooper sensed someone was there before he could actually see their shadow. It was Bull stepping into the room. He moved to Cooper and grabbed the woman. Cooper could see him looking down into his eyes. "I got her, buddy." Bull said to him and began to pull.

"No! She's got a bomb! Get everyone out!"

Bull quickly let go. He nodded and turned to the children. He looked back in the room they were coming from. "I'll be right back, Coop. Hold on," he said to Cooper as he ran out into the hall to get the people moving picking up one of the children and carrying them down the hall.

Cooper was face to face with Jodi. He could smell her perfume mixed with sweat and surprisingly sweet breath. Both of his hands were still covering her hand holding the trigger. With her other hand, she grabbed rabidly at his two and then tried to punch his face, her blows glancing off the top of his head. Cooper noticed all the shadows were gone. No one was running from the room. He only had a moment left. He knew Paul and the cavalry would be coming and more were going to die. He looked at her and smiled weakly. "We need to end this now."

She looked at him. She stopped struggling as if she couldn't hear what he said.

"What are you doing? What do you mean?"

"No one else is going to die today—just us."

"No, no, that's not the plan. You can't. You bastard!" She struggled and tried to get up, but time was leaving the room for both of them.

He could smell the sweet, cold air at the amphitheater in front of the memorial, the sun setting behind The Wall. He hadn't noticed before how golden the light was. He could see his father and mother again. They were waving to him. He could smell his mother's chicken cooking clear out on the front porch where he was sitting with friends he knew. Skinner was walking toward him, smiling. He was shaven, had on a fresh Hawaiian shirt, a pair of shorts, and Birkenstocks with socks—white socks. Others, hundreds of others, were with him.

Cooper looked to his side, away from Jodi. He could see Paul in the seat next to him. They were flying and listening to ZZ Top. There was no rush to go anywhere and even though he could see himself and his co-pilot wearing police uniforms, there was no sense of urgency. There were no calls waiting; they were just flying. He looked back at the woman. They were almost touching noses. Her hand was buried in his two. She fought to get up, but he held her down. He began to peel her fingers off the detonator.

"What are you doing?" she said almost in a panic. "No, it's not time. No one—no one's here!"

He smiled. There, on the television screen in the corner of Moreno's Bar, was George Burns and Gracie Allen in color—vibrant, intense color.

"Say goodnight, Gracie. Time to go home," Cooper said as he pulled Jodi's fingers, with the detonator, down to his mouth. He bit down hard on her fingers with all that was left of his strength, removing her fingers from the button and causing the explosives to detonate in the empty nursery.

CHAPTER TWENTY-THREE
Who are those guys?
—The Sundance Kid

The church service was full, not even standing room. People who came overflowed into the street and sidewalks to such a degree, speakers were set up so those standing outside could at least hear the service. Hundreds of people came. Moreno was there. So were Cooper's sister, brother-in-law, and nephew, tucked into the front row. The Mayor of Phoenix and the Governor were there. The mayors from Glendale, Mesa, Tempe, and Scottsdale were also in attendance. Paul wasn't supposed to be out of the hospital but between Bull, the fire department transporting him in an ambulance, a cast up to his groin, and crutches, he made it. Police representatives from every department in the state and many of the states including provinces of Canada also were there to honor him. That's what cops did. Even Allison and her husband were there. She was wearing a green paisley dress.

The casket was in the front of the hall, shrouded in the noble colors of the nation's flag. Sunlight, through the side windows, as if on cue, shone through and landed on the casket just as the ceremony started. Behind the podium stood the church's worship team consisting of a base guitarist, electric pianist, lead guitarist, drummer, and a lead singer with a couple back-up vocalists. Cooper had come to this church only a couple of times over the years. It was close to where he lived. He had told Paul one day when Paul asked him if he ever went to church. When they were planning the funeral, someone asked where to hold the service. Paul remembered the church and contacted them. They knew Cooper. The Pastor had a recent conversation with him.

The band finished and the pastor stood to speak. He was a middle-aged man of about fifty-five. He wore a suit but it was clear the church had no formality to it.

"It is with confused hearts that I, maybe many of us, find ourselves here today. We are saying goodbye to our friend, our mentor, our confidant, and part of our family." The pastor looked into the first couple of rows. "It is with confused hearts we seek solace this morning. It is also a heart which leaps for joy and the freedom this person—so long a part of many of our lives—who now walks in Paradise, free of pain, free of guilt, free of envy, feeling only the joy which comes with being a child of God ...."

Cooper looked to his right as he walked down the wet sidewalk. It must have just rained and the air was fresh and cool. There was a door. He had seen this door before. He pushed on it and walked in.

It was Paul's turn to speak. He had told the funeral organizers for the department he wanted to speak and no one was going to argue with Cooper's partner—no one. He carefully approached the podium with the help of crutches and an officer on either side. He stood for a moment, taking some notes out of his pocket and placing them in front of him. He then looked out at the audience, panning across and seeing Cooper's sister and her family, other officers, the Chief, commanders, different departments and their representatives. He looked down at his notes, then to Doris who was sitting in the third row on the aisle. He looked at her, she nodded her approval and smiled. Paul smiled at his wife then folded up his notes and put them back in his coat. "This man was me. Cooper and I, we're

236

not too different." He paused for a moment and swallowed hard. "He taught me some things and I think I taught him some things too, at least I hope so." There was pain and joy in his voice. He was looking down at the center aisle and then looked to his wife again. A smile came over his face and when he blinked, tears flowed down his cheeks.

"We meet here as a community of friends and family. We gather to support and to love each other in this time of loss. A man's past becomes his present; his present becomes his future. His destiny is set by those things that act as his compass. A true man—a father, husband, friend—have only one compass. It is this compass which men seek. The love of God calling us His adoptive children which drives true men forward—laughs with them in fun and holds them when they cry."

He looked down at the flag covered casket and smiled. He pointed at it as he spoke. "This man, the man in this box is not here. He has touched all of us. Most in this room come to honor the uniform and don't know the man. But we leave here having been changed by him. I have. We can't help it. He touched us, each of us, if only for a moment, or for years, he changed us, and if we allow ourselves to truly look inside, we will have to admit this man changed us for the good. Cooper Gardner made me a better man, I am proud to say," he paused and looked at the casket and smiled and began to choke on his words. "That old bastard was my friend. I want to be like him; there's a part in all of us that wants to be like Cooper Gardner." The crowd laughed and those that knew him were nodding in agreement. Paul was helped to his seat and the pastor returned to finish the service.

Cooper sensed the familiar smell of aged oak casks and food, *heaven in a tortilla,* he thought.

Fernando's burro was being cooked and assembled in the back. He closed his eyes for a moment and breathed in. It filled his lungs. The lights were bright when he entered Moreno's Bar. The crowd erupted in a cheer that shocked him. He felt alive, free, and playfully happy. The first faces he met were of his parents and grandparents. He walked in and people, hundreds of people filled the space in the bar. The bar appeared endlessly large. It was as big as it needed to be to hold everyone who was there, who Cooper had met, touched, or knew while he was alive. They had gone before him and it was their turn to greet the arrivals, just as they had been greeted.

"... Cooper was a friend to us and loved us in his own special way. He gave ..."

Cooper could see the people more clearly as he got closer to them. He knew instantly who they were, their names, and everything about them. The smile on his face grew into laughter.

"Officer Cooper William Gardner died, not in vain, but in the spirit of the true definition of love, which most of us will never fathom. He died for not only those he knew, but for those he did not know—"

He was surrounded, hundreds of faces, maybe thousands, he didn't even try to count. People from his past came up and greeted him. His grandfather and grandmother, along with his own father and mother, congratulated him as he walked by. "Grandfather, you're here!" he said with an air of knowing as the men gave bear hugs.

"Aye lad, we're all here. And now, so are you," his grandfather said. "I'll be right back, lad. Don't ya be going away. Oh, like where would ya want to go now? Sometimes I'm as daft as a Cornish hen, I am," he said as he turned and left back through the crowd leaving his wife, Cooper's father and mother to walk with the boy.

The band at the funeral began to play another song as the pastor sat down. As the police honor guard proceeded to the front of the hall, the one bag piper marched slowly down the aisle and took up his position in front of the casket. The honor guard, three on each side of the casket, stood facing each other. Once in position, they began to escort flag draped casket to the hearse waiting outside, up the center aisle. The song, *Amazing Grace,* filled the church. The faint sound of another piper seemed to be playing outside from some distance away, echoing the first.

There was no one there.

"Do ya hear that, lad? We're playin' the pipes," came his grandfather's voice from the hill.

Cooper could see and hear his grandfather. He could see the crowd at his funeral. "I do!" He paused for a minute and looked at the crowd gathered for his funeral. "They'll be all right."

"Aye," his grandfather said with the others looking on and nodding in agreement. "You made sure of that."

Cooper moved down the line of people. They encircled him. He recognized each of them. Music played in the background. A hand reached out and handed him a glass of thirty-year old Glenlivet, neat of course. There were balloons and pats on his back. He knew all the faces and their names, family, friends, acquaintances, all of them there just for him, to welcome him home. As he looked around, his eyes fell on Fitz and Tyrone. Cooper laughed with excitement.

"You guys are here!" he said grabbing the two of them and hugging them both. "Why here?"

"Oh, this is just *your* place," Tyrone said.

"Yeah, when I came home it was the grassy hill," Fitz said pointing at Tyrone.

"Yeah, I thought you were crazy when you would describe it. This kind of makes the transition, well, easier," Tyrone said. "Don't worry, this here ain't the end, just the beginning."

Cooper started to laugh out loud. "I don't know. I've always liked this place."

The two others looked at each other and smiled. "Brother, you ain't seen nothin' yet!" Tyrone said with a smile.

Cooper looked past the two to another face and another set of eyes. They were clear and sparkled. The face glowed with perfection of form and a light from the inside. It was Skinner, clean shaven and in a bright Hawaiian shirt. He was looking at him while eating what appeared to be a huge piece of lemon meringue pie. He had some on his upper lip when Cooper approached him.

"You're here!" Cooper said as he moved to him and hugged him.

"You, too!"

Cooper looked at him and grabbed him by both shoulders and laughed. "Where did you get that shirt?"

Skinner smiled and winked at Tyrone. "You get one when you get your first slice of pie." The men laughed.

"I suppose your comeback was at a Marie Calendars," Cooper said.

"Village Inn."

Jacob was right behind Cooper as he walked and welcomed by people, following his boy quietly as he moved through the crowd. Cooper turned to him. "Where is he?"

Jacob smiled at his son. He nodded his head to his right, to the corner of the bar, to Cooper's old bar stool. They both turned in the direction and the crowd began to part.

The casket with the American flag slowly was walked up the center aisle by the honor guard. The tone of the pipes escorted it to the front door and directly into the hearse, waiting on the other side of the door. It was parked at the end of a row of uniformed officers who lined up from the church's front door leading to the hearse.

Cooper walked through the crowd. They were laughing and smiling and waving and some reached out to shake his hand or pat him on the back. He looked to both sides but his face and eyes kept skipping to the direction he was moving—to the other side of the room, where his old bar stool was. There was a light there. It was blocked by the crowd. But he knew where it came from. He knew what it was. He knew *who* it was.

The crowd stood as the hearse passed. If they were in uniform, they saluted as it passed in front of them. If they were in civilian clothes, they placed their hands over their hearts-hundreds of people. There were no other cars, just the single hearse. The family wasn't to follow. Cooper had left specific instructions he was to be cremated and his ashes disposed of—no memorial, no marker.

Cooper had never felt such joy. He couldn't say he was *happy*. That word seemed inadequate for what he was feeling. There was an electric feeling in his body penetrating deeply into him. He wanted to reach the light and began to move faster. People around him began to laugh and cheer. They had experienced what Cooper was now experiencing when they arrived. He looked at them and laughed as well. He was sure they had done the same thing when they arrived—wherever that was. They couldn't wait to see his reaction. Suddenly—he stopped. The crowd was no longer blocking his view. Cooper could see clearly. He began to step slowly towards his old bar stool—where the light was coming from, laughing and crying at the same time. Tears rolled down his cheeks and onto his chest; he didn't care. He loved it. He had never felt tears of joy. He didn't want it to end. He knew it wouldn't. He stopped within a few feet of the source. His face was now awash in the light. It was as bright as the sun, but his eyes drank it in. Cooper fell to his knees and sobbed. "You brought me home. You really brought me home."

EPILOG
"You are one of those guys."
—Bruce Willis, *Live Free, Die Hard*

———————————

The 'Old Silverback,' called that by his friends as a term for a man of knowledge and wisdom acquired over time, played his bagpipes until the hearse couldn't be seen from the church as it drove down the street. He matched the song of the lead piper and echoed him. His intent was to bathe the crowd, soothing them only the way pipes could. Finally, he stopped playing and pulled on the corner of his curled mustache as if he was making sure the wax tips were still in place. Discreetly he slid the side of his thumb under his eye and caught the tear as it made its way to freedom and started it run down his cheek; tears of sheer joy and pride were always welcome. He pulled on his mustache again. Then he tucked the bag under his arm and, while holding the chanter in the same hand, he reached into his sporran and freed the small silver flask. He uncorked it with his free thumb and, after toasting the vacant street where the hearse was, took a long pull on the container, letting the drink slide down his throat. Cooper would have liked it, the man in the hearse, a long pull on a fine scotch with an old friend—his grandfather. There would be much of that now. He was free. He was home.

Grandfather stood for a moment and then turned and walked away. He rounded the far corner of the church and disappeared.

6261404R0

Made in the USA
Charleston, SC
03 October 2010